Praise for Adam Roberts

"Adam Roberts has got what it takes."
Peter F. Hamilton

"Roberts joins my list of essential authors."
Vector **(Critical Journal of the British Science Fiction
Association)**

"A purveyor of illusions that underscore the real, a
beguiling dispenser of cruel instruction. Heed
him. Harsh medicine is not often so
entertainingly administered."
SFsite.com

"Roberts belongs on the front rank of hard SF
writers."
SFX Magazine

"This is Roberts's best novel to date, and quite
conceivably a harbinger of greatness."
Nick Gevers, *Locus*, on *Gradisil*

SPLINTER

A VOYAGES EXTRAORDINAIRE BY

ADAM ROBERTS

SOLARIS

First published 2007 by Solaris
an imprint of BL Publishing
Games Workshop Ltd,
Willow Road
Nottingham,
NG7 2WS UK

www.solarisbooks.com

Trade Paperback
ISBN-13: 978-1-84416-490-5
ISBN-10: 1-84416-490-X

The design of this novel was very much inspired by the cover of Jules Verne's
Hector Servadac, voyages et aventures à travers le monde solaire,
first published in 1877.

10 9 8 7 6 5 4 3 2 1

A CIP catalogue record for this book is available from the British Library.

Designed & typeset by BL Publishing

To Rachel

ONE

1

HECTOR FLEW IN. It's OK, he caught breakfast on the plane. He doesn't need anything to eat, he's good. But there was a wait at the hire car desk, and this brought speckles of sweat to his face and torso. His flesh, having been starved of Californian sunshine, and infiltrated by French food for more than a year, had assumed something of the color and consistency of mozzarella. He tried this line, self-deprecating and he hoped witty, on the woman seated next to him on his connecting flight. He smiled, sticking his lower jaw out and showing his teeth. His teeth, he admitted to her, had become Europeanized during this last year. That red wine, that ink-dark little coffee in the dainty little cups, those *gitanes*, the very air in Europe, it tends to *stain*. Stains the dentine. There are reasons, you see, why everybody in Europe has such crappy teeth. But what can you do? And you know what? he asked the woman in the seat next to him. Avignon has more Italian restaurants than French. I hadn't expected that. And Montpellier has more *American* restaurants than anything else.

"You mean," the woman asked, "McDonald's?"

But Hector could tell she wasn't really interested.

"Some," he said. "But, you know, steak houses. Of course, it's a big university town, Montpellier. Students love to eat American, fast food, steaks. That's the reason I was there, actually, doing some work at the university."

But she wasn't interested, she wouldn't be drawn, and when she started talking herself it became apparent that she was married, that she had a kid, and that Hector was on a hiding to nothing. He smiled and nodded as she talked, but not sticking his jaw right out, not the big beaming fuck-me grin, just a polite smile, and a polite nod, and behind his eyes he was thinking, you could at least wear a fucking ring on your finger, you could at least give me some heads-up.

At the airport he had to queue at the hire car desk. He told himself that a year in France had accustomed him to queuing; but as he stood there, looking through the glass walls of the terminal at the wide Californian view, the perfect blue of the Californian sky, the cars with their broad paneled paintwork glistening in the sunshine as if wet, some of his American impatience started to return. He fidgeted. He started sweating a little. Anger started warming inside him, although of course he kept it in check. At the head of the queue he was told that there would be a twenty-minute wait before he could be given the keys to his hire car. At least twenty minutes, we're sorry sir.

"Why?"

"There's been an unforeseen eventuality, sir," said the clerk. "I do apologize, sir. We can offer you a coupon for a complimentary breakfast in Home Cookin' while you wait, sir."

"No, that's OK," said Hector. "As for breakfast, I'm good."

2

WHEN HE FINALLY got his car, when he finally drove out, he got lost on his route to the ranch.

The car's air-con was either too cold, or else not cooling enough. He kept fiddling with it. He made a pit stop, picking up a couple of cans and something to smoke, and then drove on out, drove east into the desert. The signs of human habitation became poorer, sketchier; the gaps between buildings opened up, and soon he was leaving the major roads and driving lonely tarmac under the cyanide blue of a perfect Californian day. He fiddled continually with the radio tuner as he drove. None of the stations seemed capable of playing two good tunes one after the other. One good song, one shit song: that seemed to be the playlist of every music station within broadcast range.

He got lost. It was probably deliberate, on an unconscious level. He told himself this with some self-satisfaction at his powers of auto-psychoanalysis; getting lost was his own passive-aggressive response to his father's passive-aggressive actions, his own subconscious way of saying "How am I supposed to find your fucking ranch? It's in the middle of *nowhere*." To sell a perfectly good house, and buy a stretch of desert miles from anywhere—how could that be construed as anything but passive-aggression on his father's part? Hector circled so completely, still, even at thirty-eight, in the symbolic orbital of his father, or rather circled the space his father occupied in his own cognitive map of the universe, that he could only understand this action (selling a house, buying a ranch) in relation to himself. What other explanation could there be? Dad was free to buy and sell what he liked, *of course*, he was free to dispose of his home, which only happened to be the house in which Hector had grown up, the house in which his mother had died—*of course* he could do that, if he wanted to. He could buy some waterless ranch miles from anywhere, if he wanted to. He could join some cult, or whatever it was, and spend all his money on subterranean whatever cables, if he wanted to. But why would he want to? Except to mess with Hector's head? And the lady on the radio was singing the song that told him, Hector, that he—made—her—*feel*, that he made her *feel*, like a na-tu-ral woman.

Hector sang along. But the next song was some Nashville crap, and he fiddled with the tuner again.

He stopped in a small town, in which there didn't seem to be a single building more than one story high. He asked in the drugstore for directions, but the guy serving there couldn't help him. He stood on the main street for long minutes, in the heat, looking vaguely about, thinking maybe a cop could help him, but he couldn't see a cop.

Above him the sky was very blue, a dark lacquered blue upon which a handful of high feathery clouds looked like scuffs. And there, tiny as a bug, was a plane, drawing two tiny scratches after it, crawling over the sky. Just visible was its boomerang wingspan, its missile fuselage. It looked like a Christmas ornament.

He bought a map at the gas station and spread it on the passenger seat. He'd parked in the sun, and the material of the seats was hot, as if it had just that minute been ironed.

3

THE TWO-HOUR drive took Hector four and a half, but finally he rolled up to the gates of his dad's new place. Hector Senior had thrown a fence around the whole area, but most of the land was in a dip or depression in the land so pulling up at the gate afforded a fine view of the ranch. There were a half-dozen buildings, including several tall barns. Heavy machines were visible, diggers, tractors. Huge spools of cable lay piled in the shade of one of the barns. Round-shouldered apricot-colored hills dominated the horizon.

Hector pulled out his mobile and called his dad's landline. After a dozen rings his dad picked up.

"Dad? I'm here. I'm at the gate."

"Yeah," replied his father. He always, or so it seemed to Hector, began his sentences with this drawly, emphatic assertion of positivity. This was more than a tic. It had become a self-caricaturing habit, a mode of West American self-identification by positivity. "Why didn't you use the intercom?"

"I'm using my mobile."

"Yeah. Well, the gate's open."

And so it was. Hector got back in the car and nudged the gate open with the fender; and, not bothering to stop, get out, shut it again, he drove straight down the side of the little hill into the declivity where the ranch house was. He parked up alongside a silver four-by-four, that was itself parked beside a truck. He could see his father standing on the porch with two other people.

Hector climbed out of the car, and pushed a smile to the front of his face. "Hi Dad, hi," he called, energetically. "Hey, you look great." But he didn't look great; his hair had thinned across the crown, and large amoeba-shaped freckles, horribly expressive of advancing age, had come into being across his brow and scalp. Old, old. Impossible, but. Even the toughest rock gets weathered. Even the most solid structure crumbles with time. Heat, a desert heat, and the sudden waft of his father's bodysmell, also hot and dry.

11

They hugged, the old man and the young, Dad's face swimming up close like an asteroid ready to crash into the world of Hector's head, but swerving to one side at the last minute. Hec Senior clapped his son's back, and Hector returned the gesture, but with a revealingly tentative touch. Hector had seen something, an almost imperceptible something in his dad's eyes the fraction before they had actually embraced. It occurred to him, with the impact of a first realization, that his father was in some sense scared by his son. Hard to miss fear in another's eyes.

Hold the phone.

This is not to say physically scared, of course. Da was still tall and lean. He still had his muscles. Junior was still his shorter, jellied, drag-breathing offspring. Not that, but something more removed, a rarer thing. A more startling thing. Because Hector's father had never been one to spend too much mental energy on abstracts. Because, because—so? It was as if, looking at his son for the first time in a year and a half the older man experienced a manner of unnerving, a tremor in the soul, and that this tremor communicated itself to Hec via the vibrating astral medium, or some kind of conceptual shit like that. This was a revelation for Hector. Reveal. For, sure, Junior had always like, totally *taken* it for granted that his father was as much stronger than he in character as in body. It was a quake to realize that this big-leggy, self-sufficient man perhaps maybe *might* look nervously upon the arrival of his son to his house. That he might not know what to say; that he might be anxious about making a fool of himself, of simply having to interact with this other human being: this had literally never occurred to Hector before. And he had the miniaturely vertiginous sense of himself as his father must see him. There: not only out-of-shape and fidgety, but his own flesh and blood rendered implacably

12

and impenetrably *other* by the process of growing up. A hybrid of his father's self and the safely alien other people in his father's life. And therefore, naturally, a little monstrous. That sort of fear. You see?

The old man stood back, and looked at his son. "Yeah, guys," he said, apparently talking directly at Hector but in fact addressing the two people standing behind him on the porch, "this is Hector Junior. Hec, that's," he added with a hitchhiker's gesture of his right thumb over his shoulder, "Tom Brideson and Vera Dimitrov, we call her Dimmi. She's," he went on, after an awkward little pause, "Bulgarian." And then, after another pause, as if the thought were belatedly occurring to him that he should warn his son away from her, he added, "Yeah, she's with Tom, they're a couple."

"I'm delighted to meet you," said Hector, relishing his chance to try on a little bit of his newly acquired, flouncy old-European manner.

"Good to meet you," said Tom.

"Yes, nice to meet you," said Vera, in accentless English.

The aluminum blue of the California sky. The heat, there.

Father and son stood looking at one another. The awkwardness betwixt was unmissable. The completest stranger to these two, watching them now, could hardly miss it. A crack in the enamel of the living bone. Something broken and not set true. "I got your book," Hector Senior said, shortly. Book? No. The book had been, in fact, one issue of an academic journal, *Art and Aesthetics*, in which Hector had published an article about late Cézanne.

"Great," said Hector, adding, superfluously, "I hope you didn't read it. You didn't need to read it."

"Yeah," said his father, meaning no. And then: "Marjorie not with you?"

Hector took this as an invitation to talk about himself. "To tell you the truth," he said, rocking back on his heels, "Marj and I are going through a more distant period right now. We're still amicable, we're still on dinner-and-wine terms, but she's in London now. I think she's seeing a guy there. We parted on perfectly amicable terms. I mean, it was never as if we were going to get *married*." But looking again at his father's face he could see that these details were of no interest to him at all. Realization dawned.

"Oh," he said, his shoulders lowering. "Did you ask that in your self-appointed capacity as the new, what, Noah?" He started into this sentence thinking it a witty observation, a chirpy son-to-father thing to say; but as soon as the words were spoken he realized how much *venom* he was expressing, how angry this ridiculous new phase in his dad's dotage was making him. His own rage surprised him. "You want us all paired off for the two by two into the ark?"

Hector Senior didn't flinch. "Yeah," he said.

4

HE HEARD THE whole story, but not in one continuous narrative. Instead it came out in a couple of separate interchanges with his father, and with some of his father's disciples. Hector Junior took his small suitcase upstairs to a bare room with a single bed, and unpacked while his father stood in the doorway. The room had white walls and a plain crucifix over its single window. There was a deal dresser with glass handles, and this dresser was screwed into the wall. There was no TV. "Yeah," said Hector Senior patting the dresser, "there's a radio in the bottom drawer. It's a wind-up radio."

"Thanks," said Hector.

"You hungry? We had lunch already. But—if you're hungry?"

"So," said Hector, "those two, the Bulgarian girl and the other guy, they are living here?"

"They live out back."

"Out back?"

"The second building. There's a group."

Hector put a folded shirt in the top drawer. "I see," he said. "Like a commune?"

"Yeah," said his father, but he was shaking his head. "You might jump to that conclusion. But they're all sorts. A dozen or so. Mix of genders."

"This end of the fricking world," said Hector, not looking at his father. He couldn't bring himself to say *fucking* in his father's presence. "It's an extreme thing to believe, isn't it? It's old, Dad. It's bent out of shape, don't you think? Are they all religious, the ones staying?"

At first it seemed as if his dad wasn't going to answer. "I couldn't lay the cables without them. Besides, we'll need them later." And then, "You want to have a look round the new place?"

"Sure," said Hector.

They walked together around the half-dozen buildings; the ranch house, and a newer barn-like building with a dozen rooms inside it. Another barn was filled with an astonishing mass of supplies, tinned food, seeds, huge drums of something or other, electrical equipment, mysterious crates. "You got a storehouse here," Hector said, "that any survivalist would be proud to own."

"Yeah," said his father.

The sun was so hot it felt like a heated cloth wrapped around Hector. It made his eyes water it was so hot. His shirt flapped against his back, weighted with an oval of sweat.

A group of a half-dozen men and women was working out back, spooling a fat serpent of cable from a large mechanized wheel on the back of a truck. The cable was going in the ground. Away in the direction of the lay, on the side of the hill, a second group was digging a hole. Hector Senior introduced the cable-laying workers to his son, and Hector Junior forgot all their names straight away.

As they walked back to the ranch house, Hector asked, "The cable?"

"A special carbon bond," was the reply. "It's a strengthening thing, yeah. It binds the land, strengthens it. The clever thing is that it has some *give* in, it's not too rigid, see, so it helps absorb the tremors. It'll keep the ranch in one piece."

"OK," said Hector, wincing inwardly to see his father so evidently throwing his money away on this crank end-of-the-world notion, "I see. For earthquakes, is it?"

"Any kinda tremor," said his father.

Inside they fetched two midday beers, and stepped out again to sit on the porch and drink them together. Two beers. His father brought out a pack of tic tacs. "Have one of these," he said, thumbing one out with a cigarette-lighter action. It was there in the middle of his father's creased palm.

"You want me to eat a *tic tac* with a beer?" Hector asked.

"Yeah."

"Dad," said Hec. "That's—no thank you. What, minty-*beery*?"

"It's not minty," said his father. "It has no flavor. It's just a pill." He popped one in his own mouth.

"What kind of pill?"

"Health kind."

"No thanks, Dad," said Hec. "I've had my shots." He chugged his beer.

But his father flicked another pill from the sharp corner of his little box and placed it in Hector's hand. The light, Hec was thinking, had a realer-than-real quality. That was California for you. The desert. The moe, the *haa*, the ve. The sky a clear film of oil behind which shone the ultimate. To stare at it was to remind yourself how sheer the sky is. Dizzying.

They talked about the old novel. Book? Yes. "I read the book," Hector told his dad. "After I got your email. The end of the world is nigh!"

"Yeah," said his dad.

"Took me a while to track it down," said Hector. That sentence didn't come out as rebuking as he'd hoped it might. "That title *Off on a Comet*, that's not the title in French. That's not Jules Verne's original title. I," he added, preening a little, "I read it in French, you know."

"Yeah," said his dad. The bright sunlight brought out the lines in his face, like acid resolving the grooves and gouges into an etcher's plate. Lines fanned from the corners of his eyes, like those route-maps airlines provide of the spread of flights they run out of their hub; say, Atlanta to a *hundred* destinations. His left cheek had a deep fold running from eye to the corner of his mouth, but there was no corresponding fold on his right cheek. Perhaps he slept always on his left side, always pressing the crease into that side of his face, every night.

"It's a pretty crazy novel," he told his father.

"Yeah," said his dad. "It's some book."

But this was not what Hector had meant. "So," he said, breezily, "the hero, this guy you reckon is an ancestor—he's in the French army in Algeria. And this comet hits the earth, and he's there with his batman and at first he thinks it's resulted in this great flood, since he's surrounded by sea which he wasn't before." Hector's father stared impassively at his son during this recital of a story that he knew perfectly well. But Hector

Junior wanted to stress the absurdity of the adventure, and hence of his father's new craze. "He searches about and finds some more survivors of this comet-hit, and they all band together, but something's gone screwy with the heavens, the sun's rising in the west—"

Hector paused, loitering over this point for reasons he didn't wholly fathom within himself.

"Rising in the west, and Venus looming large, and so on. Then it turns out they're all living on a chunk of land—*and* sea, which is I think we can agree *pretty* tough to swallow—that's been knocked off the Earth by the collision of the comet and carried away *on* the comet..." Hector shook his head. "You see how crazy that is?"

"Yeah," said his dad. "Tell me—so, how is it crazy?"

Hector swallowed the little pill in his palm, gulped it down with a mouthful of beer, and ran a knuckle along the crease of his lips to clear away suds. "Well for one thing," he said, "this comet crashes into North Africa, scoops up a chunk of the ground, and flies on... but the people on the chunk of land can still see the sky, they're not you-know *embedded* in the comet, so the chunk of ground must somehow have been flipped over through one-hundred-eighty..." He grinned goofy to convey how stupid this was. "Then they fly through the solar system, with—you know, gravity, and with atmosphere, and with the sea freezing rather than boiling off into space, it's daffy."

"Yeah," said Hector Senior.

"And then they return to the Earth at the end and they plan to float off the comet in a balloon, and then they just float into the Earth's atmosphere, *phhhw*." Hector raised his hands, palms upward, in front of his chest, as if lifting two fragile, invisible spheres. "Crazy. And then they get home, and nobody's noticed that they've even gone, and nobody seems to have figured that a comet carried off half of Algeria. I mean, what is that? Is it one of those, And I Awoke and Behold it was a Dream things?"

His father was staring into the middle distance. How he could look so long, without sunglasses, without even wrinkling his broad blue eyes, was beyond Hector.

"Then I figured the name of the guy, the title of the book in French, is Servadac, and that's 'cadavres' reversed. You see? In French. So I figured it was a trope," and revising his words *en courant* to an idiom more appropriate for his father, "a manner of speaking, a metaphor rather than a literal account. It was Verne deconstructing, you-know, Verne criticizing and playing around with the conventions of nineteenth-century science fiction. I wondered whether it isn't all about death, and spirit journeys, what are they called, astral journeys, and heaven and hell and so on. I'm not hugely experienced in reading these sorts of texts. Books I mean." Hector had minored in English, but it had mostly been Shakespeare and African-American literature. He had majored in Art History.

"It's kind of a shame," said his father, in a low voice with a burr underneath it, as if he needed to clear his throat with a strong cough, "that you didn't bring Marjorie with you."

5

OUTSIDE, ALONE, HECTOR walked over to a low concrete structure, three feet in all directions, perhaps some sort of bunker or store, and sat on the edge of this and smoked a cigarette. The fact that the ranch was in a declivity gave it a weirdly foreshortened, film-set feel; the horizon looked close enough to touch. The sky above was a pure and cyanide blue. The sunlight hot enough to feel actually heavy, as if it had mass

19

and weight. He wondered, absently, whether he shouldn't borrow a hat from his dad.

No cicadas spoiled the perfect silence.

At Yale, where he'd majored in Art History, Hector's roommate had been a theology student, a lawyer's son from Pennsylvania called Orwell Matthiesson. Hector remembered his own astonishment, imperfectly hidden behind a bottle of beer in a dim-lit bar, when Orwell had described—laughing, as if it were the biggest joke in the world—*punching* his own father during a fight. "You actually hit him?" Hector had asked, goggling. Orwell was a beanpolish, sharp-featured guy with long arms and big hands. "Sure," he had replied. "In the stomach. He saw the blow coming, he was able to tense, no harm done. He was *mad*, though. Man he was mad with me. But you know how it is when you're having a fight with your dad, you know how fierce it can get."

But Hector didn't know. He had never once fought with his dad, never so much as raised his voice, or stormed out of a room. He had barely even contradicted his father during all the long years growing up in the L.A. house. In fact, as he looked back on his childhood and adolescence from the vantage point of Yale freshmanship, he could barely remember *talking* to his father at all. What did they have to talk about?

He had given away all his money. That had made his dad angry. But that's not to actually strike him with a fist. That was more—you know—passive.

Hector had decided to study Art History because, he told himself, he loved art; but his first year at school had been a process of fastidiously unlearning all his visual tastes; or if not unlearning (for the sorts of paintings that moved him as a teenager still stirred something in him as a student, against his better judgment) then rather a process of systematic repression of his gut-responses. His mother had been an artist, producing brightly colored figurative canvasses depicting lush natural landscapes, or animals, or nudes with animals, or sometimes, Hector shuddered to recall (for these were the paintings that sold in California in the seventies) unicorns, dolphins, pumas, star scenes, zodiacal interpretations. As a child Hector had almost worshiped his mother's ability to conjure these images out of two boxes of paint and a stretch of canvas. As a teenager, he had of course acquired distance from them, which out of her presence sometimes took the form of disdain. But his taste in the fine arts was indelibly marked by his childish immersion in those images: he loved Gauguin, he admired Van Gogh, he thought Chagall beautiful. At Yale, however, after some overenthusiastic partisanship, it dawned on him that these sorts of artists marked him, they pegged him as *insufficiently aesthetically sophisticated.* And so he conditioned himself to love abstract art, to prefer Leonardo's sketches to his completed paintings, to drop names like Ben Nicholson and Karen Waldie. He just told himself that these were his preferences, over and again, until he became habituated to the idea that he actually did prefer them. He had settled on Cézanne as doctoral topic in part as a compromise between the figurative and the abstract. Compromise was one of the badges of his life. Oh, sigh. Stretch marks on his soul.

Coming to terms with the world, the world meeting him less than halfway. It was the realization that growing up was, beyond a certain point, a kind of shrinkage. That self-melodramatization! He knew he did it, and he didn't do it deliberately, he didn't, you know, *wallow.* But—still.

He had never really known what his father did for a living. Something in business, it seemed. Something involving selling, or speculating, with the now-wealthy ex-hippies of San Marino and Silverlake and Los Feliz.

Hector sat on the concrete cube in front of the ranch house and pondered as the smoke scraped into his lungs with its delicious thousands of miniature hooks, and pooled there, and came gushing out again like an excess of joy. With the nicotine his skull relaxed minutely. When he had said to his dad, about the Verne novel, "You see how crazy that is?" he had actually been saying, "You see how crazy your life is now, Dad? You see how insane you were to sell the house and buy this ranch and move here with these weird followers, these cultists, whatever they are?" But his dad had lacked the finesse to decipher that particular coded communication. There ought to be a way, Hector thought to himself, that I can tell Dad what I really feel.

Oughtn't there?

The Bulgarian woman (Hector had forgotten her name) had come out of the house and was walking over the dirt towards him. As she approached, the sound of an industrial drill started up, from somewhere well away, behind the main building, a noise shrunk by the distance and the intervening structures to nothing more than a mosquito *skirr*.

"Hello," she said. "Do you mind if I sit with you?"

By way of response Hector offered her a cigarette. "Smoke?"

She didn't reply, instead settling herself on the edge of concrete, disconcertingly close to Hector. Their hips were touching. Her legs, as long as Hector's, stretched straight out. Even in heavy-duty jeans he could see that they were good legs, shapely legs. Trying to be surreptitious, he glanced up and down her body. His intimate from-above perspective of her breasts gave her a shelf-like forcefulness of figure. Her curling hair was dark brown. It smelt faintly of candy. Her face, which had struck Hector, on first sight, as conventionally pretty in a broad-set sort of way, looked better in profile: the clean lines of her nose running down to a proportioned tip of flesh at the end, lines at the edges of her mouth suggesting a propensity to laughter. Hector's libido, or perhaps it would be more accurate to say his mere habit of bodily response, perked up at the prospect represented by this woman. He imagined her undressing. He imagined placing his hand, purposefully, on the spot where his hip was now accidentally achieving contact with hers. He speculated about the way her flesh would feel under his fingers; not too taut, not too slack. And straight away, without thinking about it, without weighing the propriety or even likelihood of success, he began wondering about the best way to get her into bed—a direct address, a sly insinuation, a slow seduction. His cigarette had burnt into a drooping hook of ash. He dropped it in the dirt.

"I'm sorry?" he asked. She had said something to him, but he'd been too preoccupied with the incipient physicality of her presence, and he hadn't properly heard.

"Je pense que vous cherchez," she said, looking straight ahead, "une simple question qui n'exigera qu'un oui ou un non. Mais c'est n'pas ça facile."

The fact of her speaking in French further confused Hector's fidgety, jet-lagged mind. "I'm sorry?" he said again.

"You have," she said, turning her head enough to see him out of the corner of her eye, and presenting another attractive half-profile, lips that Hector felt an actual physical itch to lean over and kiss, "just come back from France, I think?"

"Yes," he replied. And belatedly, he added, in his clumsily American-accented French, "Ça c'est vrai. C'est simplement que votre mots prononcés…"

"It's alright," she said, smiling warmly and the laughter lines thickened prettily at the edges of her mouth. "Only I wanted to say that this question does not exist. It is more complicated than a simple yes or no, is what I wanted to say. If you could stay here longer, you'd maybe understand."

This puzzled Hector; and piqued him too, as if he were being banished from the sexual possibilities of this woman as soon as he had been introduced to them. "I can stay," he insisted. "Why can't I stay? Does Dad want me to go?"

She was still looking at him out of the side of her eyes. "You misunderstand. I have not expressed myself well. You will stay as long as any of us. Only, if you could have come earlier, it would have perhaps been better."

Hector had an insight into what she meant. "Is it happening soon, then? This end of the world parade?"

"Tonight," she said.

The sound of the drill rose and fell in the hot air.

"Well," said Hector, trying to think of something witty and ingratiating to say to this woman, whose hip was still pressed so suggestively against his, "I guess I'll get an answer to my question soon enough. Tonight, I guess." He fiddled a new cigarette out of the packet, and slipped it up to his mouth. "What happens when, or if, I should say—if tomorrow dawns and everything's still the same as it was? I mean, like the millennium. I often wondered how the people who really believed the world was going to end in 2000, in the year, how they felt waking up the next day and realizing they were wrong."

Instead of answering this, the woman said, "I said *if you could stay here longer* because we hoped you could have come weeks ago, and then we could have persuaded you of the inevitability of this thing. But your father thought you would get into a temper and leave, and then you would be away from the ranch when it happens." Her accentless English slowed over these last three words, to give the "it" appropriate weight. "So it is better that you are here only today, although it will be a shock for you when it happens."

"*If* it happens," said Hector. He clicked his skull-topped metal lighter and placed a knob of fire on the tip of his cigarette. "I'm sorry," he said, drawing and blowing off a lungful of smoke before removing the cigarette from his mouth and holding it away from her, "I should have asked—do you mind?"

24

She was looking away from him now, which gave Hector license to peer closely at the interwoven fibers of her curly brown hair, at the snuffbox indentation in the exact center of the back of her neck. She smelled sweet, the heat and light squeezing wafts of whatever shampoo she used out of her hair straight to Hector's nose.

The drill stopped its noise, and the sudden silence was almost as startling as the sudden loudness. Hector flipped his eyes front, not wanting to be caught staring.

"I love Hector," the woman said. And for a moment Hector's heart scurried in his chest. But she meant his father, of course. The downstroke of this realization, with its release of petty annoyance, startled Hector. Spiders' eyes, bubbles in black foam. Her tangle of brown hair. He took a drag on his cigarette, and looked away to cover his confusion.

"If you'd been able to stay for a few weeks," she said, "you might have had one of the *visions* yourself."

"Oh," he said, scornfully. "Visions, is it?"

"They are very eloquent visions."

"Yeah?"

"Without your father," she said, simply, "I would be, now, in Europe, and tomorrow I would be dead. You also."

"Everybody dies," he said; but although he intended this as debonair and fearless, it came over merely as flip. Callous. He sucked too strongly on his cigarette again, and had to stifle a cough. "I used to imagine," he said, spontaneously, with a tingling in his chest of the sort he felt when he was doing something reckless, something filled with the possibilities of huge triumph and huge disaster mixed together, like asking a beautiful woman out, or attempting a risqué answer to a crucial question in an important interview, "I used to imagine exactly what it would be like to fight with my dad. I mean, you know, argue. Not fisticuffing, but the shout-argument thing. I used to lie awake at night, when I was at college, planning exactly what I'd say, exactly what his response would be, how I would cut him down to size, everything. But it never came to the right moment in actual life. There are so many things," he went on hesitantly, although in fact exaggerating his hesitancy of expression because he felt this was something he ought to express in a circumspect fashion, "so many things that I've never been able to communicate to him, about how I feel."

"Your father thinks," she said, as if replying to this confession, "that it is merely a random matter that it was he who got the visions. He thinks it could have happened to anybody. But I don't think so. I think he got the visions because of who he is."

She hopped off the ledge and turned to look at him. Her breasts moved just out of synch with the rest of her body. This plain fact of the physics of motion, inertia and tensile strength, sent jangles of electric excitement along Hector's nerves.

"Hey," he said, uncertain what to say.

"I think you like me," she said, and smiled.

Hector simply stared at her.

"Perhaps you are worried about Tom, but after tonight it won't matter so much. Tom loves me. The first child I have *will* be his, and maybe the second. But genetic mixing is an important part of this, of this whole thing, and there are only a few men here, and it would be foolish to be too exclusive."

This, Hector thought, wide-eyed, was perhaps the most extraordinary speech a woman had ever spoken to him. "Christ, you're forward," he said, gruffly, suddenly aware of his own Adam's apple, like an unswallowed lump in his throat. "Christ."

"You do not remember my name," she said, smiling again. And then she turned and went back inside.

6

HE ATE THAT evening with the whole group, sitting on the porch, scooping beans and fried potatoes and hot dogs Western-style, and watching the setting sun polish the distant round-shouldered hills a startling lobster-red. He still couldn't remember anybody's name, but it didn't seem to matter. The mood of the group was chatty, informal. "Isn't the world supposed to be ending in a few hours?" Hector asked nobody in particular, loudly, after his third beer. "You're all mighty jolly." But the only reply was laughter.

He only spoke to his father for a total of only a few minutes that evening. "I was just wondering, Dad," he said, emboldened by the booze, and by the strange social environment (and with the Bulgarian's strange words still buzzing in his brain from earlier), "about this Jules Verne book."

"Yeah," said his dad, looking levelly at him.

"I was just wondering. I don't see how it can be, you know, real. It's so wacky."

Hector Senior nodded. The Bulgarian woman's boyfriend, whom Hector now knew, after what she had said, was called Tom, was sitting close to him; and he leant forward at this point. "Servadac knew Verne," he said, smiling. "Had worked as a crewman on his yacht. When he had *his* vision, he went to Verne. That's what happened."

"Yeah," said Hector Senior, nodding somberly as if he knew what the hell this was about.

"Verne wrote it up, published as fiction of course. But, as a novel, it's so far removed from his usual thing—his usual thing, you know, is *thoroughly plausible* machines and inventions, round the world in a balloon, round the world in a submarine. It's all very much feet-on-the-ground stuff. But *Off on a Comet*, man, that's strange. *Servadac*. You read it?"

"Sure," said Hector.

"Didn't you think it was strange?"

"Sure."

"That marks it out. Its very strangeness is the badge of its truth."

"I guess I don't understand what you mean by *true*."

"It came to him, to Servadac, *as* a vision," Tom said, "a vision so intense he felt he was *living* it," Tom said, with unnerving vehemence. "It was a warning. It came a little early, yeah. But it was a true warning."

Hector played with his beer, picking at and peeling away the Budweiser label, rolling it up between his fingers into a skinny cigarette. Unrolling it. He could not think of a suitably forceful manner of expressing how absurd this sounded to him. Once Tom had moved away to talk to somebody else, he leant closer to his dad and asked, "You really believe that?"

His father only nodded.

The light faded, the red hills becoming cigar-colored, and then they were black against a carbon-purple sky fantastically replete with stars. Some people, as if to preserve the Wild West mood, were lighting actual oil lamps and suspending them from the overhang. The moon was right there, frozen in the act of transporting its small bright circle of lizard skin into the sky.

Hector took himself off to bed.

He had slept on the plane over from France, and had been able to stay awake all day without much bother. This was his patented and failsafe technique for dealing with jet lag: to push through the first full day, to resist the urge to nap in the afternoon and then to go straight to sleep at the proper time. Nevertheless his body clock was operating according to a different logic than the daytime–nighttime of California, and he did not feel sleepy.

He undressed, naked in the heat, and sat in bed to read for a while. There was no bedside table, or bedside lamp, so he was forced to read by the main ceiling light. Attempting to move his bed to be better placed underneath this light source he discovered that all four legs were screwed into the floor. This annoyed him. And so instead of reading his book he sat up, with the cotton sheet over his naked body, and fumed mentally. He wanted to jerk himself off, but at the same time he half-hoped, while more than half-disbelieving, that the Bulgarian woman would come to his room; in which case he wanted to keep (he flinched inwardly as he thought this, but it was the truth) his juices in a state of appropriate readiness. This was, of course he knew, just dumb. Plain dumb. But he couldn't block the thinking.

The lightshade threw its wineglass-shaped shadow across the ceiling.

Inside the top drawer there was a little supply of his dad's tic tac pills. A little perspexy box with a couple dozen. Little brittle white caterpillar eggs. Hector dry-swallowed one of these, thinking that perhaps it would act as a sleeping pill, but he felt no more tired afterwards.

Anger. There was some of that. If Dad had been possessed by the Bible, he thought to himself, would that have been better or worse? Possessed by the Book of Mormon, and visions that told him to build a fucking temple in the desert, or something like that? But that would have been worse, because his dad had always been thoroughly practical and material-minded, and this would be too weird a development. It was his mom who had been artistic and mystical. And his mom had died, and floated away to some mystical realm, beyond Hector's reach, while his dad had stayed right here, thank you very much, slap in the middle of the material, physical realm, living and breathing and smelling of sweat. Jules *Verne?* It was too outlandish even to be weird, like something so cold it feels hot.

He ordered the thoughts in his brain. He told himself: I'll put these thoughts in some sort of order in my brain, file them away, and then I can go to sleep. And, glancing at the inside of his bedroom door, if this woman comes, she can fucking well wake me up.

It was the *particular* book that galled him. For his dad to think that—say—*20,000 Leagues Under the Sea* was a true story would be one thing, surely batty but within the realm of possibility. Maybe some nineteenth-century billionaire could have secretly constructed a submarine, and blah-blah, and maybe it had been hidden from the world and blah-blah. But *this* book, with its kooky Hale-Bopp-cultist air, its fly-away-on-a-comet-to-paradise nonsense? And his dad had had visions, telling him *this* book was true, that the world was going to end this way?

He had not, he realized, ordered his thoughts. He had made himself more annoyed. He got out of bed and turned out the main light and got back into bed. He lay in the dark for a *long* time, thank you very much.

7

So, HE WENT to sleep. It was dark, and he went to sleep. Despite the fact that his body thought it was mid-morning rather than late at night. In fact, he fell asleep just as he was telling himself that, in a minute, he'd get out of bed and turn the light back on so as to be awake when the world ended. But, with the perversity of the unconscious, it was this that acted as trigger and propelled him into sleep. So when the world ended, he was asleep.

Que sera.

He was woken because somebody was shaking him, rocking him from side to side in the bed. The sheet was on the floor beside the bed.

Nobody was rocking him from side to side. He was alone in the room. But he was rocking from side to side.

He yelped, and woke up, or more precisely came to an approximation of consciousness.

Grains of sleep made his eyelids sticky and unresponsive.

He jumped out of the bed. At some level of his half-awake brain he knew this was an earthquake. He'd grown up in California, so he knew about earthquakes, and he told himself that the thing to do was get out of the house as fast as possible, to get the *hell* out of *there*.

He stumbled to the door and pulled it open. It felt like a live thing in his hands, trembling. Shaking with fear. *Hec* was afeared, the *door* was afeared. He flung it open, but it bounced and juddered back and forth on its hinges. The floor was heaving beneath him as if the room were about to vomit. The straight rectangle of the doorframe warped to a parallelogram as he staggered through it. It flew back to a rectangle shape.

The carpet wriggled underneath his naked feet. He half-fell, and rushed onto the landing. In the funhouse surrealism of this jelly house, and in his half-awake, panicked state, Hector acted instinctively. He ran as if he were in the Pasadena house; not this strange new ranch, but the house he knew in his bones, the place where he had grown up. He ran in the dark and turned right to bound down the staircase. But there wasn't a staircase. Instead he received a smack across his stomach, as if somebody had thwacked him fairly hard with a pool cue, and suddenly there was nothing beneath his feet, nothing at all.

His mind clarified with extraordinary suddenness. The earthquake tremor vanished from his senses. He understood instantly what he had done; he had run right through the railing along the top of the landing and was falling through space, such a *stupid* thing to do, such (he immediately believed) a stupid way to *die*. He thought two thoughts in rapid succession: one, an annoyance that he had never even learnt the name of the Bulgarian woman; the other, more self-remorseful, *I'm thirty-eight and I'm going to die without even getting tenure, for Christ's sake.*

He was weightless for the moment. For the second-and-a-half of the fall.

Then he collided with something that jarred his ankles painfully, He felt a tumble of further motion, up-down, difficult to make sense of in the dark, and then he was standing upright on the trembling floor. It took him considerably longer to understand that he was still alive than it had done to realize that he was falling. His heart was gulping repeatedly in his chest, and his nerves burned along his limbs and up and down his torso. In his mind came one thought, with bell-like clarity: *Her name is Vera Dimitrov and they call her Dimmi.*

The earthquake was still going on, but it seemed diminished in comparison with the intensity of Hector's own aftershock and fear. He turned on wobbly legs, and looked behind him. In the extreme dimness of the hallway he could just make out the crescent shape of the sofa that had broken his fall. He had burst through the railing at the top of the balcony-hallway, and had happened to land exactly on the central cushion. He had bounced up and forward and come to rest where he was now standing. Fluke.

A light went on. Hector flinched.

His father came in. "Are you up?" he asked.

"It's an earthquake falling," said Hector, through a gummy mouth. "It's outer I we should get outside."

With a precision of diction that only added to the sense of unreality pervading the night, Hector Senior said, "The house is reinforced. The house is the safest place to be right now. Go back to bed, Hec. Go back upstairs to bed."

Still trembling, Hector obeyed his father, pulling himself up the stairs by the shuddering banister and retracing his steps to his room. As in a fever-dream he clambered back onto his juddery mattress, and pulled the sheet back over himself, and lay there while the world shimmied and shook all around him.

8

HE FELL ASLEEP again, despite all the shuddering. When the earthquake subsided he woke, with the unexpected stillness of the earth; but an aftershock ruffled through the ground, and another one, and he started counting them, and soon was asleep again.

He dreamt, for some reason, of a fireworks show. He was in the Pasadena house again, with the Bulgarian woman, with Vera or Dimmi or Hot Momma or whatever she was called, and she was smiling at him over her shoulder as she walked away. But as she stepped through the door she was a different person, and dream-Hector believed that she had slipped out of her face, *Mission Impossible*-style, to reveal somebody else underneath. The door of the house had opened, with the impossibly concertinaed topography of dreams, directly into Griffith Park. It was dusk, and there were many people milling about underneath a sharkskin-colored sky. Hector tried to catch up with Vera, but placing a hand on her shoulder she turned and was a stranger, somebody he didn't recognize. "Your point?" this stranger asked. "Your point is?" "That's a pretty fucking deep question," replied dream-Hector, trying to throw a laugh into the statement but managing to sound only insincere. Somebody else (the connection wasn't clear, it jumbled) was talking to a crowd, and dream-Hector trying to push to the front, and the speaker was saying, "These fireworks are special, they are the true nature of things." Dream-Hector thought to himself, "That sounds like my dad," but it wasn't his dad, it was some dark-skinned, dark-eyed man no older than young Hector was himself. The sky had dimmed abruptly into a clear desert night sky, flush with stars like dustings of static electricity, and in between the sparkles was a purple so dark it was barely distinguishable from black. "These fireworks," the speaker was still saying, "are special, they are the true nature of things. You've heard of the Big Bang? That was exactly like these fireworks." Dream-Hector tried to contradict, because this didn't seem to him right at all, the Big Bang being ancient history not current affairs, but he couldn't remember when fireworks were invented, the Chinese wasn't it, and his mouth was gummed up, he couldn't form the words. He turned to the person next to him in the crowd, but everybody's face was angled upward, looking at the dark sky, and above him the fireworks were bursting in glory, marvelous sunflower- and lily-shaped expansions of light occupying the sky hugely, flowering with intense illumination, and then breaking into crumbs of neon red and white.

And falling away. And vanishing.

He woke to a bright window.

"Well," he said, to his empty room, "was that a *fucking* weird dream." But he knew that it had not been a dream. He knew it had all happened. The palms of his feet felt tender, as if they'd both been slapped hard. Otherwise he was unhurt.

But his mind was dancing, one-two-three, one-two-three. He'd fallen. He'd been lucky. That bang-bang, that shake-shake.

As he was dressing he realized that the whiteness of the window was the sign of a general fog. Fog in high summer in the Californian desert. How weird was *that*?

He went downstairs, but the house was deserted. The sofa looked somehow smug in the daylight; the whole scene shrunk by its perfect visibility to a comical rather than a tragic arena. Had he really believed he was going to die, just falling one story? The most he'd have suffered would have been a twisted ankle, maybe, at the worst a broken bone. Yet the terror was still there, in mental aftertaste; the genuine death-is-here terror.

An aftershock rumbled and gave the floor an odd number of shakes. Hector put his arms out, like a high-wire artiste, to steady himself. The shocks settled.

So much for the world's ending.

Out on the porch the world was milky and immediate, with an oceanic tang to the air, salty and ozoney. The view had been perfectly opaqued; Hector couldn't even see the parked cars a few yards away. So much.

Tom was sitting to the left of the front door, cradling in his lap what Hector at first thought was a cup of hot coffee, but which, looking twice, he saw was a pistol.

"Hi," he said.

Tom looked up, his grin already broad. "Good morning," he said. "Some night, yeah?"

"Yeah," said Hector. "That was some quake."

"You could say that," said Tom, blinking with what looked like suppressed glee. "You could say that."

"That one wasn't predicted," said Hector. "At least, I didn't see it in any papers. It wasn't on the TV."

"No."

"My dad, is he about?"

"He's checking the perimeter with Pablo and Esther. They'll be an hour more, I'd say."

Hector said nothing for several minutes. He took a seat next to Tom and stared at the blankness of the fog. "This is pretty freaky weather. It was so hot and clear yesterday, and now so white and chilly. I mean, I lived in California most of my life but never saw anything like this. I mean, this far inland."

"It's very striking weather," said Tom, almost grinning with delight at the joke of it all.

"But," said Hector, groping inwardly for a laugh to lighten the words but not finding one, "hardly the end of the world…"

The fog sat, motionless as cataracts. After it became clear that Tom wasn't going to reply, Hector said. "I mean, *fog* is hardly the end of the world, is it?"

"It's the Pacific," said Tom.

"What is?"

Tom gestured with the pistol. "All this."

"The fog is the Pacific?"

"What's left of it. Much of it boiled away to space, I guess, but a fair proportion of it ended up here. Most of it will distill out again, eventually. It depends how close we come to the sun."

Hector tried to listen to this, and the words made sense, of a sort. But not very much. Not very. He could have been listening to an engineering specialist explain some complex process in a technical language of which Hector was himself ignorant. Squeezing out a laugh, something more like a bark, he said, "So a comet hit the Earth last night and boiled the Pacific?"

"Something hit," said Tom, in a clear, low voice. "Not a comet."

They sat in silence for a while. The sound of two people talking became audible, somewhere away in the fog, but Hector could not pick out the words, only the fact that one speaker was a man and one a woman. That conversation, whatever it was, came to an end, and everything was quiet again.

Eventually Tom began speaking. "Something hit," he said. "Something very dense, *ve-ery* dense, and relatively small, and traveling fast. And something intelligent, I think. That's what *I* think. When—it—realized it was going to collide with the Earth it sent ahead, somehow, broadcast something to communicate with the inhabitants, to warn them maybe, or maybe—who knows?—to brag."

"Who knows?" repeated Hector, amiably, trying not to hear exactly what was being said, but not succeeding.

"I think it tried in the 1870s, to communicate I mean, which resulted in the strange and rather garbled vision that Monsieur Servadac experienced."

"I see," said Hector. He was conjuring a mental picture of Vera, called Dimmi, naked, stark naked, stark. He poured all his attention, his mental energy, into that image. He fiddled in his pocket for cigarettes, but he'd left the packet upstairs. Red ruin and the world's ending.

"The whatever-it-is," Tom was saying, "it hit last night. Somewhere a little east of India, in the sea, *through* the sea and, thwack, into the Earth. It penetrated pretty deep, breaking up the globe, shattering it into various lumps, before losing its speed and stopping—somewhere below us now. Not too far, couple of hundred miles I think. Maybe a thousand."

"Directly below us?" asked Hector.

Oddly, he couldn't think why, Hec's heart was kerplunk kerplunking. Why? It's only *fog*.

"The world was broken apart," said Tom. "Of course. But the lump we're on, it's in the best position. In terms of survival. Maybe a sixth of the globe's mass in size, but the—object—is so massive, though small, that its gravitational pull is three times that of the rock it's embedded in. If the fog cleared, you'd see. We're on a strange-shaped planetoid now, my friend."

Hector wanted to say: *I can't believe you could speak aloud a sentence like that*. But he didn't say anything.

"If the fog cleared, then it would look as though the horizon were rearing up all around us. If you tried to walk to Frisco, it would get steeper and steeper until eventually it'd be more like mountain climbing. But that's good, because it means that we're in the bottom of the concavity, so the air, and eventually the water, will settle here."

"Flood," said Hec.

"That's a year or more away. But we may have to move, yeah. We'll have plenty of time for that, yeah."

"It's a good story," said Hector, eventually.

They sat in silence a while longer.

"And this object, stuck in the soil below us, *spoke* to my dad, did it?" Hector asked, eventually. "It communicated with him? Warned him?"

Tom didn't answer.

"And," Hector went on, finding reserves of scorn inside himself after all, and able to give his words a withering spin, "and this intelligent super-heavy whatever-it-is is happy just to sit embedded in a huge fragment of a broken planet is it? I mean, why didn't it swerve and avoid the Earth, if it's so intelligent?"

"We've most of us had visions," said Tom, mildly. "Since we came here, although none as detailed as Hector's. Why didn't it swerve? Who knows? Maybe this is part of its alien life cycle. You know, a mole's gotta dig in the earth, salmon've gotta swim upstream to spawn, this thing's gotta crash into planets and embed itself, destroying them in the process. I don't know. *You* don't know."

Hector stood up, reaching for anger, although actually all he felt was incipient fear, the other emotion's close kin. "But I *do* know," he said. "I know you're all wacko. There was a quake last night—big deal, it's California for crying out. For crying out *loud*. I *know* that I'll get in my hire car and drive back to L.A. and get a room in a fucking hotel. Tell my dad I'll call later."

"Go for a drive, sure," said Tom, with infuriating patronage. "Only, belt up, and take care. The roads'll get steep sooner than you realize. Roads you think should be flat'll get steep."

"Right," said Hector, meaning *no way*. Meaning *never*.

The light was thinning, the fog growing darker. It was dusk. Dusk! Hector could see the dial on Tom's watch, on his wrist, sitting in his lap on top of the pistol; it said eight-oh-five. He must have slept right through the day, which unnerved him, because he had thought it morning. Still, he could drive through the night if he had to, get back to the city.

Yet he stood there hemming and hawing, on the porch.

"Things," he tried, "don't feel any different to yesterday."

"We're on a curious ellipse, orbitally speaking," said Tom, looking into the fog, as if talking to himself. "I've been trying to calculate it, but it's tricky to crunch the numbers. I reckon we'll move away from the sun for seven months, and up from the ecliptic, but not too far, not so far that the fog would freeze solid. Or so we hope. But then we'll swing back in and down, and things'll warm up. We need to plan to have the first children by then."

"Yeah. Right," said Hector. "I'm getting into my car now."

"You go ahead," said Tom.

"I will. I'm driving away."

"Have a drive around, sure. But be sure you can find your way back."

"I'm going now," said Hector. But he was still standing there on the porch, with the fog in every direction away from the house, as if the ranch had been domed in mother-of-pearl.

9

HECTOR HAD GOTTEN into the car and pulled the door shut before he realized that he did not have the keys. The keys were in his room. He fumed, disproportionately angry. He scowled at his face in what in France they call the *retro-vizer*. He let out a long whistle, as if he were coming to the boil. And in fact, in fact, something the reverse was happening.

By the time he had pulled himself out of the car seat and bustled upstairs to retrieve the keys, and come back down again, the fog was markedly darker. It would soon be black night, and the fog showed no signs of lifting. He checked the car's dashboard clock, but it was flicking two pairs of zeros either side of a colon, which meant that it needed to be reset.

Hector felt tired, as if in reflex to the darkening air and its suggestion of nighttime and bedtime. But how could he be tired? He must have slept a whole night *and* a whole day! He must surely have had enough sleep. He had already overslept, monstrously overslept. He'd be plenty wide-awake to drive back to L.A.

He started the car and the motor barked like a cross pooch, and then spun fruitlessly before dying. Which piqued him further. A general air of catastrophe, or of entropy, appeared to have settled over the ranch. He tried again, and the engine caught, and without fastening his seat belt he slipped the lever into reverse and he backed the car out.

He pulled the car around and started up the driveway, but found that, robbed of external visual markers, he had overestimated the turning circle and so he drove off the tarmac onto the rough ground. It took a fussy series of micro-maneuvers to bring the car back properly on the tarmac, and when Hector nosed forward he felt immediately lost. Even with the headlights on maximum he could see almost nothing. The world through his windshield shrunk to a uniform foggy gray through which, like a modern art-installation, two pale cones of light protruded and intersected. He inched up the drive, driving slowly, meticulously, but when the gate loomed up directly in front of him it came sharp and quick as a slap. Hector leaned his foot heavily on the brake.

This, he thought to himself, is stupid. I should go in the morning. I can't drive through this. Fog at night. I couldn't see my hand flapping in front of my *face* in this.

Growing up in L.A. he had sometimes known fogs; winter days when the mist would seep from the sea and nuzzle cat-like up against the frontages of Santa Monica and Venice. But he had never seen a fog come as far inland as the San Gabriel Mountains. The most he recalled from his Pasadena child-hoods were frequent fine hazes, smog that was so ubiquitous that you almost forgot there was anything fuzzy about the air; the sky still murex-blue above you, the perspectives along streets still dazzled by the light. It was only if you looked deliberately to the east, to look for the mountains you knew to be there, but which were invisible, that it became apparent how blurred and contaminated the air was.

But nothing like this. He'd never *heard* of fogs so far inland, certainly never in this season. Fogs in the Mojave? It was ridiculous. There was the fence, right in front. Stop the car. There was the fence. He pressed his spine into the plastic of his seat as the engine idled, and looked at the two circles of wire-grid cut from the mud-colored fog by his heads. As if practicing a meditative mantra, he formed the words in his mind: *the world has indeed ended.* But these words made no sense. Fog was not an appropriate indicator of the ending of the world. The ground was still there beneath his feet. The oxygen was still coming into his lungs, from its endless aerial store, and he was still blowing off his stained, useless exhaust gases. The sun was still rising and setting. Clearly the world had not ended. That was a crazy and impossible account of things. Ergo, there was some other explanation for what was going on.

He'd wait, he decided, until morning. He'd back the car along the drive, and go back in the house.

He shifted in his seat, laid his arm along the top of the passenger seat as if getting cozy with a non-existent companion, and swiveled his head to look out the back of the car. But without headlights the view was even more circumscribed. The sun seemed to have set with a Dada suddenness, and everything was dark silver, like sitting submerged in mercury, like the physical manifestation of depression. He moved the car slowly back in a straight line, and only knew that he had come off the side of the tarmac onto the gravel where the drive curved round because of the jolt of the back left wheel.

He stopped.

He saw something.

It was memory of such vividness that it appeared to have been projected onto the blank screen of the fog-muffled rear windshield. It came to him with a taste of coffee in his mouth (so, why *coffee*?), and a miniature galvanic tremor in his chest that made his heart hurry. Then it all came back to him, rushing through him, breaking over him like a surfer's wave.

This is what he saw. He remembered coming back to Pasadena, the first spring of his first year at College, after the second semester classes came to an end. Coming through the articulated corridor linking plane to the terminal with the gaggle of other passengers, all eagerly pushing forward or holding back, jittery as pigs in a chute. The sky of California, in contrast with the sky—*wait*. Fiddle-de-doo. He remembered it so vividly it was as if he could touch as well as smell as well as *see*. Sssee—

42

His first two semesters at New Haven had been marked by a kind of drabness—after, that is to say, the east-coast fall splendor of leaves in red and apricot and bright yellow had given way to its dreary winter and its pique-like fits of drizzle. For months there was only winter bleakness, a lack of color that made Hector nostalgic for the stronger visual contrasts of home. He remembered California as a place of exaggeratedly bright and vivid color; the houses all pinks and greens and whites so luminescent in his imagination that they practically fluoresced. All winter he moved about the Yale campus nostalgically recalling clear, sharply blue Californian skies, like clean new plastic. The pure silver gleam of high-rise buildings like giant swords sunk in the earth. The glorious multicolor adobe of the ordinary houses.

Then it was a *shock* when he had actually flown back home for the break and seen how *pale* it all seemed. The pinks and greens of the Angelenos' houses were insipidly pastel; the silver of the high-rises measled with dirt and rust. He had been reading Proust in translation (working, he told himself, into a French mood the better to understand French art) and although he never got past the first fifty pages it had at least given him a flattering sense of himself as a thoughtful and superior sophomore, as having *elevated* tastes. Wandering the streets of his childhood home, the roar of traffic on the Ventura Freeway sounding oceanic and epic in the distance, he had a sort of revelation, an epiphany that he considered, himself, worthy of Proust. The revelation was this: that the colors of California had been diffractions of his childish imagination rather than actual elements of the material world. This insight was accompanied not by any elation of profound comprehension, but instead by a sense of his own stupidity not to have realized it earlier; a sense of the belatedness of his own insights. His were thrift-shop insights, never new-minted, and not only not worthy of Proust but not worthy of being written on a curl of paper and baked in a fucking *cookie*. It had all been done before, everything he thought and felt had been thought and felt better by people in the past.

And sitting in the fog-bound hire car in the dark, he remembered this as well: walking west along West Union Street, the day after coming back to Pasadena that particular spring, and having these thoughts. A poem came back to him. It was one of the poems he had picked from the World Poetry course he was auditing, chosen to help him seduce a fellow student:

> *There was a time when something something*
> *The earth to me did seem*
> *Appareled in celestial light*
> *The glory and freshness of a dream*
> *It is not now as it did seem of yore—*
> *For there hath passed away a glory from the earth.*

That, of course, was what that poem was about, it was a growing-up poem; it was about the losses involved in growing up. Shakespeare, was it? Wordsworth? He couldn't remember. He hadn't actually taken the course. He'd only audited it. Nor had his reading of the poem persuaded the student, with her pleasingly reddened cheeks and the beautiful, magnetic curve of the small of her back, to sleep with him. He had felt not a joy of recognition on recalling this poem in the spring Pasadena sunshine. On the contrary he felt a sense of irruptive annoyance that some fucking English poet had *already* had the thought, hundreds of years before him. That there was nothing new under the sun. Oh, he had said to himself, how my life is *second-hand*! He remembered, precisely, thinking those words. He remembered the heat of the Pasadena early summer air going into his lungs. He remembered the sound of traffic, and, strolling past a shop, the sound of tinned music leaking into the street. He remembered the precise sensation of an atom of grit settling on the rim of his lower eyelid, and the cautious finger-maneuver he had used to extricate it, without breaking his stride, as his feet ate up the West Union.

That poem. He had tried that same routine on another girl in his second year: taking her for dinner, straining for deep conversation over glasses of wine, and afterwards settling her into the chair in his room and declaiming the poem at her. What a prick he'd been. And it had worked that time, although Hector, even in the visceral joy of his successful seduction, even as he plunged himself in and drew himself out to the mouse-squeak soundtrack of her pleasure, knew enough to read from her eagerness the fact that she would have slept with him even without the poem, the conversation, the meal—that he had put in more effort than had been necessary. And in its own perverse way this took the shine from the physical pleasure of the sex, and left him grumpy afterwards. She had been called Jill, he recalled. And her blonde hair looked so soft that it had been an actual shock, when the kissing started, to touch it and find it stiff with hairspray, like stale bread. There had been a little ulcer on the tip of her tongue, and every time she pushed it into his mouth he had felt the little corroded circle of flesh touching his own and had winced.

A long time ago. A whole lifetime ago, on the other side of the world's ending. He sat in that car, fog and night, and it all came to him. He laughed aloud and with childish delight at the vividness of the memory.

And, as he sat staring through the rear window of his stationary car at the density of fog, it occurred to him that he hardly ever thought of his student days anymore. Everything in his life had bleached away to darkness now, as if the world were mocking him. Some people looked back on college days as the happiest of their lives. For Hector it had been a blander experience; not miserable, not notably marvelous either. Except that, every time he returned to California after having left it, the color seemed to have seeped a little more out of his childhood geography.

And with a jolt like the holy spirit departing, the memories tumbled out of Hector and fell away through some invisible trapdoor cut right through the rubber mat in the footwell. Gone. Gone away! Hec gasped, and his foot twitched on the gas involuntarily, and the car lurched backwards, jiggling him. He pulled his foot away, and squirmed back around in the seat to face front, and then he just sat for a long minute in the perfect silence, with the 00:00 winking at him over and again from the dash.

Jesus, the *vividness* of that memory.

That's an unsettling thing, that sort of vividness. Like an acid flashback, only Hector had never tried acid. More like a hallucination than a memory, although Hector had never before suffered from hallucinations. Lucid dreaming. What was lucid dreaming, exactly? He had heard the phrase without ever quite knowing what it meant.

"OK," he said, speaking to the fog, to nobody, "that was weird." He was trying to fix the reality of moment, as Victorian photographers fixed their image with certain chemicals, by dousing it in words, that process of verbalization which, because spoken aloud, externalizes the thing spoken, like a spell. "That was a pretty *fucking* vivid memory flash," he said. But the words sounded tinny in his own ears. "Maybe last night, the quake, the tumble off the balcony," he said, carefully, "have shaken me more than I realized."

The utter solitude of the automobile, with fog all about, was starting to spook him. He positioned himself again to reverse the car, and inched his way back along the driveway.

10

HE HAD NO idea. He had no idea. It occurred to him, as he climbed out of the car and mounted the darkening porch, that he was not hungry. Shouldn't he be hungry? Surely, if he had slept most of the night and all through the next day, shouldn't he be ravenous? Maybe the jet lag had screwed up his body's hunger-instincts.

The lights were on in the house. Hector speculated that his father had a generator somewhere. Either that or the ranch was plumbed into the grid, which would mean that the supply had not been interrupted by the quake. Tom was no longer on the porch, but Hector nearly bumped into him coming through the front door. He was coming back out, carrying out an oil-lamp. "Your dad's here," he said.

"Thanks," said Hector, and stepped inside. Why thanks?

As he walked into the lemon-colored electric light he thought to himself, maybe it's still morning after all, but the fog is so thick it's blocking out the sunlight. Then he thought: or maybe it is a storm. Thunderstorms could darken even bright skies to midnight sometimes. And there *was* a curious electrical quality to the air, as if lightning were forming in the wombs of the black sky above him. But the important thing— he stressed this to himself—the *crucial* thing was that a combination of fog and thunderstorm did not add up to the end of the world. The world had certainly not ended.

He was on the mental bounce from his hallucination, or whatever it was, in the car. Something was disorienting Hector. Something didn't connect, but he didn't want to consider it too carefully, for fear that it would suck him back into this crazy post-apocalypse cultic what-the-fuck that his dad and these wackos were living. Whack-oes. Maybe they were infecting his imagination with their talk of visions. Maybe their weirdness was rubbing off on him. Get out of there, he told himself. Go back to sanity. One more night, and then say goodbye, politely, and drive back to L.A. Leave all this lunacy behind him on the road.

And here was his father, coming through from the kitchen with two of his followers. Hector recognized the faces, but couldn't put names to them.

"Hi Dad," he said.

His father walked up to him, and smiled. "Hec," he said. "Hec. And here we are." And Hector understood that his smile was the expression of a self-satisfaction of such profundity that it almost passed beyond the expressible: to be the prophet of doom who predicted the end of the world and *was proved right*. The gleam in his father's eyes, as much as the provoking elderliness of the man, the thin, lined skin, the liver-spots on his forehead—all this spurred Hector to a small anger. He pulled himself to his full height.

"So the world's still here then," he said, trying to toss the words with an aggressively scornful curveball delivery. But, as ever when speaking to his father, the most he sounded was peevish, as if the extinction of the world were nothing more than one of the conventional treats a father had promised his son, like a ride on the roller-coaster or a new pushbike, and then not delivered.

"Yeah," said his dad. "This piece of it."

"We made it through," said one of his two companions, a woman with a croissant of blonde hair tied neatly to the top of her skull, and a teardrop-shaped nose and droopy blue eyes on the face beneath. Her pale skin was foxed with freckles. And yet the effect of all these elements combining together was one of a rather touching beauty. "We made it through," she said again, pronouncing each word distinctly. Only with the second sentence did Hector place her accent: British. All righty-tighty.

48

"Hey," Hector replied, brightly, "I had a lucky escape last night, Dad. You'll never believe it—when the quake struck I stumbled out of my bed, and I thought I was in the Pasadena house, so I hung a right and—crashed straight through the railing." He widened his eyes, grinned, tried to draw sympathetic hilarity from his small audience. I mean, it was funny, wasn't it? But the three of them simply looked at him, placidly, waiting for him to finish. "Straight through the railing," he went on, "I fell straight down. Luckily I landed on the sofa, there. It broke my fall. Otherwise I could have been hurt."

"Yeah," said his dad, in a mild voice. "We saw the railing had gotten itself busted."

"It wasn't a very sturdy piece of woodwork, Dad," said Hector, trying and again failing to inject accusation into his voice. "I mean, a more sturdy railing and I might not have bust right through. It could have been dangerous."

"Yeah," said his dad, looking past his son. "The house is designed with earthquake in mind. It's designed to flex, you know? Too stiff, and things snap and shear, during a quake." He touched the blonde Englishwoman on her shoulder, and, as if at a prearranged signal, she and the man moved off together, out through the side door into the dining room.

"I got," said Hector Senior, gesturing at two battered wing chairs by the front window, "I got to sit down for a sec. I was up for a fair stretch of the night. I'm not as young as I used to be."

Hector Junior turned, and went over to the chairs, his dad a step behind him. And he did look tired. Spry. But old. He sat with that edge-of-collapse relief of old people settling into comfortable chairs. His skin looked dreary, thin, although his eyes were wide and in constant motion. His face somewhere between agitation and delight. As they sat, Hector Junior tried to lighten the tone between them. "So," he said, brightly, at the old man rather than to him, "you were up in the wee small hours, were you?" But this, of course, was an idiotic thing to say: the quake, whether it was the end of the world or not, would have been enough to keep most people awake.

Hector Senior sat and breathed for a short time; a minute perhaps. He did look tired. Then he said, "We're gonna have a cooked breakfast, all together. You want to join us, for breakfast?"

Hector grinned at this, as if by grimacing he could turn this statement into a shared joke, rather than a symptom of his father's continuing derangement. "Sure," he said, nodding at the black windowpanes, the foggy darkness outside, *"breakfast*, sure."

But his dad seemed to take his words at face value. "OK," he said.

And the two of them sat together, in silence, with nothing to say to one another. "You were out checking the fence, Tom said," Hector tried, to fill the gap.

"Yeah," his dad replied.

"He's carrying a gun, you know," Hector offered. "I saw it. He had it in his lap."

"Yeah," said his dad.

"I just wondered if you knew. That's all."

"You," Hector Senior suggested, "want one?"

"No," said Hector Junior, quickly.

And the silence gushed up between them again. It was Rothko; a great slab of not-quite-straight-edged silence quarried from their lifetime of non-communication. They sat at slight angles from one another. Hector cleared his throat, thought about lighting a cigarette. But his cigarettes were still upstairs, in his room. People were audible, moving around in the dining room. There were noises, too, from the kitchen. Outside it was midnight black. Hector thought to himself: this is absurd. Surely a son and a father can find something to talk about, now that the world has ended?

"I'm sorry about the railing," he said, because his eye had roved over the hallway, up the stairs and to the place where the block of railing was missing.

"That's OK," replied his father.

"I could try and fix it?"

"That's OK."

What else was there to talk about? Perhaps, Hector told himself, I should play the game by his rules. Perhaps I should go along with his end-of-the-world thing. Wouldn't that give me license to ask him shit I never had the opportunity to ask him before? About Mom and her last year alive? About his own childhood? But he couldn't think of what to ask. His eye, restless, swept past his father's form, and looked again through the window. It was divided into six sections, six panes that sat loosely in their slots. One carried a crack as thin as a crane fly's leg, cutting one of its corners, although it wasn't possible to gauge whether this crack had been caused by the quake the night before or had already been in the glass.

"We'll just," his dad said, "sit here 'til they call through breakfast."

Using the word again rubbed Hector up the wrong way; the joke wearing thin. "I was thinking of heading off tomorrow," he said.

"Heading off?" his dad retorted, a look of surprise momentarily evident in his face. "Where?"

"I thought I'd go to L.A. I can book into a motel, or something. Stay a week or so, maybe. Look up a couple of friends. But I really need to be back in Europe before too long."

Hector Senior looked intently at his son for a moment; but then his face relaxed. "Yeah, we all," he said, a little cryptically, "I guess we all deal with it in the way we deal with it."

"Deal with it?"

"That was Janet," he said, his voice louder. "The blonde lady, and her husband Jacob. Janet and Jacob Goolkasian."

"Right."

"She was originally British, but she got citizenship on marrying Jacob."

"I figured that there was an English twang to her speech." Then, because he could think of nothing better to think, "Marj is back in England right now. London, England. I was thinking, I mean, if you don't mind, I was thinking I'll call her. I say if you don't mind because I'd use your phone, rather than my mobile, for an international call. They're not cheap, I know. Not right now, calling her I mean," he continued, trying to calculate the time difference between here and London, and giving up, "not right now, but maybe tomorrow some time. Let her know I got here OK. She and I, we're still real friendly."

"London's dead," said his father. "Marjorie with it."

"Dad, that's not funny."

"Yeah."

And the silence blew between them again, prairie winds down the high street and tumbleweed.

Hector looked at his dad. There was a blockage between them, and Hec thought he knew what it was. It was money, or the way Hector had handled his money. Mishandled. Dishandled. But surely even in the U$ of A there must be more to a relationship than money? What was money anyway? He wondered to what extent the love was still there; the ineluctable magnetic tug that pulled his innards towards his dad, that familiar face. Something. The creases in his face that almost gave Hector the impression that his father's head had once been bigger and was now shrinking like a deflating balloon; and of course the dad he remembered *had* been bigger, fuller, had loomed larger and been packed more tightly with life and command and safety. It was not quite pitiful, although it nearly was, to see him so lined, his hair so thin. The tug was toward protecting him. Or, more exactly, to trying to construct his environment in such a way that he didn't have to face the desolating realization that his old mind was degrading, that he was abandoning reality for this crazy fantasy. But as he was thinking this it occurred to Hector that Dad had already done that for himself: that he had swaddled himself in this isolated ranch with a dozen disciples who believed the same strange thing, that he had effectively inoculated himself against his own reality principle. That was his dad, and it was one of the things that made him austerely lovable in his son's eyes; his complex self-sufficiency. It burnt in the middle of him, a wick converting his flesh and spirit into a flame bright and hard as amber, a flame of will perhaps, or stubbornness, that had in effect burnt down the Pasadena house and immolated his wife's corpse, and lit his way to this Mojave wilderness. But, on the other hand, it was a contaminated love, poisoned in complicated ways, like water poisoned with petrol that gives out to the bright sky both waterish clarity and gorgeous, igneous whorls of rainbow color, so that it becomes impossible to say whether it is the puddle or the contaminant which is the more beautiful. He had sometimes thought that the love he felt for the most beautiful artworks was in at least one sense an *improvement* over the love he felt for other human beings, because it was guilt-free. Standing before the ridged linen on a Cézanne, for instance, was a connection quite removed from the shame, and the self-absorption, and the embarrassment, and the fear that characterized his love for his mom, his dad. Even Marj. And yet it was the same emotion. Wasn't it? That love might break up the world in order to reconstitute it in more aesthetically satisfying combinations, like Turner or Cézanne or Picasso.

He had tried, hadn't he?—and on more than one occasion—
to carry into his actual life. The love a child feels for his parent
is like a child's drawing, boldly schematic and direct but lacking nuance. The love of the adult gains its sophistication from
the stage we all go through when we *deny* that love. It's the
painful separation, the emotional breaking away in order to
come back stronger. How to climb out of the valley? By putting your eye on the peak, of course, except that the only
point of gaining the high point is to turn and look backward,
and the act of turning jars the heel on the loose shingle, and
the body is propelled back down the scree-slope on its ass,
arms up in surrender and the skittering noise and the upthrow
of dust. Dragged back down by the gravitational effect of love
itself. The love you feel for your dad at thirty-eight is the same
horizoning thing, spiced by the same resentments and expec-
tations, as the love you feel at eight; except that the ellipse of
your trajectory away and back has gifted you with an inde-
finable something. It is the difference between an eight
year-old's sketch of a house, and Picasso sketching the house
with an eight year-old's innocency and naivety but the technical skill of a hundred year-old.

Money, money, money. Perhaps it was the time for Hector
Junior to apologize about the money.

> Apologize,
> For *what money buys*
> For *what money buys*
> Apologize,

Wouldn't buy him anything here, even if he had any.

The sounds from the kitchen and dining room were a little
louder; voices raised almost gaily, although the actual words
were indistinct through the wall.

"So," he said, angling for a jocular tone, "this is what happens when the world ends? You sit around in wing chairs chewing the fat with your dad?"

This seemed to amuse Hector Senior. "Yeah," he said.

"Food," cried somebody, and the old man levered himself briskly from his chair.

11

THE TABLE IN the dining room was nearly as long as the room, and all fourteen of the ranch's inhabitants were seated around it. Salad bowls full of hot beans, big oval plates piled with bacon and sausages, a large rack with toast stacked in it neatly like CDs; a full American breakfast. There was a cheery, summer camp atmosphere as people heaped their plates, as they moved freely around the table to scoop up sauces, before taking their seats. Conversation bubbled along. But the overhead lights were on, and the windows were black, giving it an unreal air. The blonde woman, Janet, went through to the kitchen and brought back a huge Perspex jug filled with coffee, and made her way around the table filling everybody's mug.

"Make the most of the toast," Hector Senior called to his son, over the table.

A Latino man whose name Hector didn't know underlined the statement with a half-laugh, half-whoop. "Make the *most*," he said, in a clear, loud voice, "of the *toast*. That's *poetry*, Hector!"

Hector, Hector realized, meant his father to these people. He grabbed himself two pieces of toast, already going cold. Eating breakfast at half-nine at night. It's not normal.

"Yeah, we got a certain amount of bread frozen," Hector Senior was saying, "but it won't last. And then you won't see it again 'til we get some wheat growing."

The high spirits circulating prompted a few people to chip in with extempore rhymes, as if this were a hilarious thing to attempt. "I get a rush to the *head*," said somebody, "with *bread*." "Wheat is sweet," tried someone. "Potater is greater," said a third person, in a cod-Irish accent. The laughter this provoked was genuine, but short-lived.

Hector looked over to where Dimmi was sitting, her placidly beautiful face smiling as she scooped eggs onto two slices of toast. She raised her gaze, and it connected so smoothly with his that it surely meant *something*. Hector sensed a blush chafing his face from the inside. Man, that's ridiculous. But if she believed the world has ended, if she really believed something so SF and crazy, then maybe it would be worth sticking about for a day or two, to see if she makes good on her promise (not exactly a promise, he conceded to himself, but near as dammit) to—how had she put it? Encourage genetic diversity? Perhaps she was the sort of woman who needed to wrap up a readiness to leap into bed with some guy in higher-falutin' speech—

"Hi," said Janet, her face close to Hector's ear. He almost jumped, as if being policed by a mind reader. "Coffee?"

"Yeah, I'd like,' he said, rapidly. "Thanks, yeah. Thanks, black. Black for me."

"There you go," she said, pouring.

"You're British?" he asked, peering up at her from a perspective that gave her face, in profile, a slightly bulging, ugly look: her nose pendulous, the corners of her eyes very droopy, and a barely evident, unhealthy eczematic flush to her pale skin. Her hair, yellow where it was gathered into its bun, was white at the roots where it sank into the flesh at the side of her head like quills.

"That's right," she said.

"I know England," he said. "I've worked there. Whereabouts are you from, in England?"

But he didn't really care where in England she was from. He was sexually curious about the circumstances here, the dynamic that obtained in this particular group of people. Perhaps he was even a little high on the possibilities. If this truly was a cult, if they *actually believed* the world had ended, perhaps the old monogamous sexual morality would be discarded? His glands perked at the thought. The still-adolescent core of his thirty-eight year-old body. What would it be like to fuck this woman? She wasn't as obviously handsome as Dimmi, but there was an intriguing slenderness to her wrists, her neck; a compelling depth to her blue eyes, not to mention the generic appeal of her blondeness. She was married, it was true, but, then again, hey, look, the world has ended. That had to count for something. And he was curious: what would her breasts look and feel like? How far would the small of her back curve to the top of her rear end? Would she have that little pad of fat at the base of her spine, or not? What might her turn-ons be, what would he have to do to make her eager and oily between her legs—stroking? Or biting? Or grabbing her hips? These thoughts occupied no more than a moment or two, but it was enough to stir Hector's dick a little. Then from erotics to the mundane. Adept at negotiating the shift from these mini-reveries to more conventional structures of thought he registered that she had said, "From Brighton, originally," and shifted mental gear to a state of consciousness that would generate small talk.

"Brighton, great. That's the south coast, yeah?"

"That's right."

"That's cool. I stayed in London. I was studying for a time at the Courtauld Institute. You know it?"

"I've heard of it." She stepped back, and moved behind him to offer coffee to the person sitting beside him. Two steps back. To Hector's perceptions, salted by his physical half-arousal, she looked much prettier now than she had before. It occurred to him to say so, to offer her some compliment, to say *you're so beautiful* or something, but of course he suppressed the urge.

Her husband, Jacob, sitting diagonally opposite, was speaking loudly. "I am a Jew," he announced, joyously, "but I am *happy* to eat this bacon! I am happy to eat such a delicious breakfast!" It wasn't clear to whom he was speaking. Perhaps it was a general announcement.

"I was studying History of Art," Hector said, turning back to Janet. But she had moved away. Everybody's cup was filled, and she disappeared into the kitchen, and returned jugless to take her seat next to her husband.

Hector tuned into the conversation the person sitting next to him was having with the person next to them. "The thing with Barbra R. Payne," said this individual, "is that she's a pipsqueak."

"That's too harsh," said the interlocutor.

"Pipsqueak," said the first person again, liking the sound of the word. "But that doesn't matter now, of course. That doesn't matter now."

"She'll have been in... where?"

"Rochester, New York."

"I never went there."

"I tell you where you ought to go, if it's still a place to go," the first person started enthusiastically. Hector's attention wandered.

His gaze moved over the table to where Dimmi was sitting. Tom was next to her. He had placed a proprietorial hand on the middle of her back, and with his other hand he was holding a piece of sausage speared on a fork. This he twirled, like a baton, to emphasize whatever it was he was saying to the person on his right. What a prick. Hector tried telepathically to beam the thought to Dimmi to turn her face his way, to meet his gaze, to lock her thoughts with his thoughts. But she was absorbed in her breakfast. Kismet, he thought to himself. And what if? *Kiss me*—he beamed, trying with a self-consciously goofy seriousness to concentrate his thoughts into a telepathic beam. *Come later to my room and kismet my dickmet.* Nothing, nothing, nothing, but Hec was smiling to himself with his own adolescently random mood. A shallow bowl of sugar crystals was being passed about. Not sugar, those little tic tac pills. Passed like port, *from* the starboard. Hector took one, handed it left.

Hector Senior was addressing him again across the length of the table. "*Eat*, Hec," he instructed his son loudly. "We all got to eat, keep up our strength. We're none of us stepping down from this table until *all* the food is et." Hector smiled wider at his father, but he thought: "stepping down from the table," as if we all were eight years old and sat up high on booster chairs. He reached for the cream, and mixed his coffee from black to ochre. "Sugar?" he said, aloud, to nobody.

"The early morning sun on El Capitan," the person to Hector's right was saying. "Up in Yosemite, you *just* haven't lived if you haven't seen it."

"I saw the sequoias," was the reply. "In Mariposa Grove. But we didn't get all the way up to the valley."

"Which are very pretty, yeah, the sequoias. But the *sheer face* of El Capitan in the morning light, just *sublime*. Like the prow of a huge ship. Or like a vast petrified iceberg."

The interlocutor swallowed a giggle. "I see you mean stonified," she said, "but I thought for a moment you meant afraid."

They both laughed. Oh so *warm*.

"Ladies and gentleman," said Jacob in his booming voice, standing up, and holding his coffee cup at arm's length as if it were a champagne flute. "I'd like to propose a toast—to the new day!"

People laughed, some raised their cups, and a couple looked towards the windows in the far wall. To Hector's surprise, the glass was growing pale and light. The clock over the kitchen door said twenty past nine.

12

IN THE DINING room everybody got to their feet and began going through to the hall and out the front door, leaving the breakfast half uneaten. Hector followed.

They all lined up on the porch, looking out into the swaddling fog as it bloomed from blank darkness into blank brightness; everybody in marvelous high spirits, talking animatedly, cadenzas of laughter among the chatter. The dawn, if that was what it was, was bizarrely accelerated; no more than ten minutes from murk to white. The rapidity became the talking point.

"*Man*, this's fast," said somebody.

"That's gotta mean something," said Jacob.

"I'll tell you what it means," said Tom, pulling himself up a little pompously. "From it we can deduce really interesting things about the shape of the fragment we're riding."

"Hark," said a woman, possibly Janet, in a mocking voice. "Pay attention, ladies and gents."

"No seriously," said Tom, holding his coffee cup up in front of him like a trophy, as if that would lend weight to his words. "No seriously—"

"Mr X-Ray," boomed Jacob, "he can see through the fog that surrounds us!"

"That's *Doctor* X-Ray," said Dimmi. "Didn't spend seven years at Evil-X-Ray School to be called Mister." Hec could see how the laughter lines had being folded into her face. Her smile was enormous.

"Doctor *Tom* X-Ray," said somebody else.

People laughed. Hector didn't understand. None of this seemed funny to him. The fluidity of the group dynamic puzzled him; the correlations of people eluded him. Nevertheless he was grinning, fitting his face to the social environment. He was trying to work out how the sky had grown dark and then light in such short order.

"Oh Daddy not *this* again," said somebody. Hec twitched his grinning face round, couldn't see where the phrase had come from. Or had they said, "Oh Danny not this again"?

"Seriously," said Tom. "Sunset took over an hour; it went on and on... longer than any usual fall sunset at these latitudes. But the sunrise took only ten minutes. So the fragment must have a..." he paused, working it out, "must be spinning west–east, and the land east of us must be sheared quite sharply, a cutaway, where the land west of us must curve much more gently."

"Hurrah for that," said somebody.

"Go west young man."

"Given the smaller size of the planetary fragment," Tom went on, swelling to his public-speaking role, "you'd expect such atmosphere as remains to diffract the light for longer, which should give us longer sunsets."

"I hardly feel," said Janet, "that 'planetary fragment' is the proper way to talk about *our new world*. It's so—"

"No, no, no," said somebody else, agreeing.

"—so *cold* and science-like. Can't we think of a better name?"

"Hectorworld," said somebody. People laughed.

"New Earth."

"New Hope."

"*Que Onda Guero.*"

"Let's call it *Dart*," said someone, very loud. "Or *Plymouth Rock*."

Hector was grinning through all of this, but the idiocy of it annoyed him. Or, more than the idiocy, the way it expressed a sense of community that excluded him. These people had all been together for weeks, or months, and he was not—*of*—them. It gave him a shiver of *ressentiment*, and fueled by his sense of standing outside the perfect circle of friends and lovers he was aware of an alienating perspective. Something dropped down over his usual lens like an autistic filter, and all these people stopped being human beings and became instead annoying automata, whose heads were filled with nothing but porridge and blood and whose actions were governed by computer discs spinning in their guts. The thing was to puncture their self-satisfactions.

"Presumably," he said, more loudly than he intended.

The group fell silent, and looked at him.

"Presumably," he said, "it *is* an atmospheric phenomenon?"

"How do you mean, Hector?" Tom asked.

"Well, I was thinking of the way a really intense thunderstorm will darken the air, almost to night-darkness. A really big thunderhead, black clouds, blowing over in front of the sun. I mean, I guess that's what's caused this darkness at breakfast. Now it's passed on."

The group was silent only for a moment. But then Tom started talking again, and the good-natured buzz resumed. "Another very interesting thing," he was saying, "is that we now have some sense of the rotation speed. And it's fast, and that has some problems associated with it. We need to explain why we're pulling near-as-dammit one gee, according to the spring weight in the barn. The combined gravitational attraction of the," he grinned, "*planetary fragment*, plus the mass of the collision object, taken together should give us a grav of somewhere around two-thirds what we're used to. And the spin, centrifugal effect, ought to make us feel lighter. It's a pretty rapid spin. But here we are. So maybe the collision object pulls almost exactly one gee—that's more than we were thinking, but maybe it does; that, plus the one-fifth gee of the fragments, but that one-fifth canceled out by the rapid rotation. Yeah?"

Some of the group were making their way back inside. The Hispanic guy, what was his name, was engaging Tom in close conversation. Hector saw Vera standing next to Hector Senior. He moved toward her. He needed allies, or a way into the charmed circle of people. He needed a fuck, too. It had been *weeks*. But, actually, as he stepped over, he realized that he wasn't going over toward her for any reason other than that he was drawn to her. It wasn't something within the ken of his conscious mind.

"Hi Vera," he said; and her placid, beautiful face turned toward him. For a breath he couldn't think what to say to her. It was in his mind to say *you're beautiful*, or even *I think I'm falling in love with you*, but that would be way too sappy a thing to say, especially in front of his dad. So he covered his awkwardness with an injection of extra animation into his face. "You'll never guess," he told her, "what happened to me last night, during the quake."

Her head inclined fractionally to the left, but her big eyes were still focused on him.

"I got up, not really awake I guess, and I rushed out of my room—I was in a panic, I guess you could say. And I ran, I told Dad this already, I ran straight through the railing on the balcony up there—straight through and into space!" He wanted to make the story punchier, to exaggerate his own danger, even his own stupidity, to impress her. But her expression, the calm politeness of her attention, did not change. "I mean, was that stupid of me, or what?"

"Yeah," said his dad, genially.

"It was lucky I fell straight onto the couch that was underneath."

The three of them were the last ones outside on the porch. Everybody else had gone back inside. The fog was bright all around them.

"That was," Hector concluded lamely, "some night."

Dimmi touched Hector Senior on the shoulder, a gentle, almost tender touch; and it seemed to recall the old man to himself. He stepped briskly in through the front door, and she followed, leaving Hector alone on the porch.

There was a sound of wind, but the blankness of the fog gave no visual clue to any movement of air, and Hec could feel nothing on his skin. Hector looked out into the nothingness, aware of emotional discomfort, a blend of feeling spurned and feeling stupid that he cared he had been spurned.

A bell sounded from inside the house; an old-fashioned rope-clanger-bell tintinnabulation, like a schoolmarm calling her class in from play. The noise, sounding through the spooky profileless blankness of the fog that surrounded the house, had a spectral quality.

When Hector went inside into the hall to see what was happening, he came upon his father in a different mode, commanding and decisive. Eight people were stood in front of him, and he was giving them tasks. "Pablo, go check whether the computers can be easily rebooted, see how easy that is." "Sure, Hector." "Tom, can you come up with calculations, length of day, orbit, that sort of thing?" "I'll see what I can do, Hector. It won't be much." "Harry and Asher, I need you to assemble the distillation still." And so on. This was the dad that Hector Junior remembered. This was his dad. A warmth diffused through his midriff; a sense that his dad was in control, that he knew what he was doing and he was doing it.

✳

13

THE LIGHT LASTED two hours, and then faded for an hour. After that it was dark for two hours, before the clouds parted—or the irregular chunk of rock spun its sharp edge about in a swift sunrise, Hector still didn't want to commit himself to this crazy belief—or whatever the explanation was—and it was suddenly light again. Hector lived through one of these five-hour cycles. Then he lived through another. He still didn't believe it. That he couldn't concoct an explanation didn't mean that there *wasn't* an explanation. Fog and light shrink-wrapped the house. Darkness came and hid the fog for a short space and then suddenly it was fog and light again. Nocturne. Etude in white.

These microdays fell into their pattern. At no time did the fog lift. To the eye it appeared as static and congealed as ever it did, but to walk through it (perhaps to the second house out back, where most of the dozen disciples slept; or perhaps to one of the barns or storehouses) was to be made aware of the fact that it was in constant motion, stirred by a burly wind. Hector, familiarizing his way about the compound, was hassled and pushed by this wind, and he marveled that so strong a breeze could not disperse the fog.

What did Hector do? Hector slacked. Nothing, again nothing. He moped around the house. The group didn't gather for lunch, although he himself snacked from the refrigerator; but at some point in what his watch told him was evening (or maybe morning) everybody gathered again in the dining room and had supper. The buzz was still palpable among them, excitement like a strong perfume in the air. The whole house still, Hector reflected, had the feel of a summer camp; a jolly adventure. He grinned. He looked left and right as the conversation washed around him, but he was barely registering what people were saying. If anybody addressed him, they had to repeat themselves, sometimes twice or three times. Other people's conversations became deracinated, broken into unconnected phrases and words, a wave washing over him and leaving only discontinuous droplets on his skin. Black box. Pointless. Distillation tank. Mojave. Gull. Cup light yank life. I remember when I was a boy not thirty mile from here. I'm not officer material. Devotion apprenticeship reconstituted potato recon-potato. A mobile phone whose ringtones were downloads of actual birds and of larks and of blue jays. No kidding? *You're* kidding! *No* kidding? No! Yes! Nan's surprising physical weakness effort to connect, tank of at best an imperfect engineering approach to the—Hector's forehead ached slightly.

Ached.

He smiled, he nodded, he smiled. When no meant yes...

After supper some of the group went back to the dorm to sleep. The Hispanic man was called Pablo, and he chatted with Hector for a while. Jet lag was stirring through his frontal lobes like a stiff red-hot wire. He tried to focus on what Pablo was saying, tried to process his passion-flecked syllables, but some lines of chant or song were repeating themselves in his head.

> *See the icedcream* man
> *wit' the icedcream* van
> *wit' the horn that's* honk'n
> *wit' a wham-bang-*bang—

The sky outside was dark. But instead of growing darker, as the twilight should, it rapidly reversed and lightened. Hector was tired. He could not sleep. He really couldn't sleep, despite his tiredness. He stood in the kitchen with Pablo and Janet and a man called Asher, and drank black coffee, and it felt like a normal dawn where Hector had stayed up all through the night. This, he told himself, probably has something to do with my jet lag. I'm sure my jet lag explains this, pretty much.

The kitchen was a long, narrow room, fitted out much as you might expect a ranch kitchen to be fitted out; except that there was a two-meter granite worktop next to the sink at the near end which looked as if it had been beamed in from a Manhattan apartment, and the stove was large, catering size. There was a stone jug filled with olive oil, like Europe, and that grassy olive oil smell. The clock on the wall had a flippant design, its two hands hinged behind a cartoon smiling sun that rocked side to side in the center to mark out the seconds passing.

There was nothing to do. Hector went to his room and lay down, but he couldn't sleep. He got up and went into the toilet. He pissed out a few ccs of coffee-colored urine. When he pissed he placed the flat of his right hand against the wall to his right, and held himself with his left hand.

He wandered about.

He dug out the radio from one of his drawers. It was made of blue semitransparent plastic, such that the circuitry was visible. Those little tiny toy tower blocks and crenellated chips of metal. Through blue, as if through water. A crank-handle unpacked from the back of the device, and a half-dozen turns gave the device power; but fiddle as he could with the tuning knob he could not raise a single station. If the world had ended, he thought, then that was not a surprising thing. Or if the world were still out there, on the far side of the fog, as Hector's heart told him of course it was, then perhaps the weird atmospheric conditions—whatever they were—that played such havoc with the light and dark could also interrupt radio transmissions.

He thought about money and the way it had spoiled his relationship with his father. Such a commonplace thing to happen in a family. So painfully obvious a thing to happen. What money can buy. I don't care too much for—

He thought about money.

Another three hours of light, and two of dark, and the third of the mini-days had passed. If somebody had told Hector that the ranch had been lifted, a hemisphere of rock and dirt with all the buildings on its flat side, into the sky, into the clouds and set it spinning, three hours upside-up, two hours on its back—if they had told Hector that this was why the fog was so implacable, he would have believed them. It was as good an explanation for the fog as any. Which is to say, it was no more crazy than the explanation his father was peddling.

Eventually he fell asleep sitting in the wing chair by the front window in the hallway. He dozed, and woke, and the environment was its changeless self. Because he had not noted the time at which he had dozed off, he had no way of knowing how long he had slept, except only that he did not feel refreshed. The clock in the dining room said six twenty, but that could have been morning or evening. The weirdly reconfigured day–night alternation had thrown, like dice, and come up with brightness outside. The opaque brightness of the fog. But this didn't necessarily mean it was day.

Hector stood. He had to talk to his father. He had to really talk. He wasn't sure what about, but he felt the conviction inside him that if he could just settle something with Dad, then this whole bizarre holiday could be resolved, the fog could lift, he could drive back to L.A., maybe fly to Europe and hook up with Marjorie, resume his life—anything, marry her, have kids, do the normal life things. It hinged, somehow, on having the right conversation with his dad. He addressed himself, his voice echoing in the blue-painted hollows of his own skull: *my poor brave boy*, he said. It's just another thing to work out. Find the key, unlock the door, and your normal happy life is waiting for you, just like the lives that all the other fucking sad-acts get doled out. But he didn't entirely believe this.

As he ranged through the house, he tried to clarify in his own mind what this conversation with his dad would involve, but it was hard to say. It might even, he conceded, have been grounded in some sort of sympathetic magic, as if everything that had happened to him proceeded from the fact of his dad's obsession, end-of-the-world, Jules Verne; and that if this could be countered with a more compelling narrative, then perhaps Hector could simply drive out of this odd new world. Perhaps then he could drive back to the reality he remembered.

He found his father, eventually, upstairs. It was in a room that had been kitted out as a sort of study. It was barely furnished, as every room in this quakeproof house was, denuded of the knick-knacks that might fly about when possessed by the tectonic poltergeist. A roll-top desk was set against one wall, and a single bed set against the other. There was a window, and a single electric bulb dangling like a suicide from the ceiling. The door was ajar. Hector knocked and entered.

Hector Senior was sitting at the desk, but got to his feet as Hector Junior came in.

"And what can I do for you, son?" said the older man, like a provincial attorney greeting a potential client.

"Am I disturbing you, Dad?"

"That's fine."

"I could come back later?"

"That's fine."

"I mean—really—"

"Yeah."

"*Really* not important."

"Yeah. Sit, sit down."

Hector Junior sat gingerly on the edge of his father's bed. Hector Senior did not seat himself. His son felt oddly unhappy, to be sitting on the mattress where his father's old bones lay down to sleep. The thought darted into his head of his dad and Dimmi, naked and wrestling under the blanket of this very bed. Like the tongue of an adder, out, in. Hector cleared his throat loudly, to try and distract himself from this image. He hopped back to his feet.

"The truth is," he said, "I feel like a fifth wheel. You know? Everybody else has things to do. Jobs to do. But I don't want to just drift about. Want to be useful, to somebody. Or something."

"Yeah," said his father.

This was very obviously not talking about the money.

"I mean," said Hector, feeling for the right words, but finding only, "I know I said I was going off, heading back to L.A. But I think I'll stick about a little while. At least until the fog lifts, at least—"

"Yeah," said his dad again, more faintly.

"—until this weird atmospheric shit, stuff," he corrected himself, "blows over. At least until then. I guess that might take a day or two—this fog, Dad, it's something else. I've never *heard* of fog so far inland. It's like a pea-souper out of Charles Dickens. It's like *A Christmas Carol* in the Mojave." He stopped. This wasn't getting to the nub of things. Mentally he tried out a few phrases. Dad, I don't know if I believe that the world has ended, but. Dad, to be honest I really don't accept that the world has been split like a pebble hit with a sledgehammer. Dad, I don't know what is going on, but I know it's not what *you* say it is. It was like practicing grips on a golf club before making a stroke, but the fingers would not settle right. He said none of these things.

"Yeah," said his father, his voice gruff but his eyes sympathetic. "The thing is, Hec, there isn't that much stuff *to* do. For the immediate future we're going to have to sit it out. Until the weather settles, yeah?"

Dad, said the voice in Hector's head, I want you to release me from this lunacy. Dad, the voice said, I'm thirty-eight, I deserve a life of my own. I merit an adult and independent life. I deserve it. Dad, you want me *sorry* about all the money, I know. All those lost *tokens*. But that's—only—money, yeah? This is mucho more-o importante. Dad, this is going to have to stop. I'm not a little kid, let me out of this fog-bound ranch, let me go back to L.A.—you have that power, I am sure. Let me fly back to Europe. For a moment, only fleeting, it flashed upon Hector's inner eye which is the balm of solitude that this whole thing could be a plot—a scheme—a fantastically elabo-rate scam by his dad, with a great fan sunk in the ground blowing artificial fog, such as they use on the movies, to fill the valley. And, who knows, some huge James Bond umbrella swinging on massy pivots to block the sun and simulate night in day; and studded underneath with arc lights to simulate day in night. It was crazy, young Hector knew that. He wasn't stu-pid. He could see it was crazy. But in his state of mind, at that moment, in his dad's room, with the daylight fading once again through the window—in that place and time he was almost ready to believe anything.

"Dad," he said, and cleared his throat, still uncertain how to phrase what he had to say.

But when he looked up at his father's eyes he saw that they were somehow wrong. Something was awry in his gaze, a little defocused perhaps, or misty, as if Hector Senior were staring not at his son but *through* him. Their grayness seemed bluer, stained with shadow.

Then, suddenly, horrifyingly, the old man shouted at his son—absolutely bellowed. He really yelled out loud, like a bull gored. It was a sound of such pure terror to Hector that it struck him like a massive electrical discharge, stunned him, froze him there. His father opened his mouth as wide as it would go, his eyes pulling down at their corners and a look a terror taking over his face and he fucking *shouted*, at the absolute top of his voice, two words: "*IN ME!*"

Hector could not draw his breath. He was pinned, his eyes wider than they'd ever been in his life before, the hairs on his head bristling as with static. It was like an application of essence of terror to the top of his spine. His dad had *never* yelled at him; never once in all his childhood. He had never needed to. His air of command, his manner, was enough to impose discipline without this drill-sergeant shit. Withdrawing his pleasure cut more bitterly in young Hector than any amount of shouting or hitting with a belt. And so, now, the terror of the great noise emerging from his dad's mouth lit panic in Hector's breast. His dad *never* yelled at him, no matter how naughty he had been. This was absolutely fucking un*pre*cedented. The dynamite blast of it pulled Hector Junior's own mouth open, and he almost screamed right back, although he didn't.

His father threw his arms out. Straight out. *Believe* me, he could not have been acting in a more uncharacteristic manner. His arms flew straight out, as if pulled back doll-fashion by an invisible cord at his back. He yelled again, "*i'me*," and staggered back against the wall. As he slumped to the floor, his limbs straight out like a starfish, he yelled again, and Hector realized what he was shouting: *Dimmi*. It chimed with Hec Junior's own inchoate desire and guilt, as if his father were screaming up a tower of flame in accusation and rage. As if he had gazed with clear telepathic gaze into his son's sordid imaginings, and that these had stapped him and bowled him literally over.

"Dad?" Hector croaked. He could not breathe properly. A terror was in him. His heart scurried in his chest like a spider at the destruction of its web. He had never seen his father like this. Downslumped the da. C'est fort étrange.

And Hector Senior was folded now into the coign of wall and floor, his legs straight out, his arms straight out, his eyes bulging like eggs. Oh the color was yanked clean *out* of his face. It occurred to Hector that his father was dying, expiring right before his eyes, and the thought brought a shuddering breath into his lungs. "Dad!" he cried. But he did not move, did not step towards his father's form.

Dimmi came silently through the door. She pushed past Hec, and swooped down upon Hector Senior with a practiced ease, scooping him and moving him smoothly into the recovery position on the floor. She loitered a moment, bent over him, her face near the floor, checking his airways, and then she rose to her feet.

"My God," said Hector, feeling tears pushing behind his eyeballs. He blinked, blinked again. He blinked again. "My dad."

Dimmi came over to him, stood right in front of him. "It's an epileptic seizure," she said, in a calm voice. "Do you understand?"

Hector's heart was thrumming. He nodded, oh, and his eyes were wide, wide. Hector Senior was on the floor, lying on his side. Hector Senior was shuddering very slightly, as if cold, except that the shudders were oddly synchronized in his arms and legs. His eyes were shut and his mouth tight, with a pearl of spittle in the exact middle of his lips. Hector thought of a dreaming dog. "Christ," he said, vehemently. Not so much speaking the word as venting it at high pressure. "He's had them before?"

"Yes," said Dimmi.

"Jesus, I didn't know. I never knew—*this*. He never had them when I was younger. When he was younger. I mean— Jesus. How long ago did these start?"

"What you can do," said Dimmi, in her mild voice, "is fetch a *glass of water*. He'll want to speak as soon as it passes off, and his mouth may be dry."

"He'll want to *speak*?"

"He's perfectly comfortable. There's no danger. As long as he doesn't bite his tongue, and he hasn't bitten his tongue. It'll pass off in a little while."

"How long?"

"He'll want to speak," said Dimmi, "when he comes round, to tell us what he's seen."

Hector sagged back, sat on the bed again. Dimmi returned to the twitching figure on the floor, and sat herself beside it, folding her long legs beneath her ass in one graceful movement. She laid a hand on his trembling hip, and then she just sat there.

Hector did not want to look at this scene. This had nothing to do with his father. Hector did not want to see his father looking like this, shimmying unconscious on the floor. He got to his feet and stepped through the door, thinking of going back to his own room. But once he was in the little dim corridor outside, the stretch of unlit passageway that led to the upper hall, he stopped. He leaned his left shoulder against the wall. This was not a good thing. His heart rattled a devil's tattoo in his breast. He brought up a hand to his brow, as if to hold it in place, physically to prevent the thoughts of blame—for if his father had *such* power? To read telepathically in Hector's mind his thoughts, doubts, the Hollywood mist-generator sunk in the scrubland out back somewhere, the Bond villain mechanical parasol? Had such thoughts prompted a fucking *epilepsy* in his father? "Steady," he told himself in a voice so low it was almost a sob. "Steady, you're a little overtired, is all."

Or, hallucination. Something in the water—something pumped into the air, the wood of the house steeped in *something*, that prompted this mad mass-hallucination of sunset and sunrise over five hours. He was thinking it was all

74

happening: it was not all happening. Those little pills, like white rice grains, that they kept taking all the time. And who knows what else was cached in the food, what else we all swallowed with the coffee? Dad's nebulous "dealings" with ex-hippies and ex-drugsters and ex-weathermen and ex-dreamers over the last decades—had he acquired the wherewithal to convey his own fantasy of the end of the world to his little coven? This new possibility, in its very plausibility, steadied Hector. That would explain so much. That would surely Occam's-razor through the cord binding him there. He would get into his hire car and drive very slowly through the fog, inch along the road, put a hundred yards between himself and his father, two hundred, five hundred, a mile, ten. And slowly the poisonous chemical effect of the *something*, whatever it was, would wane, its little claws would retract their hold on his neurons, and the world of Southern California would reassert itself. He would drive clear-headed into L.A.

But the light-levels outside the house had now sunk to a midnight darkness. There was an electric light, somewhere in the front hall, but only wisps of light found their way to the base of this first-story corridor, where Hec was standing; an ambient gleam just enough to throw a grainy indistinctness across everything.

14

THE DOOR OPENED behind him, and Dimmi came out. Hector pushed himself away from the wall to stand straight up. "How is he?" he asked. "Is he OK? How is he doing?"

"He has recovered a little," she said, in a voice modulated to match perfectly the crepuscular half-light of the corridor. She put a hand on Hector's chest, right there, palm flat against his ribcage. "I helped him to his bed, and he's lying there. Did you get a glass of water?"

"Was it, like, a vision?" Hector asked.

"He has not said much. Sometimes he needs a little while to gather himself after an episode. He'll tell us shortly."

"I," said Hector, "had one myself."

Dimmi's beautiful face, made more beautiful by the semi-darkness, looked calmly at his.

"I had a vision," he said. "I think it was a vision. I got in my car, yesterday or the day before, and drove to the gate. But I couldn't drive, because the fog was so intense, I didn't think it was safe." He stopped, disconcerted a little by the absolute focus of her gaze. She did not drop a comment into the pause. "So," Hec went on, "so I decided to back the car along the drive, and turned in the driver's seat. Then I saw—or, *saw* doesn't do it justice, it was a much more immersive experience than just seeing. I re*visited*," and again he stopped, because having built up this account he was afraid of the anticlimax of reporting what it was he had seen.

"What did you see?" she asked.

"You've had them?"

"I've had three visions," she replied, in a level voice. "Since living with Hector."

"What did you see?"

"Tell me yours," she prompted.

"I saw myself, or rather I *was* myself, wandering along West Union in Pasadena. I was visiting home during my first year at Yale. It was the spring, a beautiful day, and I think I was going to the Norton Simon. The museum. I say I think I was going there, because that wasn't the point of the—" he was still unhappy with the word, but he couldn't think of another, "—the vision."

"And what was the point of it?"

He shrugged. "Just the vividness of being there. The trees set in their little concrete rings right in the sidewalk, with all their furry foliage, straight up and down like lances. Like corn cobs when the corn's been bitten off them. The blue of the sky, like in a Courbet canvas. Music playing inside a shop as I walked past. The traffic. And I was thinking of a poem I'd memorized, only not memorized it very well, because I'd hoped to use to it get this girl I knew into—to use it as a romantic prop, you know, to set the mood on this date. And thinking how Pasadena wasn't as vivid a place as I'd gotten in the habit of thinking it was, during the New Haven winter. I mean, I used to sit in New Haven and imagine that California was all bright blue and sunshine, and when I got back I was always struck by how much less vivid it really was." He stopped. Was that all there was to it? "I'm not expressing myself very well," he added, lamely. "It wasn't the *content* of the vision, if you see what I mean. It wasn't that. I don't know." She was still standing with her hand on his chest, a gesture somewhere between reassurance and a more sensual sort of intimacy. He reached up with his own right hand and placed the fingers there, pressing her hand to his heart. "What do you think it means?"

"Why do you assume it *means*?" she asked, mildly.

"Well, doesn't it?"

She stepped closer, in that enclosed space, such that only an inch separated their bodies. Hector smelt again the almost candy smell that came from her hair. Her eyes reflected more of the attenuated ambient light than the rest of her: her clothes, her hair, even her skin seemed matt, to soak the light in, but her eyes were clearly visible, as if lit with some element within them.

"It," she said, and Hector knew at once to what she was referring, "is interested in our memories. *I* think. It often prompts them; a matter of stimulating certain areas in the brain." Then, perhaps registering some barely conscious flinching in Hector, she swayed away from him a further inch, and slipped her hand from his to let it dangle at her side. "I think so, anyway. Surgeons operating on the brain," she continued, a little stiffly, "report it a simple matter of applying an electrical current to portions of the brain to result in the conscious patient experiencing intense and vividly experienced memories."

"Is that what *your* visions were?" Hector pressed, sensing that the intimacy between them was fading and wanting to reignite it. Wild ideas rushed through his mind of reaching over and kissing her, of grabbing her in a tight embrace. But that would not be right, that would not work, no. No meaning no.

She took a step further away, until her own back was against the opposite wall. "Some of the visions are of the past," she said, in a dull reportage tone of voice. "Some of the present and some of the future. Hector, I mean your father of course, he has the most complete visions." She turned back to the door. "Bring a glass of water from downstairs," she ordered, and moved back inside his father's room. And cursing himself inwardly for the missed chance, and for all the missed chances, every single one of them, Hector went uncertainly through the dark and down the stairs and into the kitchen.

TWO

1

So, THIS IS what happens after the end of the world. There is a lot of hanging about. There are meals, where everybody eats together, and there is a camaraderie among survivors. The initial euphoria which had buoyed everybody up, the helium of apocalypse, the hilarity of doom, that dissipates in the inevitable, ordinary, day-to-dayness of the world's ending. There is food from stores, and fourteen people eating two large meals a day, and snacking from time to time, all of which makes surprisingly little impact on the supplies. Hector Senior had thought ahead. Wise man. Looking ahead, frontwise, forward. There is water to drink, and even bathe, although the group agrees to limit washes and to reuse bathing water.

There's this little pill. It's cute as a tic tac. It is white and has no flavor at all.

There's coffee, the real ink, not instant. It gurgles through this black plastic box and into this Perspex jug. Young Hec takes the metal coffee filter from the machine and spanks its bottom against the side of the sink until it coughs up all its old grounds. There's water to rinse it in. Plenty!

There is electricity from the generator, and fuel to run the generator, although Hector Senior decides after a week to ration the electrics and so people grow used to the natural pulsings of darkness and light. This accelerated rhythm of dawn and dusk. Either they stop what they are doing and rest, or nap, until the light comes round again; or else, if they must be active in the dark, if the need for light is a pressing one, then they light candles. But it soon becomes wearisome to bother with candles, and people grow used to the dark. The goose drank wine. Swallow this, and beer is a good swallowant, swallow-agent, a good swallowfacent. And *down* we go—

One thing that people do, one of the sorts of things that of course people are going to do, is to impose order on the new environment, to the best of their various abilities. Day, dusk, night, sudden dawn: the whole cycle happens in a little under five hours. Five of these periods, which are called "dawns" to distinguish them from pre-end-of-world days, make a "day": a twenty-five hour day: five days. Monday to Friday, each twenty-five hours, and one day "Saturday" a truncated twenty hours, and then the week begins again. Every few months another hour is dropped, on an ad-hoc basis to keep the pattern whole. Nobody mourns the passing of Sunday. For some on the ranch the old concept of days becomes altogether irrelevant. They adjust easily into a new circadian rhythm: wakefulness and work for three hours; a nap for two—a new constant progression, turning their lives into one long day interspersed with multiple naps, rather than the older manner of humanity, gorging on wakefulness for sixteen hours and gorging on sleep for eight. Others do not find this transition possible; they sleep through a dawn and a half, and wake irritable because a twenty-five-hour day simply does not mesh with their old habits of flesh. Hector Junior is one of these people.

He finds himself awake an hour before an evening dawn, or during a mid-morning period of darkness. Hector can no longer even translate the time into the old pre-apocalypse horology. *C'mawn butterbelly, get with the program*! But he cannot. Many in the ranch are asleep, slumped in chairs or dropped like hypnotized subjects onto beds fully clothed. For those who have adapted, sleep is a near-instantaneous thing; no tossing and turning, no shuffling under the bedclothes getting comfortable, no mulling over thoughts while staring at the ceiling. Some fall asleep before their bodies are prone on the mattress; or they sit down and are instantly asleep like narcoleptics. Those remaining awake, the minority, at first tiptoe around the sleepers; but experience has taught them that there is no need for this courtesy, the nappers are deeply in. They lie like drunks, their eyelids bulging and twittering with veiled rapid-eye movement—for dreaming comes on much more quickly to these new sleepers, after no more than ten or fifteen minutes sometimes. Then, when the windows lighten to their foggy brightness, the sleepers awake; sometimes grogged, but often fully awake, snip, snap, up. Hector's father is one of the new sleepers. Dimmi too.

In fact, after a month or so (for old-style calendars are hard to use precisely; and perhaps it was less; and it felt longer) there are only three of the group stuck in the old-world grooves. Those three: Janet, a man called Leo and Hector Junior. They cannot sleep in what their bodies stubbornly insist on believing is "the day"; so they move like ghosts through the darkness. They light candles, coaxing the liquid nubbin of flame from a match or lighter onto the singed wick until the almond-shaped and almond-colored flame swells and takes. Hector Senior has decreed (increasingly dictatorial, is Hector

Senior) that it is a waste of electricity, which is to say of generator fuel, for the lights to be turned on for the benefit of only three people. Everyone else, after all, is asleep, and the sleeping need no light. It is accepted, though unspoken, that in time these three will adopt the new sleeping patterns too. But Hector has tried it; he can't do it. So he is condemned to walking through the darkness by candlelight, at a loose end.

He smokes carelessly at first, but then it occurs to him that he will soon exhaust his supply. Nobody else in the ranch is a smoker. There are no cartons of cigarettes in the storehouse, packed tight like gold-tipped bullets into their cardboard cartridges. The exquisite cellophane on each pack, like a brand-new pack of cards, and like the first unsheathing of a new pack of cards; pulling that cleanly off was always for Hec somehow touched with gorgeous possibility: the open-ended future. But now—count the days 'til they're all gone. Angrily, Hector is reduced to hoarding his last packet; to smelling and fingering the unlit tubes of white rather than wasting them in a smoke; to allowing himself one a day, and then one a week. The boredom is made much worse by his withdrawal.

So what do people do after the world's ending? People play cards. One or two strum at guitars, or perfect elaborate fingerpicking runs up and down folksy arpeggios, like a sort of aural knitting, generating nothing, nothing at all but air, and sound waves, and the spread of a soap bubble of sound that dissipates. The radios pick up nothing but the sore-throat grumble of ethereal static. The phones do not ring. It feels like a retreat, as if the fourteen of them have founded a new religious order and foresworn all contact with the outside world. But the outside world is surely there, nevertheless. This is what Hector Junior persists in believing.

From time to time there are tremors in the earth beneath them. These never have the severity of the original quake, but they shimmy the floor as you try and walk over it, or they wobble your knees as you stand, or they give the bed you are lying on a hearty shove. As the months pass they decrease in frequency.

Hector Senior's visions, on the other hand, increase in frequency and intensity over the same period. The buzz circulates. Haven't you heard? "*It*" communicates with him in his dreams. Well, half the time in his dreams, half the time *it* comes to him with more vivid and detailed immediacy during an epileptic seizure. These seizures increase in frequency, and Hec don't like it. Hector Junior cannot adjust his view of his father to accommodate this shuddering, tight-faced invalid. The fits are too redolent of physical vulnerability as he surfaces from one with a heave and shudder. *I'm sorry about the money, Dad.* A stony, buried, anthracite quality to the pupils of his eyes. Opening his mouth to reveal a cat's cradle of spittle linking lip to lip. He comes to with a shuddering moan low enough and sensual enough to remind Hector, obliquely but horribly, of sexual release. These are not the ways he wants to think of his father. Le vrai mort, la vraie morte: e, not e, not sure. He hurries from the room if his father's eyes glaze, in that distinctive manner of somebody withdrawing from the conscious world. He tries never to be around when the old man flips to the floor with locked limbs. But there are occasions when he isn't able to absent himself, for whatever reason. Time when he must attend: must help maneuver the stiff, trembling body of Hector Senior into recovery position; must sit with him as he mumbles and shudders; must help him to sit up and take a drink of water as he opens his frothy mouth and moans. On one occasion the moan caught exactly the cadence of the "o" that the Big Bopper sang as the intro to "Chantilly Lace," *hell-o-o bab-ee*; and ever after Hector cannot disconnect his memory of that song from this uncomfortable experience of nursing his fitting dad.

It is widely known that Hector Senior prefers Dimmi to attend to him at these moments. Dimmi's calm gaze and confident stride have taken to themselves a fuller and a stronger aspect. There is a little more bounce in her walk, a prouder set to her face. She is the uncrowned unofficial queen of this group. Her partner, Tom, is increasingly lost among the technical equipment, trying to delineate the shape and nature of their catastrophe, of their orbit, of the object buried beneath them. Dimmi reigns. Hector Junior has long since abandoned himself to a complete and a hopeless love. He has never loved a woman so completely (and he has loved many women, or thought that he did). He thinks about her all the time. He daydreams, and night-dreams. But erotic reverie, or sentimental imagining, or obsessive working-over in his mind of all the contours of her body, all the features of her personality—all this chafes him up against the thought of Dimmi fucking his father, and that thought brings on him a physical nausea, actual sickness and pain in his gut. Sometimes, in his room, trying to sleep during the evening pre-dawn darkness, or else awoken by the middle-of-the-night brightness, he will roll from side to side like a whale in pain, begging himself to stop thinking about her and his dad naked together, unable to stop thinking about that. And he will moan too, startling himself with the closeness of his noise to his father's post-epilepsy groaning.

Chantilly Lace and a pretty face

Dimmi sitting cross-legged on the floor, Hector Senior's head in her lap, cooing to him. Hector touches the base of the door with his toe, and it swings closed, and the scene is shielded from his sight. Some things aren't supposed to happen. He believes this, because it carries with it the unspoken correlative that some things *are* supposed to happen, and that thought includes within it a grape-seed of hope. But it's all a game he is playing with himself. His heart aches. His heart has suffered a greenstick fracture, and it hurts the way a broken bone hurts, and he's *nearly forty years of age*! But the simple thought of her. Dimmi. His young and copycat heart throws its own epileptic mini-fit when he sees her.

A wiggle in her walk and a giggle in her talk

The seizures themselves have started to acquire an almost religious, or at least a ritualistic, quality in the eyes of the group. In the period following one of Old Hector's epilepsies they all gather in the dining room of the main house; and, sometimes, the patriarch is guided in to sit at the head with a cup of coffee, or a beer (depending on which dawn has just passed) he will tell them what they need to know. I saw the present. I saw the future. I saw what "it" is doing. The visitor, the "it," the cannonball, the bullet, the meteor (yeah, they've names for it) is putting out feelers, growing into the fractured granite and cooling magma like a tuber. Hector Junior doesn't like the thought of this. *It* is growing, or rather expanding: its extraordinary density is relaxing, like a long breathing out. There will be tremors. The world has not finished being refashioned. Long faces all around the table, a few ponderous nods, people digesting this new holy writ. Where will it end? How will "it" refashion the world? This has yet to be vouchsafed.

That makes me act so funny
Makes me spend my money

Hector ponders whether one of the more palatable things about his father's new cult is precisely its lack of a theologico-mystical component. "This thing," Old Hector announces, not once but several times, "I don't think it's God. I take it to be a purely material thing. Yeah, I guess it's an object in the universe just like we are." And although several of the group have religious-obsessive backgrounds (Pablo spent years as a ferociously believing and

85

proselytizing Mormon; Amiot had been an evangelical Christian, screaming at others on the Toronto sidewalks that they *must* be *born* again) they all accept this materialist pronouncement. This end of the world has not been engineered by God, it seems. Or if perhaps it was, then God has not intervened *personally* to bring it about, He has harnessed natural forces, as He always does.

Hector's own constitutional atheism finds balm in this thought. But, then again, this eventuality, this world's ending, this red day, has been so thoroughly anticipated by religious discourse, and those discourses are (of course) so well adapted to human habits of thought, that it becomes hard to rid oneself of a quasi-religious, almost unconsidered, almost superstitious belief that providence, or the supreme being, is shaping events. And Hector Senior is Its prophet.

The fog does not lift. It's foggy as Old London town. That's where Janet is now, a town older than America. But then they are all of them older, far, than this entire new world.

2

THE FOG IS so complete it baffles sight. And then there is the actual mystery itself, the nature of the thing. The group, moving about between the two main buildings, making their way like confident and experienced blind men and women through the fog, will break into twos and threes from time to time to speculate on this. It is, clearly, key. Hector pictures a black cannonball, or a sphere of perfect oily blackness, with shudders and ripples of dark blue and cupric-green, like the breast feathers of pigeons, fleeting across its black surface. It occurs to him that he has lifted this image from a science fiction film he once saw, long ago, before the world's ending: a Michael Crichton film, he thinks. It depresses him that his imagination is so secondhand. It is an old sore in his thoughts that his natural affinity is for popular culture and not the higher arts: that when he closes his eyes and tries to recall the exact organization of details in a Gauguin canvas he finds he cannot; yet he can visualize Disney's Simba, or that little orange-white Nemo fish, down to every last little detail. He can no longer remember even the themes and tunes of the great symphonies he used to listen to, though he had concentrated hard upon them, trying almost to breathe them in as embodiments of European culture. Yet his head is continually jangling unprompted with pop songs. How much does this lessen him?

The tendency among other members of the group is to talk in quasi-mystical terms. Their understanding still inflected by the unspoken religious assumptions they all, in one form or another, shared. A stocky Bostonian called Raymond says: "I think of it as lacking dimension. A black hole lacks dimension altogether, yet it has mass, and acts in the world."

"It's putting out feelers," points out Pablo. This information has after all been revealed through Old Hector's visions.

"But even *feelers*," says Raymond, unwilling to let go his vision of a material object lacking material features, of a zen-like contradiction-in-terms, a notion which satisfies his subconscious yearning for a godlike flavor to the whole circumstance. "What are they? That's the point. We don't know what Hector means by *feelers*."

Hector Junior tends to think of tubers growing under the ground, of bindweed roots fat as a man's arm, reaching and connected and branching off again, filling the space of the old world entirely. He thinks of sinking a gardener's fork into soil you believe healthy and rich in order to lever out a well-grown dandelion, say, and wrenching a great glob of earth, the earth dry and falling away, and in fact you hold on your fork a head-sized tangle of roots, albino and ropy. That's what he thinks of. The burial of the dead is handing over corpses to the whims of these sorts of roots. He's known that since he was a kid. It's deep knowledge in more than one sense. The thought that he would lie in the coffin until these nerveless, restless feelers broke through and knitted themselves wholly around his head and face—that was so horrible a thought to him, so upsetting, that it might even (when he was younger) make him cry. Burn me, rather, he thought. That's what I want, cremating is what I want. Those feelers of flame whose action is so much more rapid than the hideous vegetable tentacles, orange and yellow wrapping themselves closely around my sightless head and squeezing it with such suddenness that it is reduced in moments to hot ashes.

He doesn't say any of this, of course, *much* too down, too morbid for the conversation.

"Feelers," Raymond continues, "could be lines of energy spreading through the earth. Couldn't they? I picture it as skeins of energy, a *web* of energy, binding the world together and making it safe, preventing it fragmenting further. That's what I think."

"Oh but we *don't* know," says Pablo, his small, pugnacious eyes flashing, bright umlauts to his chunky nose, "we don't know it's *benign* like that. Do we now? No, we don't. You're *assuming* it's benign."

"Surely," Raymond offers, making an impatient gesture with his left hand, "I think we can assume that. It's not just a *mindless force of destruction*, after all."

"It," Hector chips in, tentative, "*did* destroy, though, I mean—"

"Well, yes. *But*—it also created. If it was a mindless force of destruction, then why did it contact some of the inhabitants of this world? Why does it communicate with Hector, even now? It's smart, it's intelligent, it wants to reach us, to bond with us. It *loves*..."

This is too much for Pablo. "That's crazy," he says, with passion. "We can't *know* that. That's pure guesswork, you're just guessing."

"I believe it," Raymond says, doggedly. "I feel it."

"I don't. It's not the God of Love, this thing. It's Shiva, more like, the shatterer of worlds. It's the end."

"I wish people wouldn't talk that way," says Raymond, peevishly, as if there were still a widespread population in the world, and as if this population were given to expressing these sentiments as a general and odious bigotry. "It's just being negative. That's *all* it is. We can't get through this if we surrender to negativity. Why believe the negative? Why *not* believe the positive? Why not believe that it feels love, that it is drawn to us—that it warned us of its inevitable collision *because* it loves us?"

"Who says inevitable?" fences Pablo. "I don't believe it was inevitable. I don't believe we can just sweep under the carpet so many billions dead."

This thought is a conversation-snuffer. Billions. Fancy! The three of them sit in silence for a while. But Raymond, with his short-trimmed apricot-colored hair, and his narrow, precise little features, cannot surrender his belief in the benignity of this thing. "But you can't explain why it should *contact* us," he insists, after a dutiful pause to register the terrible loss of life that was involved in the ending of the world. "You haven't explained that."

"Who knows?" says Pablo. "There could be several explanations." But the heat has gone out of him now. He is no longer so energetically keen to win the argument. And the truth of the matter is that he, Pablo, in his gloomy apperception of events, can no more generate *real* feeling for the billions of dead than can Raymond, in his sunny look-to-the-future positivity. Like all men, Pablo has gone through life knowing rather than in any sense *feeling* that billions crowded the same stage he himself occupied. He had never really let the fact of the teeming multitudinousness of humanity penetrate to those parts of his brain where his truest feelings were stored; for to do so would naturally capsize his mind. Accept instead the sort of understanding that flows around without touching the core emotional belief we all share, really: that only oneself and one's immediate acquaintances truly exist. Since those billions had for him always occupied that spectral Schrödinger's-cat existence of alive-but-not-alive, it is hard now for him fully to translate his understanding just because they are dead-but-not-dead. It all amounts to much the same.

"I wonder," says Hector, again tentatively, "whether it *needs* us, in some way? You know what Tom thinks—" But he hardly needs to go on; because everybody knows what Tom thinks, the physics major, the rationalist interpreter of Old Hector's darker visions. Young Hector carries on anyway. "Tom thinks that its collision with the world is part of its life cycle; that it passes through space, perhaps for unimaginable lengths of time, accreting, slowly drawing in matter to itself until it is large enough to effect a suitably destructive collision."

"Hm," says Raymond, unimpressed with the loneliness of this notion. It doesn't sound correct to him, not because a creature of love would be incapable of destroying a world (for we all know the heat of love can be a wild and destructive thing), but rather because he doesn't think a creature of love could exist so long in the wilderness of vacuum without going mad. Tens of thousands of years of solitary sailing. Or perhaps it is mad?

Would explain a lot.

"So I was thinking," Hector says, "that maybe it—I don't know." He can't think how to phrase this without it sounding like something he is parroting from an old episode of *Star Trek*. He casts about for a way of putting it that would sound truer to actuality, but the discourse has been too thoroughly overgrown by sci-fi. "Maybe it seeks out worlds with intelligent life upon them," he says. "That could be why it sends out visions, it's testing the waters. So to speak. Casting out a net to see if there are minds to snare. It needs us," he says again, lamely.

"How do you mean?" prompts Pablo. "How do you mean it needs us?"

Hector is thinking, without any exactness, in Discovery Channel mode; of wasps that seek out particular animals in which to lay their eggs, or flowers that grow into the shapes of particular breeds of insect so as to attract them and pass on their pollen. But he cannot think of any specific examples. His natural history education has been too televisual. There are no *names* in his head. He has only a nebulous impression of the workings of the natural world, of the boggling *specificity* of its interaction: insect fitting to flower, parasite to host, predator to prey. So he says, "Maybe it's like this. Maybe the life cycle of this—thing—needs intelligent life. It needs to collide with planets to bury itself, to…" He is going to add *lay its eggs*, but that's too maggoty and unpleasant a thought, so instead he says: "propagate itself. But maybe it needs to preserve intelligent beings upon the planet to help fling its next generation back into space to continue the process." Having articulated this notion, Hector finds that it doesn't sound as stupid as he was worried it might. "Maybe," he goes on, "it'll pass on knowledge to us, through the visions, or whatever. Knowledge about how to build rockets, or spaceships, so that we can send new seeds into the cosmos."

Raymond likes this. "It *could* be," he says, nodding earnestly. "Yes. Couldn't it, though? It could be a mutually beneficent arrangement. Like a bee and a flower—the bee gets the pollen, the flower gets to pass its seed on to another plant."

"And the pollen is...?" asks Pablo. He is scowling. A hand-washes-hand universe? No, no, no-meaning-no.

"The knowledge that it passes on to us," says Raymond immediately. "Don't you see? Can't you—who knows what it may be about to teach us! It could give us the knowledge to become interstellar creatures. Giant starships, communities in space, the next phase in human evolution! This could yet turn out to be the necessary disaster that propels man to the stars!" But he senses that he has gone too far, and rests three fingers on his upper lip, covering his mouth. "All I'm saying," he concludes, speaking less distinctly, "is that we don't yet know."

Hector doesn't know anything.

There are times when he is so completely absorbed by the habits of living of the group that he no longer even questions the idea that the world has indeed ended, that they are all now living on a rapidly spinning chunk of the former globe. All of them sitting round the main table, monochrome contour maps and peacock's eyes and Jupiter-spots in the grain of the wood, and they pass a cup around between them. In the cup are the pills. Crystalline caterpillar eggs. One each, wash it down with wine. Nothing sacramental about it. Did you say Sacramento? I lived in Sacramento. Puddle. Hey, I spotted it from. Does anybody recall the coverage of the Chernobyl thing? Did. I spotted it from the upstairs window. No. The place was really called Chornobyl, not Cher but Chor, not Cher-Chor but. The goose drank wine. How might a goose drink wine?

And down it goes.

But in more solitary moments he reverts to his skepticism. Lying in bed during the dark–bright–dark–bright passage of what used to be the night he stares at the ceiling and is astonished that he has actually started thinking like the rest of them.

The end of the world? A tremor in the earth and some fog surely cannot add up to the end of the world. At such moments he
rehearses all the explanations that do not involve apocalypse.
Collective hallucination. Bizarre atmospheric and geological
freak. Elaborate hoax. He revolves the notion of the new environment as *The Truman Show*, in truth nothing more than a
huge reality-TV game. And hidden cameras dotted about the
houses, and their every response to their new life watched by
millions. They were all chloroformed on Hector's first night at
the ranch, and helicoptered to an L.A. studio lot, and *hence* the
fog, to disguise the fact that their world is now wholly artificial.

Is *everybody else* in on the hoax, except for him? Cher, chor.
Cher, chor.

The dawn comes up as rapidly as arc lights flipped on and
warming to their brilliance. Hector gets up. He has slept poorly, and now he faces another day of meandering, or hanging
about, of nothing at all. This is the way the world ends.

3

IT IS AN hour before an evening dawn. A new day, probably a
new week, perhaps a new month. Who knows? Most of the
group have dropped into their instant slumbers, in chairs, on
beds, some even curled on the floor. Janet is sitting in the wing
chair in the hall by the front door, and Hector sees her there
from the landing. The candle on the table is blowing out a
fragile bubble of light that only just encloses her. He comes
down the stairs, picking his way carefully from shadowy step
to shadowy step, barefoot-in-rock-pools walking, who knows
what poisonous spines are out of sight in the black shadows to
stab the feet. He goes over to sit with her.

"I'm just summoning up the courage to go back to the dorm," she says, looking at the black windowpanes. "It's always a little spooky in the darkness. The fog makes the darkness so complete, doesn't it?"

"I know what you mean," Hector says.

"Darker than dark. It's windy, too. It's gusting strongly today."

He nods. This means that droplets of rain are knocked out of the mist, such that moving through it can leave a person soaked very thoroughly. Many drops of water are visible adhering to the far side of the black glass, quivering slightly, sometimes dribbling downwards to disperse against the wooden frame at the bottom.

Now that he and Janet and Leo are the only ones stuck in the old sleep pattern they have started spending much more time together. Janet's husband is asleep in their room in the dorm right now. Leo is there too, in his room, probably awake, probably looking at the black blank windows too.

"I tell you what," says Hector. "Let's have a glass of wine. Why not? There's a bottle opened in the kitchen. It's evening, as far as our bodies are concerned, yeah? Let's have some wine. Why?"

"That would be nice," she replies. "Did you say why?"

"I mean *why not*? I sort of swallowed the last word." One nervous snicker, *chor*!

They take themselves and the candle through to the dining room and sit, just the two of them, at the big table. A wooden mirror-candle burns its wooden mirror-flame underneath the actual candle. The wind outside rattles the panes of glass in their frames, but gently. Hector fetches two glasses, and pulls the plastic stopper from the half-drunk bottle, and pours two glasses with a *gulglc* and a *shloguloc*.

"Thanks," she says.

"You're welcome. Hey, should we go get Leo? I could run over and get him, see if he wants to join us?"

"Just the two of us," says Janet, looking directly at him with her droopy blue eyes.

Hector feels something. His stomach tingles. "OK," he says. "Just the two of us."

"I don't feel I know you," says Janet. "We've become so used to one another—don't just mean you and I, I mean everybody in the group. It's as if we've known everybody here all our lives, but of course we haven't. There's so much we take for granted that we shouldn't take for granted. I don't know, for instance, what you used to do before the—before now."

"I was an academic," he replies. "A university—teacher, I was going to say, but I was more the eternal student. More that."

"You see," says Janet, warmly. "I never knew that. That's really interesting. What was your subject?"

The wine is tart and a little bitter in Hector's mouth, but he can feel the tang of the alcohol on the roof of his mouth, down his throat. It has an almost petroleum and igniting sensation. "This isn't especially nice wine. I was in France until a few—" weeks? months? He can't remember. "—until a little while ago. And the wine there, something *else*. Of course."

"I knew you'd been in France," she says.

"My subject is History of Art. I did a PhD on Cézanne. You know him?"

"Of course," says Janet, in mock outrage at the idea that she might not have heard of Cézanne.

"I was working on an article on Cézanne and his milieu. That's why I was over there, looking into some stuff in Provence. But I can't really describe myself as an academic. I never got tenure, or a proper teaching post." He is going to add, *not yet*, but you know, in the present circumstances—

"Why Cézanne?" asks Janet, looking very intently at him. There is definitely, Hector thinks, something happening here.

Definitely something sparking between them. He starts, almost without intending to, calculating how long ago the sun went down, how much longer the darkness will last, before Jacob wakes and starts moving about. How much longer they have together, unobserved.

"Oh," he says, hurrying his pat answer. "I was originally attracted to the exquisite balance between representational and abstract elements in his paintings. His landscapes that really beautifully capture what southern France actually looks like; but which at the same time are these fantastic, abstract arrangements of blocks of color and shade. Halfway between Poussin and Ben Nicholson." He is aware that he is sounding pompous, and doesn't want to screw up the chance of a more intimate connection by snaffling the focus too much to himself. "But, look, what about you? I don't know anything about you, except that you're British. That you're from," and he can't remember. "The south coast," he says.

"Well what do you want to know?" she asks, sitting back in her chair and angling her head. There is a ghost of flirtatiousness about the gesture.

"Anything. You tell me."

"I'm positive," she replies. For a moment Hector misunderstands, tries to connect this statement of her certainty to what he has just said. But then he registers her meaning. He says: "Oh." He can't help shrinking back into his chair.

"I've got, I have HIV," says Janet. "You know what I mean. Of course I told Hector, because I didn't think he'd want me along. We have to breed after all. We need to breed. But he told me to come anyway. I love him." She says this so simply Hector finds himself almost moved. "It's OK," she continues. "Jacob and I sold the house, and bought years' worth of supply of drugs, all I'll need. And Trojans. Jacob," she says, smiling as if at a fond memory, "used to be ticklish around the subject of condoms. He used to wear two when..." She casts her eyes down, as if defusing the intimacy of her revelation with a charade of modesty. "Now he's much more comfortable with, a function of the days, of the days, of the days we, of the days."

The wine in Hector's glass does not seem to be so much a red fluid as a space in the imperfectly lit room where the shadows happen to overlap into a curvingly conical shape. The candle-flame kinks and stretches, making the shadows in the corner of the room bulge, making the shadows threaten and recoil, pulse as if alive. Hector literally does not know what to do with this intimacy. He has no idea.

Really, no idea.

His head has this song running through it, but it is a song that relates neither to the specifics of Janet's communication, nor to the general mood. *Three, six, nine. The goose drank wine. The monkey chewed tobacco on the streetcar line.*

"Well," he says, looking at the table. The lines and knots of the timber are so pronounced they look as though they have been inked on. The wax is shiny under the candlelight, like a mirror-layer of varnish. "I'm sorry," he says.

"Thank you," she replies.

When he looks up he can see that she is looking straight at him.

"HIV," he offers. "That's hard. That must have been a shock to hear."

"It was," she says.

Hector can think of nothing to do but drink his wine. The rain and wind scuffs and rattles at the window in a soothing pattern of crescendo, diminuendo, crescendo. The candle-flame moves as if tugged from all four corners of the room in turn. *The line broke, the monkey got choked.*

"I suppose," he says, in an awkward voice, "I wonder—I don't know how to ask this." Vanilla skin, and rosé in her hair.

"Just ask," she says. Her simplicity is very close to the core of her, he believes. It defines her, surely, and its purity draws him. It helps, of course, that the candlelight flatters her bad skin, its velvety patches of red eczema set against a corpse-pale ground dissolved in the roseate light into something warm and inviting.

"I wonder," he says, slightly bolder, "how it comes about that a person. A person like you, a smart person, with a good mind, and a life. I wonder how a person like you decides to give up everything in your life, sell everything, and devote yourself to following..."

"It seems strange to you," she offers, "because he's your father. But try to see him as somebody might see him who didn't grow up with him."

Hector nods. But of course this task is beyond him, like looking directly at the back of his own head. *And we all went to heaven in a little rowing boat clap hands.*

"My life before," she says, in her refined English voice. Maybe her voice would not sound refined to another Brit, but to Hector it seems pure Jane Austen, clear and somehow sunshiny. It makes him think of green apples. "It was a good life. I lived in a town not far from London, a wealthy little town. I had a husband with a very well-paid job. We enjoyed a good quality of life." Hector can sense the scare-quotes around this last phrase, although she makes no gesture, she does not inflect her voice, she just keeps talking in the clear, fluid progression. "We had a cottage in France. It was in Normandy, and we'd holiday there, or just pop over for weekends. I played the cello. I worked part-time on a PhD, on English Literature. I wrote poetry."

"You did?"

"I had a circle of friends and acquaintances. Paul and I were planning children. We were going to have children, after his lump was checked out. The lump was on his shoulder blade, like a mole, only larger, it was more ragged than a mole. The lump was there. But, Hector, mine was a life running in grooves, comfortable. It was a good life. And it genuinely was."

Trying to see ahead into the narrative, Hector offers: "The lump was...?"

"It wasn't the *lump*," she says. "Not that *that* decided me. I'd already decided. Of course, perhaps I already had a sense of what was going to happen, but I don't think so, it didn't *feel* so. I was just sitting in my kitchen one morning, and I was drinking a cup of coffee, and the radio was on, but I wasn't listening to the radio. It had been raining, and now it was sunny, so that the patio doors were dotted all over with these beautiful glass pimples, and each drop was touched by the sun with tiny miniature little shards of rainbow. The lawn was exhaling after the rain. And I thought of the little author bios you get on the front page of books. Or on the back flap, under one of those doleful little photographs of the writer."

"Bye-oze?" queries Hector.

"You know the sort of thing. The author was born in Rochester N.Y. in such-and-such a year. He grew up on a farm in western New York State. He was educated at Deerfield Academy, and then at Harvard, and then at Columbia. He moved to New York City in such-and-such a year. He married and had one child. He is married and lives with his wife and three children. He published this book, and that book, and this book. He died in such-and-such a year."

"OK," says Hector, uncertain where this was going.

"Well," Janet says, "it seemed to me that there was something simply *desolate* in summing up a whole human life in that way. A whole life, with all its various experiences, its pains and ecstasies, boiled down into a little paragraph of ten-point type. But that's the truth of it, isn't it? That in fact those author bios are *more* than most people get. That's what life does boil down to. More than that, perhaps that's all a life—all a life *is*. Maybe it only seems more to us because we're so myopically close to our own existences—in the larger perspective, perhaps a life doesn't even merit so much detail as 'born in Rochester' and so on?"

"That's a rather nihilistic way of looking at things," Hector says. But he's not trying to argue with her.

"It's liberating, in a way. Because I realized that I was actually simply ticking off those markers, that was all. Touching the bases as I ran round the baseball diamond just because the bases were laid out and linked by a line. I had been born, and therefore I would get educated, and get married, and die. It's conformism, but that sounds more dismissive than I mean, because that's being *hu*man. Isn't it? Being human is just conforming to the things that define human."

"I see. I think I see. I."

"But that revelation, it seemed to free me up somehow, to shake me loose. So I got on a train, and I went straight up to London. And I was walking along Charing Cross Road, and on a whim I stopped off at the library, there on Charing Cross. Hector was giving a talk, and purely serendipitously I stopped off."

"He was giving a talk?" This is something Hector had not known. It was something he had not realized his father was capable of. Giving public *lectures*? In libraries in strange cities to strangers, passing on his crazy gospel? That really doesn't sound like the father Hector knows.

"He was giving a talk. There was hardly anybody there, of course. But his words went straight to me, they flew straight as an arrow and connected with my heart." This more flowery idiom seems false in Janet's mouth, a departure from her simplicity, more cult-like. But he is leaning towards her as she speaks.

"And then?"

"After he finished I talked to him. He recognized that he had made a connection with me, I think. I invited him to the house, to come and stay with us in Tunbridge, if he ever needed a place to stay. Instead of coming he gave me his card, and told me to come to America, to come to Los Angeles, and stay with *him*."

"In Pasadena? I grew up in that house. Was it in Pasadena that you stayed?"

"I took the train back to Tunbridge, and when I got home Paul was waiting for me in the sitting room, drinking whisky, and he told me that the lump was Kaposi's sarcoma, and that he was not only HIV positive but starting to develop the full disease. He'd never been tested. He'd never thought there was a need. I guess he caught it a decade and a half, or two decades, earlier. From some partner or other. But he'd never considered that he'd placed himself at risk, and it had never crossed his mind to get tested, until the lump. He cried so much, and I don't think it was only self-pity. I got myself tested, and I was positive, and that was that; but Paul had had the virus for a long time, and he got very sick very quickly. Treatment didn't seem to reduce his viral load. So he died."

"I'm sorry," Hector says, reflexively. But his being sorry is not the point of the story. The table is between them. The candle-flame winks its eye at him.

"I flew to L.A. That's where I met Jacob. He already knew Hector, had already been touched by the connection, and he and I got together. We married. He and I got married. I sold up in England, and Jake and I pooled our money to buy a house, in San Marino." Hector raises his eyes, to indicate that he knows this area. His face communicates a "?". "Just off Garfield

Avenue," she clarifies. "Then Hector told us of his latest visions, and we sold up after a year to come... here." She smiles.

"That's very interesting," says Hector. It tells him nothing about why this woman gave up her life to follow his dad. He doesn't say so. *His dad*, that's the nub of it, that's the hard-to-swallow part. He swigs some wine. "Thank you," he says, somberly, "for telling me your story."

"It's one of my stories. Do you want to tell me your story? Or one of your stories? I guess you told me one, about studying Art History. But I'm thinking of another of your stories about the person you *are*, not what you've done."

But the mention of Jacob, Janet's husband, of his special connection to Hector Senior, has put Hec off his stride. He tries to decode the mood of this meeting; the seemingly romantic candles, wine, the *à deux* intimacy, the wind and the rain safely on the far side of the window. He thinks it may have a sexual component; it may be her way of expressing her desire for him. And yet there is her husband, real, there is her love for him, apparently. There is also the virus, of course, like another husband. A less forgiving one.

"I had a disagreement with my dad," says Hector, not meeting Janet's eyes. "He gave me some money on my twenty-first. A whole bunch of money. A pile of it. I was sensible with it, too. I bought a car, and paid some debts, and had a whole bunch of it left over. I invested it." It sounds such a lame way to start a story.

"Money," says Janet, in as neutral a voice as a Britisher ever uttered.

"It was a lot of money," says Hector, shrugging. "I'd grown and... What I'm trying to say is that my mom and dad didn't *lack* for it. And I was the only child. And it seemed a natural enough thing. And this wasn't my *inheritance* or anything. Dad was clear about that. But it was a lot of money. Anyway, I found myself thinking about it a lot. I promised myself not to let it change my life, or become a, you know, a cliché, yacht, playboy, cocaine." He says this word with a very short first syllable and very long second one. K'cayne. "And then I... well, I took it and..."

It's crazy. He feels an embarrassment about this.

She is waiting to hear what he did.

He shrugs. "I gave it all away."

"To whom?"

"To charity, mostly. A couple of deserving people I knew personally, but mostly to charities."

She smiles. "You gave away all your money? What, are you a saint?"

But this is exactly what he's worried about. He leans forward, "No," he says, vehemently, "precisely not that. I don't mean to be weird about it, but I'm just not. I didn't do it for anything, I didn't do it *to be good* or anything. I mean, it was a lot of money. Some of the charities were like real grateful pooches, and wanted me to come to dress-dinners and have my photo taken and so on, but that wasn't the point of it at all."

"So what was the point of it?"

He doesn't answer this. Instead, sitting back in his chair, he says, "One unintended consequence was that it pissed off my dad. It hadn't occurred to me that it would, but it really did. He was furious. It was a waste, he said. I might as well have nailed it to a board and burned it up in an avant-garde art experiment. It caused a breach."

"A breach."

"Between the two of us. I mean, we still talked and stuff. I still went home for Christmas. But things were never the same. Always his disapproving eye on me as we all sat at the table. And after my mom—" but, no, as he is speaking he realizes that he doesn't want to talk about *that*. So he says: "I didn't need the money and other people needed it. I couldn't see the logic in hanging on to it, but my dad saw it differently. He's still mad, you know. I still can't find a way to explain to him why I did it."

"And why did you do it?"

"It was about," says Hector. "It was a *weight*, and." But he can't think what else to say. So he goes off in a different direction. "I was supposed to bring a woman to this end of the world party," he says, speaking too loud. The window is starting to brighten away to his left. "I was dating this woman, Marjorie, she was. I'd been dating her for a couple of years actually, but it was an elastic sort of relationship. It tautened, it slackened, we were cool."

Janet is looking at him.

"She's in London," he says. "She teaches. If Dad is right about all this, she's dead. But on the other hand..." Oh, there is no other hand.

Janet says something unexpected. She does something unexpected. What she says is: "There's no coming to terms with death—terms? That's a vocabulary from the battlefield. There's no war between life and death." It sounds like a prepared statement, like a quotation, but she delivers it with such ingenuous spontaneity that Hector can believe it's just that moment come into her head.

This is what she does next: she pushes her chair back and stands up, and steps round the table. Hector's heartpulse increases. He looks up at her, for now she is standing over him, her face foreshortened, her nose less pendulous, the candlelight flattering her skin. She says, "Stand up."

He stands. It is fully light outside. People will be waking all over the compound. The wind is still bothering the panes in the window, *churrr*, and to the accompaniment of their rattling, and the background hush of the weather outside, she drops to her knees before him. Hector nearly gasps out in surprise and joy. He can't believe it, but here she is, pushing the metal button of his jeans through its tight denim buttonhole and sliding down the zip like the cover of a Rolling Stones album and hitching the pants around his hips so that they can slide down to concertina at his knees. He gasps. He can't believe it. He doesn't want to say anything that might break the spell. It's pure and perfect anticipation. He daren't even draw breath. His dick is solid; it is a vertical brass rod; it is painfully tight and hard, the end pressing up between his stomach and his pant-elastic. The feeling of her hands touching his waist as she slides her fingers underneath the elastic waist of his boxers is so very good; the ticklish deliciousness as she slides them down to pull his pants is so very good; and the sensation bubbles all through his torso and up his throat and he says, "Oh God." His boxers slide down his thighs under the gentle pressure of her fingers. The windowpanes' rattle seems to increase in frequency. A scurry of rain drums the glass. Her head goes into his lap. Hector looks down, and there is the center parting of her shoulder-length brown-blonde hair, and her scalp, and from above her nose like a little pink hard-on of her own.

She seems to be examining him, looking closely. He wants to grab the sides of her head and pull her in. But he doesn't do this, and the wind burlies and bustles against the window, and he can't think of a form of words to urge her on that doesn't sound either cajoling or pathetic.

She gets to her feet, smiling, a warmth in her eyes. What's happening? What's she going to do?

But she only leans in and kisses him lightly on the lips. And then, before he can say anything to call her back, she slips away and he is alone.

So, he is bewildered. She seemed to disappear through the door with such speed, and now there *he* is, with his pants down and his dick out, all alone in the dining room. The window is bright. People are waking up. Upstairs, his father is probably waking in his room, directly above. What is she thinking? Is it a tease? *How could she?* he thinks. He thinks: *what's she doing?*

A complex of emotions squeezes through him, a queer peristalsis. Was she just toying with him? How could she set him up like that, and just walk away? He feels the beginning of humiliation, and a growing anger, and yes he is still horny. But at the same time he feels anxious, and he feels insecurity growing in him, and the fretful thought that perhaps it was something about him that has *driven* her away, that he is too dirty (washing is not something he is able to do every day), or his potato-white skin is too hideous, or he is otherwise disgusting. But that cannot be right. His own desperate urging desire carries him past all that, he must have it. He *must*. There's no maybe here. So he grasps himself, running his right hand up and down his own dick, and it takes only a few strokes for him to come, so ready he is. He suppresses a shout as he comes. He shuts his eyes as if he is sneezing, and—

Outward it flows.

He is sitting. He *sees*.

This one is much more intense than the vision he had in the car. Some part of his mind is worrying, with that post-come flexure of self-disgust and the need to cover up what he has done—to tidy up, fetch a tissue from the kitchen or something, for Christ's sake, people might be coming through here any moment.

But he doesn't do any of this, because the vision possesses him completely. It is more immersive than the earlier one. It takes him back not to his student days, not so far, but just to France a few months before. One summer evening, the evening before Marj left for London.

—They are walking, together, they are discussing art. In fact, he thinks, they are using the language of art to talk about the clogged, blocked, *fucked*-up *something* that they have been pretending for years is a relationship. And are we adults? Let's get past the blaming you, or blaming me, let's face it. Shall we? Except that every attempt to articulate what's going on between them runs into silence, and they fall back on pointing out to one another aspects of the South French landscape that strike them as beautiful. Like tour guides. Sad, really. Linking it to the artists who have tried to capture it on canvas.

—From where they are, on the road, the hills rise gently, broken, to the horizon. The countryside is broken by a few villas. It is a proper sunset, a slow settling of the red sun behind the west.

—Trees lamppost the hill under a lager-colored sky. The trees are cypresses, following the line of the road. The most beautiful trees in the world, says Marjorie. She says this sincerely. He can agree with that.

—He can hear the cold cooing of birds, as if they were in the dining room with him there on the ranch. He can hear it with an almost painful clarity.

—The late evening shadows are strengthening in their slots and hollows. It is a barely perceptible tuning-down of the light.

—The ceramic tessellations of Provençal rooftops.

—The lavender field changing from mauve to blue-black. And then the color thickens to pure black as the light withdraws itself. Together they stand silently for a while watching frozen droplets of stars chill miraculously into view.

—The cypresses take the form of flames. He says this.

—You sell yourself, she replies. You do a good job. In the dining room of the ranch, in that ridiculous position with his pants around his knees and his limp dick out, sitting in the chair, Hector can nevertheless see and feel all this as if it is real. The real real.

—The fading light deepens the color of the trees. The more distant ones are stubs on the horizon, dark lit green.

—But all the *money* in the world, she is saying, is not enough. All the confetti in the world. This relates to something they had been talking about before the start of his vision, but the oddity of his hallucination, or alien memory-recall, or whatever it is, the *oddity* of it is that Hector cannot remember *what* they were talking about before. That memory is part of his conventional mental structures, and like a match-flame in the glare of an arc light, it has been bleached to nothing by the incredible immediacy of this experience, now, this now-experience.

—Oh, the shine of your bright wit, she says to him, part-mocking, but affectionately. Oh, the edge of it, the *blade* of it.

—Walk alongside you forever, he says. I could. It's nice.

—It's lovely here, she agrees.

—And the sun goes down between blood-orange and plum clouds. It tucks behind the trees.

—So

—Good night. *Good night.*

—And, is he really going to leave her, to let her go to this house, her friend's house, and sleep alone in their spare room? Is he really not going to beg her to come back to town with him, to share his hotel bed? Is he going to let it all end, here?

—And

—hh,

—breath shading pale in the darkness.

—The cypresses, now, are merely bellbottomed gaps between the stars. Hector and Marjorie banter a little more.

—You say van go, she tells him. She hawks, but doesn't spit, to illustrate what she says.

—I'm sorry

—*I'm sorry*

—No, it's me, he says. I can be a real cunt in July. It's the heat, or something. I'll try, I'll be better tomorrow. Let's get lunch. We can talk it through. She smiles at this, and although she doesn't say yes, she doesn't say no either. But they won't meet tomorrow. She'll go to London. He'll never see her again. The world will end.

—So

—Good night again. *Good night again.*

HE COMES TO, gasping, like a diver breaking in to the light.

Janet is there, standing over him. She is looking down at him, sprawled in the chair in his state of partial undress. There is puzzlement in her expression. "Janet," he says, rasping a little.

"What are you doing?" she asks. But it's pretty obvious what he's been doing.

"I," he says, confused, embarrassed, hoicking up his pelvis in the chair to pull his pants up, to pull his jeans up. "I thought you'd gone away, I swear to God I thought you'd left me all alone. I thought I was quite alone."

"Jesus," she says, in a small voice, looking at the floor. "Jesus, I'm standing in it."

"I'm really sorry, Janet, I really am. I thought you'd gone. Then I had a vision—Christ it was vivid. Let me," he tries to struggle from the chair, but his trousers aren't quite right about his haunches, "let me get a tissue."

"A vision?" says Janet. The expression on her face is a sort of hurt-disdainful. Hector has violated something between them. And of course he has. This is disgusting. He is disgusting, to be found like this, with his pants around his knees and his *stuff* all over the floor.

"Christ Janet I'm sorry," he says, pulling his pants on right and getting up. "Oh Christ I'm sorry. But I thought you'd gone. I thought you'd gone off and left me, in the lurch, you know? Where did you *go?*"

She holds up a little wrapped rectangle, like a boiled sweet. "I went to get a rubber," she says. "My jacket is on the chair in the hall."

"A rubber?" he says, gasping. "For a blow job?" But he sees.

"You got to be cautious when you're positive," she says, distractedly. The fragile thing they had, the thing that bloomed briefly at the candlelit table before the rapid dawn, has been wrecked now. He has wrecked it. He can feel that he is blushing. He can feel the corrosion he has caused breaking them apart. He can't believe this. This is the worst thing.

"I had a vision," he gabbles. He dashes through to the kitchen and returns with a sheet of tissue from the roll; and, as he's down on his hands and knees, cleaning up his own pearlescent fluid, he says: "Janet, it was incredible. It was so vivid, I had one before, in the car, the day after I arrived here. But this one was much *more*. Much *more*."

She is sitting in a chair, looking down at him as he cleans. "What was it of?"

"It was of the past," he says, getting back up and sitting in the chair next to hers. "But the recent past. A few weeks before the—it happened. When I was in France. Christ it was *vivid*. Are your visions like that? Are they really vivid, so that you feel you're living them again?"

This, he realizes as soon as he speaks, is the wrong question to ask. There is grief in her face now; her blue eyes sagging further at their corners. She has been fiddling with the wrapped rubber in her hand, but now she puts it into her pocket. "I've never had a vision," she says. This is a painful admission for her to make.

"Never?" he asks, breathless. Then: "I thought everybody here had had one. I thought that's why everybody was here."

"I had one once," she replies, after a short silence. "It's Hector, with him is where the focus is. Closeness to him does it. Once. My second night here on the ranch, when I was with him."

Hector Junior digests what this *with him* means. He feels a float of clamminess in his chest. He can't believe it, just can't still can't believe that Janet came back into the room to *find him like that*. But as if needing to transfer the vileness wholly onto himself he refuses to imagine that Janet and his father could have done anything. Done. Are there any ordinary working-joe words in the entire English language that *don't* mean fucking? Doing, having, knowing, all of that intimacy. But she goes on speaking. She isn't about to stop speaking, actually. In his jangled, upended mental state, it is like a blow. She says: "It was one night, the only night when we were a little careless."

He knows what this means. He is watching her again pocketing the rubber, unused, that embodiment of caution and safe-sex propriety. He can see her from above as she kneels below him, her face an inch from his crotch, and he cannot help himself. Some part of him tries to salvage the situation. To defuse this revelation for his own benefit. The sentence, taken as a sentence, could mean any number of things, after all. It could mean something wholly non-sexual. But of course, it doesn't. And, as a second blow, a subsidiary revelation, he realizes that her sentence imputes not only the one occasion of careless, rubberless contact; it also carries within it an unknown number of more careful encounters, couplings where Janet has wielded her prophylactics and preserved the hermetic healthiness of her sucking and her fucking. Now: how much does this realization hurt? Much, although he cannot say whether it does so because of the bitterness of the image of his father in this connection, or whether it is a jealousy at the thought of Janet with another man. He is still trying to gather himself. She is still talking.

"I had a very, this was my vision, a *vivid* memory of my childhood, on the beach in England. It was intense. But I thought it was just an especially vivid dream. I woke up from it, and I woke up Hector, and told him I thought it was a dream, but he seemed certain it was a *vision*." She is not looking at him; not, he realizes, because of shame at this confession of a sexual relationship with his own father, but because she grieves that this one ambiguous event, half dream, is the closest she has come to sacred vision. She craves a fuller sign of grace. How very human that is.

"You," he croaks, trying to distract his train of thoughts, trying to move the conversation away from his dad. "You never had a vision anytime else? Then? No?"

She shakes her head. But she says another sentence, and it squeezes his mental pain markedly. He had not believed it could have been made worse, but she manages to multiply his jealousy and agony by simply saying: "Dimmi has had loads of visions with him."

This double confirmation of what he has suspected, feared, is such an emotional body-blow that he doesn't even especially feel it, at first; like a motorcyclist whose legs have been snap-dragged off in a traffic accident who, at the first, is purely numb below on the waist, lying on the tarmac and staring at the sky.

"I see," he says.

"He's the receiver," she says, and Hector's disordered, traumatized mind thinks, at first, she means wide receiver, like in football. But of course she means like *radio*. And of course she gets to her feet, and walks away.

4

LATER ON HE happens upon Tom, and tells him about the vision. He's still wandering around, that pre-shock moment which stretches, before the impact. He's still the fly, hovering on the freeway like in the song. The windshield has yet to intersect him at fifty-five. Sheer hard parallelogram of glass sweeping out its corridor in space-time. "You should talk to your father about it," Tom says, his face serious. He is impressed. "It's a more complete vision than *I've* ever had. It sounds as if it was more immersive, more direct, than anybody here has had—except Hector, of course. But if it's a DNA thing then it shouldn't surprise is that... anyway, anyway. Hector will know what it means."

Do they even make windshields out of glass anymore? Isn't it some kind of plastic?

But the thought of even seeing his father at this time fills Hector with a sort of existential terror. He can't do it. He can't tell his father about his vision. He flees the house, for very fear of meeting his dad. Outside.

The wind has gotten much burlier. He forces his way along and it pulls and pushes his body like a boisterous crowd. The rain, either squeezed from the fog or else falling from some-where else into it, splatters and rattles into his face, wetting his clothes. Just as the fog shrinks sight to a few inches, so the rain reduces the other senses to a tightly wrapped helmet of sensa-tion: sound becomes the thrumming and hissing in his ears, touch becomes the sparkling wetness, warm on his skin. He follows the path from ranch house to dorm, and then breaks away to tramp over the pathless ground. What had been parched Mojave dust and dried mud is now, after weeks of moisture, scattered and covered with pale moss growing in clumps.

He must leave. When this thought arrives crashingly in his brain he realizes that it has been coming, inevitably, for a long time, his seabed-mind awaiting the impact of an ocean liner that has slipped beneath the waves many leagues above, perhaps days ago, drifting down and down. He can't stay. But as soon as he thinks this, cocooned in splashy, bristly rain, fog, dimness—as soon as he thinks this he realizes he cannot. He cannot leave Dimmi. He loves her with a sudden but total love. His passion is as all-surrounding as this weather.

"The world has not ended," he says aloud. He stumbles over one of the pillow-like clumps of moss, and falls to his knees, ripping his trousers a little on an intervening patch of gravel. The rain feels like the pressure of the whole cosmos coming straight upon his head. His understanding of his father is now fully overwritten by a newer, two-dimensional portrait. The crazy cult leader, the mad old man who seduces a group of young followers into a desert hideaway with stories of the end of the world—and, in Hector Senior's case, going to elaborate lengths to convince them that the world has indeed ended—in order to indulge his lusts, for power, for sex. Hector is crying. He is sniveling, rather. It is this word, sex, that is the trigger. He cannot believe how upsetting it is to think of Dimmi and his father naked together, lying together on his bed, to think of his father lying between Dimmi's long legs, to think of his dad pressing his wrinkled, liver-spotted features against Dimmi's beautiful face. It burns his mind to think of this, and yet he cannot stop himself reaching for the thought of it. How could she do it? And Janet too, although this thought lacerates him less. He slumps forward so that he is on all fours, his left hand on gravel, his right pressed into the fuzzy yielding mass of a clump of moss. The rain pounds his back. The heavens collapsing upon him. The wind rocks him back and forth, making his hair wriggle against his scalp like worms. Why did you give all that money away, boy? Why give it all to charity? You think it's helping them *now*?

It was my money, Dad. But this's a pretty fragile point to make.

It occurs to him to make a deal with whatever forces are presiding over this end of the world charade, the forces of apocalypse or the forces of pastiche and fraud, whichever. His father can have Janet, he offers, if he, Hector Junior, can leave and drive back to L.A. with Dorothy. His father can continue getting his fucking jollies with Janet, if he, Hector Junior, is allowed unique and sole and father-free access to Dorothy. He, Hector Junior, will give up the ranch, give up his father, give up everything if only—He stops. *Dorothy?* This is idiotic.

Did he say Dorothy? He's not thinking straight. He meant Dimmi. He rocks back until he is sitting on his haunches with his arms at his side. The spatter and rush of rain and wind and fog is all around him. He could be a million miles from the ranch instead of a few yards. It's like Psychology 101. It's banal. Who even buys into that sort of slip-of-the-tongue Freudianism anyway? The verbal rubble of hasty thinking, of stressed and rushed expression; of the brain sagging under the load of input and social repression (don't say fuck, don't say nigger, don't say what you really think about this person's clothes or that person's picture). It's a simple input–output logic, really: under calm, unstressed circumstances people do not perpetrate slips of the tongue. It's only when the input load rises, and the brain-mouth network cannot cope with the increased load. Nothing to do with revealing secret and hidden desires, no, of course *not*.

Rain on his face, and in his eyes. Dorothy is the name of Hector's mother. But she looked nothing like, and *was* nothing like Vera. Dark hair, yes; long limbs, pretty face, but not in the same specific look as Vera, nothing like it. Her family was Irish-Scottish. Her maiden name had been McCormack. But her family had been in California for four generations, and in the U.S. for six, dating back not to the potato famine but to a wealthy Dublin Protestant who had sailed for New York in the early 1800s to set up a silverware manufactory.

Marjorie, seven years Hector's senior, had used to tease him about his predilection for mother figures. But it's just a joke, that's all, one of the many levities liable to be exchanged between young lovers. Or, at thirty-eight, not so young. If the thirty-eight year-old Hector were given the chance to travel in time back to a younger incarnation of himself, to himself, say, at seventeen: and if he were able to tell that younger Hector, "You think you'll mature and settle as you age, but the truth is the same insecurities, the same wildfire all-consuming desires and crushes, the same sense that everybody else is more competent and assured than you are yourself—all these things will still be true in two decades' time," then the younger Hector would not believe it. The older Hector can hardly believe it even now, and he's lived through it. What is he doing, out here in the rain and the fog?

He gets, slowly, to his feet. His trousers are torn over his right knee, a rip in the fabric of the jeans like a mouth, the torn-off edges of the strands of denim like miniature teeth. A hint of red is visible. Grazed his skin. He should not have fallen, operatically, to the ground as he did. It was a thoughtless act. He hadn't really tripped; or, more exactly, he'd been primed, in this all-consuming weather, to fall because the tumble had matched his mood of self-inflating doom and suffering. But, annoyed now by the damage to his trousers, he looks back with disdain on the fucking high-drama, high-*camp* drama, of his rush into the rain. What was he thinking? So his dad has had sexual relations with that woman. So what?

116

The tug and the wetness of his clothes, flapping heavily about his body. He wishes he had not come out in the fog and rain.

Worse, when he turns to retrace his steps, he cannot remember the route he took to get out here. He stumbles around, over the irregular upholstery of moss, in the sense-baffling weather, until his feet strike the tarmac of one of the paths. Following this, head down to minimize the sting of rain against his eyes, he eventually runs up against one of the storage barns. Its metal doors are padlocked, groaning in the wind. Reversing his steps takes him back to the dorm, and from there he makes his way to the house.

5

OF COURSE, OVER the next few days Hector does speak with his father, and of course he does so *without* exploding at his pain and his irrational sense of betrayal. Of course he speaks with Dimmi without breaking down and begging her to flee away with him into the mist. He has the completely ordinary, bland, everyday conversations with these two people that adults have with other adults. The one person he finds it hard to speak to is Janet. He slinks away whenever she comes into the room.

Word that he had had a vision makes its way back to Hector Senior. One morning (or evening, or *whenever*, Hector can no longer tell whether his seven-hour sleeps coincide with what used to be nighttime)—say instead, a little after one of the dawns, his dad knocks on the door of his room. "Hec?" he calls, through the wood.

"Hi Dad," Hector replies. He is sitting on his bed.

"Yeah, can I come in?"

Hector is, almost despite himself, rather touched at this reticence. Had his dad simply walked in, as befits his position as patriarch and panjandrum, Hector Junior wouldn't necessarily have felt invaded. "Sure," he says.

Hector Senior comes in. He looks older by the week, these days: the lines on his face deeper, his eyes seeming more sunken and panda-ringed with darker skin. The skin of his cheeks seems to have changed in texture, bubbled with numerous miniature undulations like cheese under the grill just starting to cook. Perhaps, thinks Hector, it's the burden of responsibility. Or perhaps it's the physical strain of having so many attractive young women to fuck, And he says, "Take a seat, Dad. Take a seat and—how are you?"

"Yeah," says Hector Senior, sitting on the edge of Hector's bed.

"We haven't had much time to—you know."

"Talk," agrees Hector.

"Yeah." His father rubs his forehead with the palm of his hand, a vigorous gesture as if he is trying to scrub away layers of skin. When he finishes he widens his eyes. Man, he looks *tired*. "Hey. I heard you had a real vivid image."

"Image?"

"Vision."

"Oh," says Hector, as if being reminded of something he has forgotten, although in fact he has thought about little else for three days, going over and over the terms of his vision, trying to decipher it. "Yeah. I had a sort of—it was a pretty vivid one."

His father is looking at him. "Tell me about it," he says.

Hector doesn't want to come anywhere close to the circumstances in which the vision happened; certainly not the picture of him with his pants around his knees, and not even the fact that he had been alone with Janet in the dining room while almost everybody else slept, drinking wine and flirting with Janet. So he only says, "It was a couple of days ago, during one of the pre-dawns. I saw—more than saw, I felt—being back in Arles."

"In France."

"That's right. It was after a long period when Marj and I were growing apart, when it didn't seem to be working. She'd suggested she go and stay with these friends of hers who had a villa in the countryside outside Arles. Very beautiful country-side, real van Gogh countryside." He pronounces this name in the American manner, and at once he gets a tremble, a near-flashback, of the vision itself. "Anyway," he goes on, his voice quavering a little, "we agreed. We spent the day in the town, we had lunch, it was nice. We looked round some shops. They've got an arena, and we did the tourist thing."

"Yeah," says his dad. "Arena."

"Roman. They do bullfights there, and stuff. You can just wander round in the day."

"Right."

"Then in the evening we went out to the countryside and walked out to where Jim and Hermione's place was. I knew them a little too, but through Marj. So we just walked through the sunset and dusk, and that," he concludes abruptly, "was what the vision was." He feels a little spurt of bitterness at the fact of his telling his father this. What business is it of his? But then again *why*, his subconscious bickers with him, did you have to let Marj go, anyway? She understood you. She loved you with her complicated love. He clamps his teeth together and looks at the wall, because tears have suddenly threatened his eyes.

How stupid! *Alors.*

Hector Senior seems to be digesting what Hector has told him. He nods slowly.

"Yeah," he says, eventually. "It likes to provoke strong memory. It prefers that to prophecy, but it'll do that too, sometimes. I reckon it finds it easier to tune in to strong mental pictures. That's what it's doing, Hec; it's tuning in to your thoughts."

"I'm not sure I like the sound of that," says Hector Junior, primly. "That sounds pretty invasive."

"Yeah."

But, having recalled the vision for the benefit of his father, Hector does not now want to discuss it in these terms. He refuses to force all his previous life into the procrustean bed of his dad's strange apocalypse. If he has experienced this parting with Marj so intensely that it was almost like reliving it, then it must say something to him about his life.

"The funny thing about it," he says, still not looking at his father, "is I experienced a sort of stereoscope-view. I was there at that time, and I was here looking back at that time. I mean, *at the time* Marj and I talked about painting, and talked about cypresses and stars and shit, stuff, and then she wandered up the garden path to her friends' front door and I wandered back to the village to get a taxi to Arles. The point is that at the time what I felt was mostly just relief. I was relieved that it had passed off without a big scene, that Marj and I were still cool, or seemed to be. I felt this load off my shoulders, you know? As I walked back I was thinking of this girl that I knew that I could..." But he doesn't want to include his dad in this part of his memory, so he snips this sentence off. "But *looking back on it*, I'm aware of the fact that this was our last meeting. She went back with Jim and Hermione to London. The last I heard from her she said she was seeing one of Jim's friends, a guy called Andre or Andrew or something. So looking back on it, I have this sense of regret, you know? And what was so odd about the vision was that I was intensely aware both of the relief and the regret, *at the same time*."

He stops. This long speech has, strangely, tired him. He wants his father to leave him. He'd like to lie down and get a little sleep.

"It's been tuned into my brainwaves, or whatever the hey," says his dad, "for some time now. I think it's got me down pat. I think it may even be using me as some kinda benchmark. Maybe the fact that you're my son—" He stops. Then he says: "Tom thinks that it may have something to do with my DNA. I don't understand much of what he babbles about, but apparently my DNA can act as an accelerant, as a tuning coil, or something."

"Your DNA," repeats Hector Junior. "Like from your blood, or your—" But he doesn't so much as think to the end of this particular sentence, snap, close-down. A rush of anger smothers the more precise understanding. He thinks: *I'm opening my heart to you here, Dad.* He thinks: *Can't you put your fucking stupid cult-fantasy to one side just for a moment?* He grinds his teeth, and stares more intently at the wall. The light is starting to fade at the window. Instead of giving unmediated voice to his spurt of anger, Hector Junior says:

"I know you were mad about me and the money, Dad." Surprising how effective the form of apology can be at containing other emotions, like anger.

There is the faintest of blusher-smudge red in the center of Hec Senior's saggy old cheeks. But he doesn't say anything.

Hec Junior then goes for the double, to capitalize upon his success in throwing his father by apologizing. Passive aggression is an art. "You know I'm sorry about that. Dad."

"Yeah."

Then he asks: "What do you think *it* wants, Dad?" He articulates these words with rather more vehemence than might be thought warranted by the content of the question, but his dad does not seem to notice that.

"That's a good question, Hec," he says, getting creakily to his feet. "I wish I knew the answer to that question." He straightens up, and his knee-bones crack like popguns, one, two.

He wants to say, come on, Dad, there's no it, none of this is *real*. But he doesn't say this. And then his dad has gone through the door, and it's too late to say anything. Which is often how things go. You know that as well as I do.

6

ANOTHER DUSK, AND a mini-night. Now it's dawn, and Hector Junior is starting to get tired. He returns to his bed and lies there, thinking once again how his father might have orchestrated this whole elaborate hoax. Keeps coming back to this. Because, while he feels increasingly certain that it *is* a hoax, he can neither explain the mechanism by which it has been perpetrated, nor even understand his father's motivation. He tries to put himself in his dad's place. Let's say you reach your sixties with plenty of money, with a wife dead and in the ground nine years, with nothing much to fill your life. Oh, sure. Hec Junior can imagine wishing for a place of his own, far from civilization, with some adoring followers, among whom are several attractive young women to share his bed. But there are easier paths to that goal, surely. Piggyback on Christianity, for instance. Declare yourself the new Christ, or the new David Koresh, and you'd have your pick of any number of long-limbed Californian and Nevadan young men and women. You could gather a hundred around you, so that when you get tired of laying with Janet and with, whoever else, you could move on to a dozen more. But this path his father has taken is *bizarre*. An intelligent fucking *asteroid*, nothing less? It's scooting through deep space, makes contact intermittently on its journey towards Earth... two centuries ago, a century ago, before making its pre-impact connection with Hector Senior. The only way to survive the ensuing catastrophe is to join the old man on a ranch in the Mojave Desert. That's such a lame story. I mean, to tour America and Europe lecturing with *that* story? It's amazing he picked up even a dozen disciples. It's amazing that anybody believed him.

Except (he thinks at breakfast, watching his dad's face), except that there *is* something charismatic in the old lizard. The bright blue eyes, like Sinatra's. Stained-glass blue. Christmas-decoration blue. And his quiet certainty, his "yeah." Perhaps spending time with him *would* wear down skepticism. Janet in some dusty London meeting room, listening to his drawl, his underinflected spiel.

The meal over, the group passing around the pill bowl, one each. Tic tac toe.

On the other hand, there is the question of balance of equations. On one side is Dad's version. On the other hand is, say, Marjorie. If Dad is right, Marj is dead; if Marj is alive, Dad is wrong. The two brass saucers, with these two weights in them, pivot smoothly across the fulcrum of his emotional need. *Of course* Marj is alive. She and Hec left it too ragged at their last parting; they'll meet up again, probably in the near future. They'll smooth their parting, or else—perhaps—they'll reconnect, as they have sometimes done in the past. They'll go for a meal, and Hector will make her laugh, and they'll end the evening embracing in the back of a cab. Who knows?

He tries calling Marj several times, but the landline doesn't seem to be working, and he can't get reception on his mobile. The fog, and continuing storm, probably. But that doesn't mean anything.

In fact, the very persistence of the storm rather tells against, Hector thinks, his father's catastrophic story. The original blank white fog has been replaced by a relentless slanting rain, most definitely falling from somewhere above. The darkness must be being caused by this dense cloud cover. Perhaps it's a world-storm, like that *Day After Tomorrow* film. Which is to say, perhaps there *is* some sort of global catastrophe happening, just not the shattered Earth of his father's imagination. Walking between the buildings is an inundating experience. You need raincoats and good boots, and you need to hunch forward so as to brace yourself against the capricious and strong-muscled gusts of wind that carry thick hard raindrops with them. Visibility in daylight is as truncated as it was with the fog; and it's even possible (though scarcely credible) that the fog is enduring despite the rainfall, for there is a hazy edge to the air, the same ozone-flavored seaside tang. But the question is moot, because the constant rainfall blocks vision.

It comes in great swirls and crashes, precipitating diagonally down from what feels, with its smack and sting on the skin, like a great height. "It'll clear," says Tom, confidently. The whole group has recently had its first collective round of haircuts. Most of the men have been shaving their faces with rechargeable electric shavers, but their head hair has gotten shaggy and tramp-like. One afternoon the group gathers in the dining room and spreads a paint-spattered sheet, a Pollock-lite relic from whitewashing a shed or white-ceilinging a room, on the floor. Everybody takes turns cutting everybody's hair. It becomes an occasion for general hilarity; and laughter has been a rare thing these last few weeks. Everybody gets sheared except, of course, for bald Old Hector, who presides over this chaste saturnalia from a chair at the far end of the room. Scissors flash under the electric light. "Turn all the lights on," Jacob booms, "to save us slicing off one another's *ears*." The hilarity at this idea is disproportionate, as if the idea of taking bright scissors to the flesh of the housemates is a fantasy not too deeply buried in the collective subconscious. "Slicing off," booms Jacob, capitalizing on the success of his jokes. "one another's *ears* and *noses*." Cuttees can nominate cutters. Jacob requests Janet. "She cuts my hair all the time," he announces to the room in general. "She's a natural hairdresser." Tom requests Dimmi. But Dimmi and Janet request one another in turn, as if reinforcing their common bond. Hector Junior, on the edge of the group looking on, as always, keeps thinking of this. Their common bond, he thinks.

When it is his turn to wade through the piles of blonde and black and sit in the chair, he is grinning. Oh, he is anxious on the inside. The good spirits feel too high-pressured to him. The beaming, staring faces all around him have something of the medieval witch-trial about them. And he feels that social tug inside him, that warping of his solitary ego in the direction of the group, such that if they all pressed him he would confess to traffic with the Devil, or being a member of the Communist Party, or whatever else was required. He looks all around. "Nominate!" says Jacob, holding the scissors aloft. People chatted, giggled, people grinned at him.

"Dimmi," says Hec. And then, not meeting anybody's eye, he adds: "Hey you did a good job with Tom."

In fact Tom's haircut is uneven and urchin-like, a scrabbly fringe that makes his boyish features look even younger. Dimmi steps forward, moving her long strong limbs gracefully, collecting the scissors from Jacob to take up her place behind Hector's chair. He tries to compose his features. It *would not do*, as they say (or said) in England, to reveal how utterly possessing and utterly hopeless his passionate love for Dimmi is, not here, in front of these people, as her long fingers touch the sides of his face, his scalp, his nape. He focuses deliberately to prevent his eyes glazing over with pleasure, like a puppy rolling over and twitching its hind-leg as its tummy is scratched. Like his Da rolling over and twitching with epilepsy. But it is difficult. When she slips two fingers between his right ear and the side of his head, separating them just enough to slide the clear hardness of the scissor-blades in and snip, and snip, it is the most sensual, erotic sensation Hector can remember experiencing since coming to the ranch. He cannot prevent the ends of his lips curling upward. The hair flutters past his neck, bounces and falls off his shoulders, joins the promiscuously messy pile on the sheet. As if mainlining something narcotic, Hector sees the faces of the observing crowd distort. They stare at him, their grins widening impossibly, their skulls elongating, their bodies swaying. He feels a powerful urge to yell something out, Tourette-style, some terrible obscenity, or some obscene truth: *I love Dimmi* or *Fuck you in the ass* or (and this thought acts, to some degree, to pull him back towards reality) *My dad's a fraud! He's taking you all for a ride!* His smile, paradoxically, widens. A hand darkens his vision and the snipping passes across his forehead, and shards of his fringe stick on his shirt and fall to the floor. When his vision returns the room looks normal, and his haircut is finished. He brushes spastically at his shirtfront, apelike with his knuckles, to dislodge strands and tufts of dark hair, and stands up. "Thank you," he says, aware too late of a considerable hard-on, and so not turning to look at her as he speaks. "That's great." Leaning a little forward as he walks away.

Afterward, when the hair had been gathered, and a few spurious or facetious suggestions proffered as to what they should do with it, Amanda brews up enough coffee for all, and everybody settles in the hallway, some in the sofa (the sofa that had

126

saved Hector's life the night of the end of the world), some in the wing chairs, some on cushions, some on the floor, two—Janet and Jacob—sitting on the bottom step of the staircase. Hector Senior has a wing chair to himself, of course.

Tom, with his impudent little face underneath its urchin haircut, is holding forth, in the most pompous manner he can manage. "Guys," he is saying. "I've an announcement. It's kind of important." The burbling and laughter dies, and all faces turn sunflower-like to Tom on the couch. Hector, still a little high from the sensual intensity of the haircut, throws occasional glances at Dimmi.

"The nights are getting longer," says Tom. "It's not by much, a few minutes at the moment, but it is significant."

"Winter is dra-a-awing in," booms Jacob in Dracula voice.

"Seriously," says Tom. He holds up his palms to the group to command attention. Hector boggles. What did Dimmi, beautiful poised Dimmi, ever see in this jerk? This doofus, this *kid*, with his adolescent and nerdy earnestness? "Seriously," says Tom again, and Hector feels a spin of bloodlust dash through his veins, a desire to sheathe a sword in this fucker's *chest*, to stab and stab at him, to leave his corpse unrecognizable.

"What does it mean, Tom?" says Hector Senior, from his wing chair. From his throne. His voice quells the schoolroom inanity of the group's mood. Everybody settles, somewhat, to attend to Tom, who lowers his hands to register the fact that he has the floor.

"Well," says Tom. "It means one of two things. This may be a function of our new orbit, and of the inclination of our spin, the same reason the old world experienced longer nights in winter. Maybe we're settling into our permanent orbit. But I believe the explanation is otherwise."

He waits, to be prompted, and a couple of the group obligingly prompt him.

"What? What?"

"I think it is—it," he says, dropping his gaze to the floor so that there can be no doubt as to the subterranean object of his sentence. "I think it's shifting. I think it's moving up toward us, or toward—" He does not conclude this statement with words, but instead glances over at Hector Senior, in his wing chair. Many eyes follow his lead. "Remember," Tom goes on, in his lecturer mode, "that it contains a hefty proportion of the mass of this new world, our brave new world, more in fact than the remnant of granite and iron from the old globe."

"Possibly," puts in Pablo.

"Probably," corrects Tom, prissily. His right hand has come up again, palm out, as if he is swearing some sort of oath. "The effect of that is it unbalances the spin of the sphere, or quasi-sphere, upon which we live." Hector Junior wrinkles his face with disgust at *quasi-sphere*. And Dimmi truly prefers this to him? She'd prepared to part her legs to this little jerk? But his outrage is compromised, even in his own head, by the knowledge (however much he wants not to acknowledge it) that it is not Tom who is his sexual rival for Dimmi. That it is not Tom with whom he is angry.

"So for that reason," Tom is continuing, "the rotation becomes irregular. Imagine a wheel, with the spoke in the dead center, and a dot marked on the rim." Hector cannot believe how furious he feels at Tom's patronizing fucking schoolteacher voice as he says this. He wants to yell out *We're all adults here, you little runt. Talk to us like adults*. But a second voice contrapunts in his mind: you're no adult, Hec. He shudders.

"In that case," says Tom, "the dot will pass round the wheel regularly, half its time in the top half, half its time in the bottom. But imagine the axle is not in the center of the wheel, but an inch below that, and that the dot is placed at that point on the rim closest to the axle-point."

"Like a clown-car!" puts in Jacob, although nobody laughs at his image.

"Exactly, so then when the wheel turns the dot spends proportionately more time in the top half than in the bottom. For our purposes the top half is the shadow side, and the bottom half the sun. You see?"

Hector Junior breathes in and takes the plunge. "That's very clearly put," he says, trembling a little with the agitation of public speaking; or with the sheer buzzing completeness of his rage. But, despite that, his voice sounds mild, and even sincere. He can see several people nodding their heads in agreement.

Encouraged, Tom speaks faster. "I think, like Hector says, it's spreading out through the underground, putting out feelers. Who knows what shape it's assuming, a baobab tree, or a shield-shape, or whatever. But I think its center of gravity is shifting up toward us."

"Yeah," says Hector Senior. "It's coming to get me." Then, to make clear that he is speaking flippantly rather than ex cathedra, he adds, "Or something like that. Or maybe it's coming to get somebody else." But Hec Senior can't really do comedy. That's not his mode.

"Maybe it's coming to get Dimmi," squeaks his son, surprising himself with the statement. And immediately he blushes, and drops his face to try and hide it, for it is surely as obvious to everybody in the room as it is, now, to him, that his whole yearning is focused on precisely this one idea. Getting. Getting.

7

THE STORM CONTINUES. One day something bursts through the exterior fence; a boulder, big as a car and surprisingly round.

Nobody heard it come in, over the howl of the increasingly insistent rainfall and wind; but Tom spots it on one of his roundabout wanders. A group of them go take a look. Shuffling together through the bad weather like the penguins in that movie: those Morgan Freeman voice-overs, those Antarctic landscapes. "Can it have been blown by the wind?" wonders somebody, shouting above the wind. But no, apparently not, the general opinion is that it's too bulky to have been moved by anything except a seriously heavy-duty hurricane, and the wind, though burly, is not so devastating. "It rolled," shouts Pablo. "It just rolled." The fence is knocked over, lying juddering in the wind against the moss—moss, Hector notes, that now covers the whole ground.

"This moss," he bellows, at the person next to him, anonymous in their windcheater with their head down. "It's everywhere. I guess there's lots of water," he continues. "Lots of water everywhere, so it grows." But it feels oddly stiff under his soles, wiry and convoluted like an agglomeration of oven scourers. There is no indication that the person to whom he was speaking has heard him.

The group, or the eight of them who have coated-up and come out to look at the boulder, quickly get bored. Pablo and Hans and a couple of other men are struggling, in the wind and rain, to heave the panel of fence upright again, its wire flapping with ponderous sinusoidal momentum, slow-motion footage of a flag in the breeze. It is hard to handle, but the others are trudging back to the main house, and Hector falls in with them.

The boulder, he thinks as he disrobes and hangs the sodden Macintosh to dry, is a good touch. Lately he is increasingly certain that not only his father but several of his disciples are conspiring together to preserve the post-catastrophic impression. It is all so obviously a hoax. The fact that he can't see how it's done doesn't mean that it's real. The best conjuring tricks are the ones where you can't see the prestidigitator's sleight-of-hand. But what's most certain is that the whole world has not come to an end, it must still be out there.

Evidence that there is indeed life out there comes three or four dawns later. The phone rings. The phone! The landline, its receiver tucked away in an alcove in the hallway, surely obsolete in this new world, bursts shockingly into brassy purls and knits of sound: twin trilling chimes followed by a repeated syncopated pause of silence, and then two more rings, horribly strident, the same rhythm as the step-step-stop, step-step-stop of the throttler advancing on his victim in the stage play.

It rings and rings. People in the house seem too startled, at first, even to register it. They gather in the hallway. Staring in the direction of the sound. Finally Pablo plods over and picks it up. Others come out upon the landing, and in from the dining room, like shy woodland creatures, to peer at him as he talks. "Right," says Pablo, loud. "Right."

Hector Senior has emerged, summoned from his room by the hubbub. "What's going on?" he demands, theatrically positioned on the balcony above.

Pablo presses the receiver into his broad chest, and addresses the patriachus, "A guy named John. It's a guy. He says he's in Las Negritas. He says he knows you, Hector."

"Negritas is forty miles from here, towards the coast," says Hector Senior. He looks cross, as if this unexpected voice from outside the compound is a threat, something threatening to degrade and defeat his fantasy. But mightn't there be other survivors even in his fantasy? "Let me speak to him."

"He says can we come get him?" explains Pablo, holding the receiver out as Hector Senior steps down the staircase. "Says he knows you."

But when the patriarch picks up the receiver and puts it to his head it is blank, voiceless. All it's doing is humming. The receiver is filled with aural, as the air with visible, fog. "Yeah," he explains, handing it back to Pablo. "Line's dead."

Pablo presses the call-tracer button, but that facility does not seem to be operating. "It comes out of the central L.A. exchange, the call-trace thing, I guess, and that's dead," says Tom.

"Then how come the phone rang at all?"

"Maybe the local exchange is still working. I guess it'd be automated, but—yeah, it's kind of surprising."

"There's no signal on my cell-phone," says Leo, trying to be helpful.

"It's like a ghost phone call," says Hector Senior.

"What shall we do?"

"What? What to do?"

Hector Junior, emerging, asks what has been happening, and listens eagerly to the explanation. "Well let's go to this place," he says, at once. "To this Las Negritas."

"It's forty miles," repeats his father.

"The weather's not good for driving," observes Pablo.

"I'll go," says young Hector. "I'll take one of the four-by-fours. Who'll come with me?"

"It's not just the weather," says Tom, sniffing. "The terrain will be all messed up. Not just the aftermath of the quake and the destruction, but also the distortions of gravity."

Everybody is waiting on Hector Senior's judgment. "Yeah," he says, finally. "Pablo, Tom, you come with me."

"I want to come too," chirrups Hector Junior. "I wanna come along."

"It'll be hair-raising," says his father, in the voice of an old prospector. But he is not denying his son a seat in the car.

The four of them gather some things, and hurry out to where the cars are sitting on the drive, rocking slightly in the wind and speckled with a thousand evanescent warty spots of water, wriggling and changing in the continual downpour. The doors are opened and the four men pile in, panting hard even though they have only dashed the dozen yards from the house. Pablo is in the driver's seat; Hector Senior next to him; young Hector and Tom on the back seat. "Let's go then," says the old man, immediately. "Everybody belt up, back seats as well as front."

The car scrapes to life, lights dotting the dash and the wipers waving in a leisurely, then a frantic, series of gestures, waving not drowning in the huge quantity of falling water. The four-by-four is a stick-shift car, but Pablo handles it smoothly; fog lights on, reverse engaged, and an easy turn to face the drive. It moves along the driveway, but the ubiquitous moss has overgrown this roadway with its tough strands, and the passage is bumpy. "This moss," says Pablo, in an exclamatory voice. "It's getting everywhere."

"There's a great deal of water," Tom observes. "A whole bunch of water. It could be seeds that lay in the Mojave for decades until there was enough water to germinate them."

"But it's like the Mojave was ever dry," says Pablo. "It rained here, time on time."

"Nothing like this!" exclaims Tom, as if that were explanation enough.

The car rattles to a stop in front of the gate. Pablo opens his door to an atmospheric roar and an inrush of rain. He is only out of the car, pulling open the gate and tethering it, for moments; but on his return he is drenched. The torrent and the kling-klang of it all. Hector Junior, half-repenting his decision to come along, says, nervously, "This is some weather, heh? Blow wind and crack your cheeks, you hurricanoes blow."

Tom looks queerly at Hector Junior, as if he is spouting this flowery speech for no reason other than sheer eccentricity; but Pablo, drying his face on a paper tissue before driving off, looks round and grins.

"Seriously, guys," young Hector continues. "Are we sure this is a good idea, in this weather?"

"Yeah," says Hector Senior. "We'll see how we go."

Pablo puts the car in gear, and they drive out of the compound. The road here is smoother, not overgrown with the fungus that is covering the ground of the ranch.

For long minutes they make their way along the road. Spray throws up huge dynamic ruffs of water into the cones of the headlights. It leaps with a scary white-rapids vigor from the tarmac. Leaning forward, Hector peers over the driver's headrest to see the illuminated speedometer reading less than twenty miles per hour. Nevertheless it seems to him that they are careering crazily along. He wishes now he were not cooped up in this car, rocking precariously side-to-side on its axles even as it moves forward, with these three men.

He sits back, and Tom says to him: "You were quoting?"

"Yeah."

"I figured you were quoting. At first I thought it was a pretty weird thing to say, but then I thought." He has to speak loud, and slow, to be heard over the storm and the noise of the car.

"It was Shakespeare," says Hector.

Tom, his boyish face shadowed, only partially and eerily lit by the lights from the dash up front, makes an "oo" with his mouth. Hec takes this for mockery; the little prick. But perhaps he only meant to indicate that even he, a scientist, should have been able to recognize a quotation by Shakespeare.

Hector turns to gaze through the glass; but he can't see anything in the dark except his own half-reflection, and the ever-changing glass-pimpling of the rain outside. The car moves along. Hector does not know quite what to expect. When he made the call he still half-hoped that a drive out of the grounds of the ranch would move into some terrain that directly contradicted his father's fantasy: out of the shroud of cloud cover, perhaps; into sunshine, and a normally functioning East California. Towns with people working and living; police-cars cruising the freeways. The spread of L.A. as you drive west down through the San Gabriel Mountains to see the sparkling quilt of streets, punctuated by the bristling spires of high-rises away toward the coast. But they drive for twenty minutes and neither the darkness nor the rain lifts. Hector had figured, when he called, that it must be afternoon outside; but he reflects, dolefully, that he may have gotten out of synch with the real passage of dawn and dusk. As they move, a mile, another, away from the ranch it is still black. It must be night. The storm must be general everywhere. Worse, they seem, against all the geography that Hector can remember, to be driving uphill.

Pablo suddenly swerves the car, and Hector's face bangs against the glass at the side, *smk!*, ow. Pablo swerves again, swinging wildly left, then right, bouncing Hec, bouncing them all violently in their seats. "Hey," Hec calls, annoyed. But, looking forward, he can see why Pablo is hanging hard left, hard right, hard left: there are ghostly *somethings* hurtling down the road straight at them. They fly straight at the windshield like specters. First an angular object composed, perhaps, of triangular lumber followed by a more conventionally figured ghost, complete with a moaning open mouth and a body that spreads to flapping jellyfish tendrils of ectoplasm. They are only in sight for a moment, before Pablo's deft shimmy sends one down the right side, and the other down the left.

"What was that?" Hector squeals.

"That first one looked to me," says Pablo, matter-of-fact, "like a piece of somebody's house. And the second..."

"Somebody's body," says Tom, in the same tone.

"Yeah," says Hector Senior.

"Jesus, is the wind that strong?"

"Gravity assist," says Tom. "They may have started in L.A. itself, or even San Fran. The incline at L.A.'s probably forty degrees. At San Francisco it might be as steep as fifty."

"Those are pretty extreme figures," says Pablo, in the blandest of voices, like a scientist querying a colleague's findings. "If it got that steep that quickly, and if the ranch is at the bottom of the funnel, as it were, then we'd be buried in rubbish by now."

"Well," replies Tom, levelly. "There's a lot of stuff for loose rubbish to snag on between L.A. and us. The mountains for one."

"L.A.'s broke off," says Hector Senior in a sepulchral tone, looking through the passenger window at the darkness outside. "San Andreas, snap, gone. This stuff isn't from L.A."

There is silence in the car for several minutes. It's not clear that Hector Senior is speaking with the authority of vision-delivered knowledge or not, but Pablo and Tom clearly take his words as if they have that status.

"I was thinking," Tom says eventually, by way of breaking the silence. "That boulder, the one back in the compound, it's too smooth a sphere to be a natural formation. I think it's a large-scale ornament, like a garden thing. Or maybe a work of art. Desert art, perhaps." The car shudders and bounces over what feels like a series of potholes.

"There's a turn to the left here," Hector Senior tells Pablo. The car slows, and the deceleration gives Hector's body the impetus to rock him forward a little in his seat. As they turn a cross-blast slams in to the side of the car, swinging it up off its far-side wheels completely and holding it precariously on the nearside two for a long second. The wind howls like a bear, with prey in its grip. The blast is accompanied by a hailshower of gritty somethings that crashes against the windows like buckshot. Hector squeals, covering his head with his right arm, and as the car rocks back down and bounces onto its four tires again he cannot prevent himself for crying out in a high-pitched voice: "Oh let's go back, let's go back to the ranch!"

"We're going to this guy in Negritas," boomed Hector Senior, speaking too loudly for the enclosed space, even with the clamor of the storm outside. Perhaps he too, even ineffable he, had been rattled by the car losing its traction.

Pablo was still driving, but the speedometer had dropped to less than ten mph. "How far is it along here?" he asked.

"It's some miles," says Hector. "Nine, ten."

"And when we get there," presses Pablo, "how are we gonna find this hombre? He didn't give me a meeting place. He could be *anywhere* in Negritas. He rang off pretty quick, or else the connection got broke."

"It was me!" cries Hector, hotly, miserably, "It was me, didn't you *recognize* my voice?"

This admission is greeted with silence. Pablo slows the car, stepping down through its gears, and they come to a halt. Hector, now, is crying. The car is a soundbox to the roaring white noise and throaty undertow outside. Ridiculous phlegmy tears sliming his face.

"Jesus," he screeches, "I made the call, I went through to the dog-leg at the back of the house, where there's an extension. I pressed the cradle twice and made the other phones in the house ring. When Pablo picked up I gave him this story about Las Negritas. I only know about Las Negritas because I drove through it on the way out to this fucking ranch." He appears to be (he is startled to discover) swearing in front of his father. He has never before sworn in front of his father. "I spun out the story, and then rang off." He takes three or four lurching in-breaths as the sobs work themselves out of his body. Lacking a handkerchief he wipes his nose in the crook of his elbow.

The two front-seat passengers have swung about in their seats to face him. Tom is looking frankly boggled. The car is continuing to rock, though stationary, as the wind and rain buffets and burlies against it.

"Hey, man," says Pablo, in a soft voice. He says it again, a little louder, perhaps worried that the first utterance had been drowned out by the noise of the storm. "Hey man, why did you do it?"

"I wanted a ride outta there," says Hector, miserably. "In this weather, I couldn't take my hire car. I wanted to hitch a ride in a four-by-four."

"To Negritas?" says his father, in a baffled voice. "What good would that do you?"

A spurt of self-pity and anger carries him over the hump of inhibition, "I figured that once we left the ranch the weather would clear."

His father still doesn't understand. "But—"

"I *thought*," Hector wails, "we'd drive out to normalcy. I figured that the world was going on in its normal grooves—I thought," he adds, his voice failing, "that we'd see your whole end-of-the-world thing was just," but he can no longer summon the moral courage to use the word *fucking*, certainly not directly to his father, and he resorts to a milder self-conscious Britishism, "bloody *fantasy*, just nonsense. You made it all up, Dad, it's attention grabbing, it's a complex *illusion*." His head is buzzing. He can't seem to focus properly. Did he add "You only did it to be able to have sex with these young women"? Or did he only think of saying that? Either way, he feels a corrosive sense of his shame growing in his torso, hideous, percolating up to his face and down along his limbs. Some part of his brain is scrabbling to think of a way of reversing this appalling situation; to un-speak the words, to turn them toward comedy or irony. But it is too late.

His dad, almost sweetly, is still not quite getting it. "But how could you think that?" he asks, in a wounded tone. "After the object *struck*—"

"You don't believe there *was* a strike?" Tom says, more for old Hector than for himself. "But in that case how about the changes? The day–night alterations? The gravity. The mist?"

"I don't know," says Hector. He leans forward and presses his face against the plastic-leather of the set in front. "I don't know, I thought maybe that was all a hoax."

"A hoax?" repeats his dad.

"It could be, I *figured* it could be a combination of things— freak weather. Little nudges to people's gullibility."

"You think I'm a hoax?" his dad says once again. His tone is more sorrow than anger, although the anger is there, unmistakably underflowing under his words.

"Oh Dad," says Hector, to the plastic-leather of his seat. The other three occupants of the car don't know what to make of this. It is as if, Hector thinks, an athiest were to die, and go to heaven, and meet Saint Peter and God Himself, and still insist on an atheistic view of the cosmos. They are waiting, he thinks, for him to say sorry. But he doesn't do this. Not that.

"Well," says Hector Senior, in the tone of voice of a disappointed schoolteacher. "I guess we should drive home."

8

BACK IN THE ranch Hector is led through the front door like a police suspect. He is steered toward the couch, the same couch that had saved his life on the night of the quakes. He sits and Pablo takes the place next to him. Young Hector now is high and almost giggly with mania, on the upsweep after the plunge of shame he had experienced in the car, and he finds it agreeably ridiculous that it is Pablo, with his sturdy Latino shoulders, and his unflappable combination of small eyes and big nose, that has been appointed unofficial bodyguard, rather than the nerdy, pigeon-chested and boy-faced Tom. In a surge of self-confidence Hector decides that he hates Tom enough to kill him. If he gets the chance.

Soon enough the whole group has been gathered, all filing into the hallway with puzzled and even anxious countenances, to see (he almost laughs aloud) this apostate, this unbeliever. Infidel. Unfaith. As they gather themselves preparatory to Salem witch-trying him, Hector feels his elated mood slipping away from him. The pressure of so many eyes, eating up his image over and over, splitting slivers of himself into each of so many hostile minds. He looks into his own lap.

"Yeah," says Hector Senior, and at once the mumbling and shuffling ceases. All eyes are on him now. "You'll have heard we got a phone call—we figured there might be a survivor in Negritas. But in the car, going out there, Hector here—" And all eyes swivel back to Hector Junior. "Hector here admits he made the call."

An *ou* goes through the crowd. Hector, his face hot, tries to summon the energy to call out something defiant. But he doesn't speak.

"Why?" asks somebody.

"Yeah, I'm not sure I do understand," says Hector Senior. There is a puzzled expression on his face that goes beyond his words, as if there is more in this world that passes his understanding than just his son's behavior.

"He doesn't *believe* the impact even happened," says Tom, in a tone of pipsqueak outrage. The sound of his voice gives Hector a focus for his scattered consciousness. A clarifying anger, ahh! To pop his head with a high-powered rifle shot. To slam a rifle butt into his face, over and over again. Lurking

140

behind that thought is the almost subliminal apprehension that Dimmi is in the group, looking at him. He does not cast his gaze about him, precisely for fear of meeting her eyes.

"Hector, hey," says somebody, in a caring-concerned voice that is, really, most *extraordinarily* grating. "How can you believe that?"

"Don't you believe the evidence of your own eyes?" somebody else cries out.

"He said it was a *hoax*," whines Tom.

The *ou* sounds through the group again, like a ghost's wail. This, Hector realizes, is their whole life now; they are as immersed in this playacting of the end of the world as any staring-eyed religious fundamentalist. To say what he has said is the primary heresy of this new world order. Anger, though by its nature immiscible with the abject sense of worthlessness and shame that is mostly in his soul now, nevertheless swirls and flurries through him, like bubbles of oil in a vinegar salad dressing. He takes a deep breath. He takes another.

Breathing.

"I'm not on trial," he observes, in a quavery voice.

"Nobody is suggesting you're on trial," says a woman. It is, Hector realizes, Janet speaking. "It's just that we all assumed you *believed*."

"It's not, come on, it's *not*," Hector complains, sounding even to himself more like a surly teenager than a man nearly forty, "a religion." His tone of voice would equally well carry sentences *it's not fair* and *I'm not a kid anymore* and *you don't understand me*. "You saying it's a matter of blind faith? Blind?"

"Of course it's not a religion," says Janet, shocked. But of course it is. Of course, it governs all these people's lives exactly as a religion would, and old Hector is its prophet. His dad. And Hector Junior wipes his nose with the back of his hand, and glowers into the middle distance. The real punch of the truth is that they don't even understand him. He has forfeited Dimmi's love. He should—and tears glisten alarmingly in his eyes as he thinks this, suddenly, from nowhere—he should have kept his mouth shut. He should have played along with them all, and then the possibility of Dimmi would still be open for him. He cannot quite believe the sharpness of pain that sheathes itself in his chest as he thinks: she hates me now. She hates me now.

And, as if on cue, Hector Senior slumps to the floor in one of his bibble-babble divinely inspired fits. He doesn't even have time to call out Dimmi's name; he simply drops and starts twitching, as if the perfidy of his own son's betrayal was so extreme that it chopped him straight down, pierced him with a fatal crossbow-bolt, poleaxed him. The focus of the whole group swaps instantly to their fallen leader. Everybody hurries to crowd about him, and with brine swimming all about his eyeballs Hector watches Dimmi move to offer her usual ministrations. In silence they lift him and bear him, their temporarily fallen Caesar, up the stairs and away to his room at the back of the house. In moments Hector is alone on the couch.

The life-saving couch.

Without an audience his tears dry, and a sense of his own ridiculousness grows upon him. This is crazy. He's not beholden to this ragbag of cultists and gullibles. He should just go. Walk back to L.A. If necessary. By any means necessary. Who said that?

But from being certain that the whole show was a put-on, a collocation of coincidental elements and artfully organized sleights-of-hand, he is now starting to doubt his own doubt. What if it was all true? That would make him a doubly ridiculous figure. How to explain the unprecedented persistence of this storm? Of the dark and light alternating as regularly as clockwork? And the car ride—it had been uphill all the way from the ranch, but that hadn't been the lie of the land when he had driven here.

"So," he says aloud, trying to pull himself back from this precipice of belief, "so they drove me up into some hills. They knew I had my doubts—they were trying to hoodwink me." He says this aloud. But it is very hard to make himself believe this.

And again the thought comes of the spectacle he has just made of himself. Dimmi must hate him. The tears tickle at the back of his eyeballs once more.

9

RATHER THAN REMAIN in so public a spot Hector removes himself. He slouches first to the kitchen, takes a little water from the tap, swallows a pill, tic tac, down the throat. Then he makes his way up the stairs and into his room: its bare, screwed-down bed, its single dresser, its window into which the dawn is hurriedly pouring fuzzy light. Sitting alone up here, self-banished to his room, makes Hector feel even more like a delinquent teenager. To be crying at his age! It's a bad joke.

But it is the undertug of imminent doom, the pressing vigor of darkness and depression, that most recalls him to his own adolescence. That teenage instinct that every little setback is in fact Disaster with world-ending big-D. That if a girl turns you down for a date she must hate you and you'll never ever get laid. That if you do badly at one set of exams then you'll never go to college, never get a job, you'll be doomed. It feels like that now. He is morbidly and wholeheartedly convinced that Dimmi will never speak to him again.

He recovers his last packet of smokes from the deal dresser, and carefully extracts one of the remaining five cigarettes. He is hoarding these last pleasures, ruling himself severely to repress those cravings that flutter and itch at his body. Nobody else in the compound smokes. He sits on the bed, and looks for a long time at the little hyphen-shaped tube of white. It goes into his mouth. He flicks the lighter to life, and, carefully, places a knob of flame on the end of the cigarette. The draw of breath is as sweet as ever it has been. Ahh, the air soaked in tobacco smoke, warm and heady and rasping like Johnny Cash's voice. He holds it inside his lungs, and, putting his head back, breathes out a straight spear of smoke that plumes into upward feathers and drifts for the ceiling. But the second drag is less distracting, less absorbing, and the thought of what he has just done begins to intrude. The third drag and the fourth drag are taken automatically as his mind slips back into its wearying grooves of self-recrimination and of shame and of bitterness. He has effected a breach with Dimmi. He feels sure it is a permanent breach.

The chain of association leads him back to Marjorie. How did he ever let her go? How could he ever have been *grateful* at the thought that she had gone off to London to sleep with other men? He was a fool and he is a fool and he'll always be a fool. A true, prating fool. He constructs an elaborate castle in the air, lying on his bed, an alternate timeline in which Marj had come with him to this ranch, in which they slept in this bed together, and faced the ending of the world together. Marj with her strong face, its large dark features and its heavy mass of dark hair above. She used to say that, to sketch her, all that was needed was to write ° L ° and draw a line underneath, and there was her face. But she did herself an injustice, for her features were always clear and handsome rather than cartoony. Her body, with its stocky waist and with two sets of broad, wide muscles on her calves and shoulders, sometimes seemed almost mannish to Hector; and her breasts had been small and underfilled, hanging in a slightly deflated manner from her ribs. But the curve of her hips and thighs was an aesthetic wonder, a perfect Matisse-esque pair of lines swelling and tapering perfectly to her knees. He used to love stroking her back when she lay, face down, on the mattress. And she was catlike in her love of being stroked. The triangular pad of fat at the base of her spine; the twin babyish dimples in her buttocks; the smooth warm skin of the back of her thighs.

He feels the pang of lost love, but of course the pang is tangled up with his present desire for Dimmi. The truth is that, at the time, he had been glad to get rid of Marj. The brutal fact of this, of his own callousness, brings the tears back to his eyes. At the time, and especially toward the end of the relationship, he had seen her as plain. As she sensed his withdrawal, she had become clingy and slightly desperate, which had, of course, only increased his ambivalence. Clingy didn't suit her anyway. And Hec had looked at other men's girlfriends and wives, and at women passing in the street, and almost all of them seemed more comely than his own woman. He had believed that he could do better. That was the truth of it. And in that ancient human self-delusion, that grass-is-sweeter, he had let his relationship slide and slide until it expired altogether.

He is crying again. Ach, ach, ach. He crushes the cigarette to death under his heel against the wooden floor. It is as if some faucet has been opened inside him, and he is not sure when it will stop pouring. He curls himself up on the bed and sobs himself into a sleep. Sleep.

And he really sleeps.

When he wakes he knows he has not been asleep for very long. Dimmi is sitting beside him, her hand on his shoulder. "Oh," he says, startled, hope like a headache ringing his gong-like head. "Hello." Is *she* here?

145

"Hello," she says.

Her face carries neither disappointment and disapproval, nor especial pleasure to see him. Hector hauls himself into a sitting position, and rubs his face with his sleeves. "I sort of fell asleep there," he says.

"I can see."

There's no disguising it, so Hector attempts to jolly through the fact of his weepiness. "I've been crying," he says, grinning. "Isn't that stupid? Isn't that the stupidest thing you've ever heard?" He wants her to say *no it's far from stupid*, or perhaps *I like a man in touch with his feelings*, or *it's been an emotional few hours for everybody*. But she says none of these things.

Silence settles between them like snow falling. It lasts a minute, or more; and, of course, silent time is longer than time touched by speech.

"The rain is lessening," she says, eventually.

"Is it?"

Silence again. Hector can smell the odor of her hair; that sweet, almost candied smell that he had previously assumed was a shampoo or a conditioner, but which—since few people shower more than once a week these days—is presumably nothing more than the intensification of her own smell. Her musk. It stirs something beyond words inside Hector's head, or his heart. There is a gorgeous taint of spice, of rosemary per-haps, in among the sweetness of the smell. It's a heartbreaker. And the light does seem to be beaming more brightly than usual through the quick dawn of the window. He can see every strand of her hair clearly, each one thick and black and each one dense with this extraordinary smell. He stifles the urge to throw himself upon her, to embrace her. He knows that if he does he will simply burst into tears, he will simply explode into tears, and he cannot bear the thought that she will witness his collapsing in that way. She is looking coolly at him. He finds it

hard to remove his gaze from the double-rounded completeness of her chest. The folds of cotton drapery trace the
contours of her figure as eloquently as any Quattrocento Old
Master's paintbrush. He's losing it. He pulls his gaze up by the
root, and it makes a tinny mandrake-shriek inside his head.

He focuses on her eyes. Beautiful eyes. Those café-lait brown
irises, those polished mahogany pupils. "You probably think
I'm crazy," he tries, in a light tone of voice. When she doesn't
reply, he adds, "I mean because I don't really believe, crazy,
yeah. Despite all the," he pauses minutely to place invisible
quotation-marks around the next word, "evidence, despite *all
that* I still don't really believe." Having started to talk, he finds
it easy to carry on talking. "I'm almost clinging to my disbelief, it's almost the thing that keeps me going. It's the
photographic negative of faith. Non-belief can be as sustaining
to a soul as belief, you know."

"You don't believe," she says, softly and without rebuke.

This stems his flow. "I," he says. "I don't know. Sometimes—
it makes sense. Other times, it all seems a total crock. Yeah? I
mean, how does *he* know? That's what bothers me."

"He has visions," says Dimmi, with the clear-voiced certainty of a nun.

"But how do *we* know?" Hector replies, speaking suddenly
rapidly as if her words have unblocked some repressive bar
inside him, "How do we know that these visions aren't lies—
they could be lies, they could be untrue, couldn't they? I
mean—you trust him, that's fair enough. But how do we—"
He stops speaking. He feels an inhibition, although he can't
quite locate what it is.

They sit in silence for a while.

"Anyway," he says. "I'm sorry."

This word is, perhaps, a word for which Dimmi has been
waiting. She smiles, gently, and reaches out with her hand to

touch Hector's hand. His heart jumps up at the connection, his teenage despair alchemically transmuted into teenage possibility. Perversely the happiness presses tears just as hard against the backs of his eyes as the sadness had before, and he crumples his face and hides his eyes behind the back of his free hand.

"I used to have a lover," says Dimmi, looking past Hector at the bright window. "He had an unusual sexual kink. He could only come, with a woman, when he was weeping. Only when he was in real tears. So he used to upset himself, to get himself worked up, to be generating this intense storm of emotion in his head as we got near to going to bed, until he was crying like a baby. The intensity of everything, you see. And then he would embrace me, his face all wet, and clasp me close like a drowning man, and kiss me and kiss me, and then he would put himself in me and come, like that. And really he could only come that way."

Hector's mouth has dried. This verbal account of her sex life is an intimacy so sudden and exhilarating it's almost frightening. He does not know why she has said it. But he doesn't want to spoil the bloom of his new feeling, so he nods, and appears to think about what she has said.

"He doesn't," he says, a little croakily, "sound like a very satisfying lover." Has she told him this because he, Hector, *reminds her* of this previous lover? As if he, Hector, is just some sort of sniveling crybaby in her eyes—but that's not fair. Hector is no crybaby. Come *on*. And, worse, Hector hasn't even had the chance to show Dimmi what sort of lover he could be—she's prejudging him, she's dismissing him without even giving him a chance. He feels he has to defend this nameless previous fuck-buddy, this other ghostly rival for his love. It stings him inwardly to say this, but he says, "Although, you know, I can sort-of see the logic of that."

"Can you?" asks Dimmi, neutrally.

"As opposed to other sorts of," (what word had she used?) "perversion." Hector stops, because that isn't the word she had used. Now he sounds too judgmental. But he presses on. Part of him thinks, *at least we are talking about sex, she and I.* There's a kind of closeness just in that fact. "What I mean is that there are plenty of, ur, sexual practices that I don't see the point of. Sadism, or some of the fetish gear that gets people excited, that kinda thing. Those gimp costumes, or gas masks, or whatever, I really don't get that at all. But what you're talking about…" He grins. "I mean there is something *teary* about orgasm, don't you think?"

She inclines her head a little.

Feeling he is losing command of his own little speech, he hurries on. "Not that it's how I… but that's not what I'm saying. All I'm saying is that this makes a sort of sense to me. That a man could link the sweeping intensity of weeping with… I read once about this guy, and he'd been," so difficult to choose the right words, "masturbating for the first time, as a kid, and he'd gotten himself snuggled under a rug, slid right underneath this rug, and as he came for the first time his mother happened to walk in and tread upon him. You see? And later, as an adult, he could only make it to orgasm if a woman in a certain kind of shoes were walking on him. Maybe this crying thing… actually, now that I come to relate that story, about the guy under the rug, it smacks rather of an urban myth. It doesn't sound like a real case history. But you see what I'm saying?"

"Hector," she says, softly, disengaging her hand. "You *can* believe, if you wish to. You can believe. After all, it is the truth."

"My dad," Hector replies.

She gets to her feet. This time Hector cannot censor the thought, and he blurts, "Is that it? Is that it?"

"It?" she queries, turning toward the door.

"You're *going*?" He cannot believe it. "You can't go."

"Hector," she says, with a crushing directness, "I am not going to sleep with you today."

"But," he splutters, "but we were—you were telling me. There's a *connection* here, Dimmi, Vera, there's a connection between *us*." And now, hearing their cue, ten hundred tears come hurrying out to parade down Hector's face. "Oh God, look," he pleads, knowing he is losing it, that he is losing her, "please don't go. Please stay with me. I can't be alone now, please don't go." But even he is disgusted by this sniveling abjectness. Dimmi does not even shake her head, she looks down at him with a Virgin Mary loftiness; she turns her back; she leaves.

10

HECTOR PUTS HIS face in his hands, but when the hands come away moments later he is no longer crying. The reservoir is ashy. It's all bound up with the frustrations of her simultaneous closeness and inaccessibility, isn't it? But what follows from this, as Frankenstein is followed by his monster, is the thought that if he were to break through her defenses and she were to become his lover, then he would eventually tire of her strong-limbed, rather overwhelming body; of its perfect proportions and its tough joints; of the weighty double-armature of her breasts in their cream-cheese perfect skin; of the solid almost manly heft of her two buttocks; of the sheer inescapable solidity of her being-in-the-world, like a natural feature of landscape. If he could possess her, she would cloy upon him. It goes something like this. This is about *you*, you know. For you love her, and you love her for her perfection. So what do you want? You want her husband to divorce her, her boyfriend to leave her, so that she can be yours. And when she's yours, and you say "I love you," or "I've always loved you," or "I will always love you," *that* is the exact moment your love starts to blister and peel away. Because your love is a function of her perfection. And if she's so perfect then why did her husband divorce her, her boyfriend leave? You don't even need to be presented with material examples of any actual imperfection in her. The *idea* of her imperfection, in your mind and without reference to reality, is enough. Because perfection is the most precarious and emotionally unstable of tyrants, and cannot permit even a crumb, even a peck of dissatisfaction. Perfection is a high-strung suicide bomber prepared to eliminate himself in a flourish of fire at the least thought that *it might not be so*. That another man might fall out of love with her means that you might, and the phrase *you might stop loving her* is the same phrase as *you will stop loving her*. All this comes crashing onto you at the moment of consummation, as if consummation and disillusionment are synonyms for the same, entropic emotional state of mind. The only pure love is the love that does not reveal itself. So the world turns.

The consuming passion he feels for her! He yearns.

There is a rushing sound in Hector's ears, as he sits messed and mournful, pitying himself, with his back to the door; a cascading hissing gush that sounds as if somebody has flushed a toilet inside his skull. His eyes are blanking with light, tinged with pink. Pink? Really? Yeah, odd, but: a great wash of white touched at the edges with these downflowing ribbons of exquisite pink and cream light, like a kitsch aurora borealis. As if the aurora borealis weren't kitsch enough already. And, and, much more slowly than an orgasm, a wash of visionary emptiness and purity comes into possession of his mind. He even has time to become aware of his own jaw slackening, of his own knuckles tapping the floorboards as his arms go limp, and then he is gone. Solid gone. He has slipped, slips, will slip into the future.

THREE

1

THIS VISION, AS it goes on, will have a much greater sense of something controlling it than the previous ones: something guiding Hector's thoughts, slowing to focalize certain events, hurrying to fast-forward others. This is the vision that will prove to be his fullest and his final one. There will be something freer about it, too, a visualization more Pollock than Dutch Master. What *about* all those photorealist and disconnected Dutch Master paintings? All feathery and hallucinatory, expressive of a disconnection from the body, art more spiritually extreme even than, say, Fra Angelico. No. But Pollock was something else. There had been a moment of understanding for Hector about Pollock, when he was still back at Yale, and he came early into the department and stepped into the washroom for a piss. The steel slope of the urinal was coated in blue bleach, and Hec angled his member as he pissed to score Pollock-like lines out of this, like cutting into the wax for an acid engraving. Like peeing the letters of your name into new snow, and he'd found himself thinking, with the physical relief swelling his sense of original insight, *that's* what those monumental Pollock canvases actually mean, with their tricolor spaghetti intertwinings on their white ground. That's why they're so effective as art. It's precisely because they imply this actual line from world back to body, the same fluid cord that men spool out when they make their water. It's all about connection.

This vision will remind him of that. This most complete vision. The elements of it, drawing together, or *growing* together, will relieve themselves into being, and as they clarify in his buzzing brain the lines will look less like dribbles of paint, and more like seams, the place where reality and reality are stitched together, the meeting place of before and after. The healing of wounds and coming-into-being of newness.

He sees that he will run out of the front door because he, and several others (Esther, Jacob, Pablo) hear a jet plane flying through the sky, its unmistakable gravelly scraping noise, a weighty trolley pulled on castors across the blue linoleum of the high sky. They are not going to be able to see the jet, and will spend fruitless minutes gazing at the sky. They will see only clouds.

The air will be perfectly clear of fog or rain—an amazing horizontal clarity stretching to the near horizon, but pressed down by the tight-fitting Tupperware lid of low clouds over their heads. Looking into the future, Hector now is even startled by the whiteness that the great arch of sky will assume. The rain and storm will have cleared with that surreal suddenness that characterizes so much of the atmospheric phenomena of this new order. That's all it is: one dawn the rain will stop, and the fog will have raised itself a hundred meters or so above them, and that's where it will stick, moving continually and heavily in the slowest of curls and waves. To look up at this lower sky will give Hector a strange sensation of optical illusion, as if he has been living on the ceiling of the world for so long that up has begun to seem down to him.

The new horizontal clarity in the air will reveal a landscape utterly different to the one that had existed before the fog. Hector will remember, though only imprecisely, the orange and ochre dust, the red humps of distant hills bouncing back the sunlight with plastic vividness. He will remember the flawless blue of the sky ironed smooth by the relentless slow procession of the hot metal sun. But that will be all in the past. Stepping out onto the porch with the rest of the group, Hector will be confronted with a desolated and tangled landscape, bleached of pastels into a muddy series of grays and greens and diarrhean browns, under a Northern European rather than a Californian sky. The view will be clear to the fence, one ten-meter panel of which, imperfectly mended by Pablo and Hans, gapes a little, suspended only by a top corner. Every visible element in the middle-distance will stand out against the egg-white ground, placed in sharper relief as by an artist's trick. All the intervening ground, including the macadamized roads, will be completely covered by towering growths of moss, of a variety Hector has never seen before. Tight-packed bushes half as tall as he is himself will be everywhere. Wiry fronds curled tautly. The myriad bunches of this moss will give the ground an upholstered look, and yet when examined individually each bush will strike Hector as prickly, sparky, like the strands of static discharge within an electric egg.

Wandering among and treading upon this fantastic outgrowth of moss, the more adventurous members of the group will find local variations on the pattern. Some bunches will contain lengthy, narrow, trumpet-shaped ganglia right in their heart; others will display pale yellow knobs at the end of their wire-thin branches, or foxbrushes of bristly jags like stiff old paintbrushes in a jar, or oddly square or rectilinear pads of growth. Tiny leaves or buds or brown and black, like waxed boot-leather.

Tom will say: "This isn't like any moss I've ever seen before. This is no lichen—look at the size of it, for Christ's sake."

"But what is it?" James will ask. "How come it's grown here?"

"There's been a tremendous amount of water fall in the last few months," Tom will say, uncertainly. "And the rain has had a higher salinity than is usually the case with rain." But this will not answer the doubts in the group's minds.

"It's weird," somebody will suggest. And they will be right.

"Not like any moss I've ever seen," is all Tom will be able to say. As if he is some kind of expert on mosses. *Not*, Hector Junior will think. But he won't say that out loud.

Still, it will be a relief not to be accompanied at all times by the drumming of the rainfall. And more than that, standing outside the ranch house, it will be possible to see the movement of the sun, though veiled by the clouds, as a shift of emphasis of the illumination above, like a torchlight being passed on the far side of a sheet of thick cotton. It will swell further and further west, and then after two hours of daylight it will drop down, and darkness will swallow everything.

Over and over, this veiled and speeding sun.

2

BUT HECTOR WILL not be part of the group any more, in any meaningful sense. His continuing willful atheism will serve to alienate him from the others, not least from his own dad. He will walk about the compound like a specter. People will sometimes stop their conversation when he enters a room, and resume as he leaves; or they will continue talking as if he isn't there at all. Sometimes he will join the group for the evening meal, and while they will not expel him he will not dare engage anybody in conversation. Often, to avoid the simple social awkwardness, he will eat alone, in his room.

His father's fits will become more and more prolonged. He will have them in the hall, in the kitchen, on the stairs. Often Dimmi will come down to tell them all that he is lying fitting on his bed and cannot join them for dinner. But at the same time, his ability to report what his fits are showing him will diminish. Sometimes the whole group will gather, in expectation of some tablet of stone from Mount Sinai, and he will simply sit and gape at them, as if he doesn't know who they are. On other occasions he will be cryptically laconic. "Cities," he will say. Or: "It's taking the shape of a, of a, hell, what's the word, what's the word?" Or: "This was how it mooned the moon, yeah?" People, too in awe to press him for explanations of these odd little statements, will debate them hotly among themselves when by themselves. "*Yeah* I'm gonna lie down and die," he will say, "but not *yet*." What might *that* mean?

It will become clear, slowly but inescapably, that his mind is losing sharpness, infected perhaps by the prolonged fog and rain and unable now to shake off the blankness when the rest of the world is being reborn. He will start to forget people's names, or to muddle people's identities up. He will call Pablo "Xavier," and there is no Xavier in the group. He will get Paul and Tom mixed up. He will call Jacob "Jewboy" without shame or apology, almost as if he hasn't realized that he has used this offensive term. On one occasion he will refer to Dimmi as "Dorothy." Hector Junior will find himself almost glad that he is not too close to this man. He will say to himself: nobody need be too upset by this visible deterioration. The battered old bird is protected by his very alienation from the pain of his encroaching senility. No longer son and father, now merely observer and patient, the way popes go senile and die slowly in plain view because there is no mechanism for a discreet retirement.

The trick Hec will have learned, a lifelong lesson, a lesson for living: give everything away. That's always the best strategy.

One day, taking advantage of the windless and clear air beneath the ubiquitous cloud cover, a group will go out in the four-by-four to scout around, to see what the land around the ranch looks like: it will be Hector Senior, Pablo, Tom. Hector Junior pointedly will *not* be asked to accompany this exploring party. They will maneuver the auto awkwardly over the masses of non-moss, or whatever it is, that has grown over the driveway, and they'll be gone, away, away, over the close horizon and gone.

Standing on the porch, looking over the weird Jurassic landscape, Janet will say to Esther, "It's funny this *stuff* hasn't grown on the roofs as well. The buildings' roofs are all clear."

"Rooves," Esther will say, testing the word. "Roofs. Yeah. It's strange."

"I mean," Janet is going to say, "why not?"

Esther will say, "The thing that freaks me out is that it broke through the macadam, that it *rooted* in tarmac. What if it breaks up the foundations of the buildings? What'll we do then?"

Hector Junior will be loitering at the far end of the porch, watching these two women talking. The ivoried, cloud-filtered light will be enough to his dark-adapted eyes to give their skin a striking, gleaming beauty. Neither of them really see Hector there. Janet's skin will have worsened a little, little patches of eczema like red felt standing proud of the skin of her neck and hands; but from a distance these imperfections will be less perceptible, and Hector will see only the compact figure, the mournful purity of her eyes gazing out across the ruined landscape. Esther, a tightly plump woman with very white skin like curves of porcelain and hair the color of black coffee, has never been very communicative with Hector; and after his public apostasy she will withdraw even more completely from him. He will think to himself: this is my life now, standing on the margins, watching. This thought will not upset him unduly. This, after all, is what life is bound to be like after the end of the world.

After a sunset and night and a new dawn the car will return, and people will gather as excitedly around its occupants as if they were astronauts reporting back from a trip to a new planet. "Yeah," Hector Senior will say, looking tired, "it's pretty much growing all around the ranch—"

"The moss," Tom will put in.

"—the moss, yeah," Hector will say, with a glance of weary annoyance at his lieutenant; "but about a mile west it starts to thin a little. It's still there, all about, but it does thin out some. It's like—what's that word?" Then, crossly, at his disciples: "What in tarnation you all gawping at?"

This will alarm the group into anxious silence. After a moment Tom will clear his throat, and everybody will look at him.

"The slant seems less, as well," Tom will announce, in his pompous little voice. "Slightly less than the last few times we've been out. I think *it* has spread itself more evenly under the earth. I think it has concentrated its mass less, uh, singly."

Hector Junior will try to disguise the scorn at the goggle-eyed ingenuousness with which the others greet this news.

Young Hec, tenaciously, will continue to *refuse* to believe. This refusal will become his talisman. It is all a hoax, or all a delusion. He will incline sometimes to the former hypothesis and sometimes to the latter. He will not be sure how the trick is being pulled off, but he will be sure it *is* a trick. Everybody else will go inside, but he will stay on the porch.

Sitting on the porch for two hours is enough to watch the emphasis of light shift, like the brightest of gods turning over his radiant sleep above the white mattress of clouds, from east to west. At the new dawn the western horizon will be muddy and mauve; but whiteness will seep swiftly into every corner of the sky and a general milky light will fall softly; it will be creamier and brighter than the light the fog had permitted to pass, and will create a new mood of hope, howsoever cautious, among the group.

One project (from which Hector will, naturally, be excluded) will see Tom supervising a half-dozen others in the business of clearing away a patch of ground to do some planting. "Do some real farm work" is Tom's phrase. See if there is enough light to enable crops to grow. Plastic sacks of compost, like huge yellow pillows, wait in the barn, ready to be mixed into the Mojave dust and watered. Long-term, Tom will explain, they must be ready to grow their own crops. They can't rely on stores forever. What about their children? They must learn, as a group, to become self-sufficient. Planting some seeds is the first way to do that.

But the clearance of even a modest half-acre will not go well. The moss, or whatever it is, will prove hideously difficult to cut; the stalks and strands intensely tough, and the metallic green and brown nodules blunting shears after only a few minutes' work. Metal bladderwrack, or volcanic cacti. And the root systems of these bushes will seem to go down forever, fibers that knit and sprawl and grasp and will be even more resistant to cutting than the stems: a tough plastic consistency that denies the spades and shears purchase. No matter how far the team dig down they will be unable to reach the final tapering tips of this system of roots;

and after two hours of sweat-popping work the sun will set quickly on a dismally small pile of harvested moss-clumps. The men will come back inside, and wash hurriedly, before joining the rest of the group—Hector Junior too, on the edge of things—for food and a round of pills. Tom will have brought in a sprig of the stuff, this strange plant, to examine at his leisure; the rest will have been left in an ungainly pile until the following dawn. The diggers, hungry, will grab some food before going off to snatch an hour-and-a-half's sleep. Hector, for whom his personal nighttime will not yet have arrived, will wander the silently dark ranch. Of all the group he will be the last one, the very last, to have resisted the general conversion to the new sleep patterns. All the others will be taking five naps, an hour-and-a-half each, out in every day. It will seem to suffice for them.

With the next dawn, the group will gather again, this time in the front hall. The electric light will be on, even though it will be daytime, the better to help them to minutely investigate the cut bough of moss they have brought inside. They will pass the frond of moss from hand to hand, examining it, as if it holds some secret to their new life. A golden bough to grant them entrance to some new realm. "Come on guys," Tom will say, peevishly trying to rally the diggers. "Let's get *at* it. Let's get out and clear some ground, and see where we are. Let's extend the patch we cleared yesterday, if only a little way."

But outside, under the milkmoon-colored clouds, they will find that the patch of ground they had so laboriously cleared has overgrown again. Watching from the porch, as seven or eight of the group thread their way awkwardly through the great bunching blooms, Hector Junior will feel a strange sense of superiority. That they can get so caught up in this idiocy! That they can be fooled by such obvious props and artificiality!

"They're gone," Tom will cry, his voice cracking with an odd combination of annoyance and fear. "All the pieces—"

"What do you mean?"

But it will be true, all the severed pieces of moss thrown into a pile will have vanished. Blown into the air by a sudden, secret wind, some will suggest. Grown back into the ground, others will say. But the earth that had been cleared only a few hours previously will be found to be closely overgrown again.

From this it will be apparent, to those who had not already made this connection, that the "moss" is no conventional growth. A powwow will be called in the dining room, chaired by a worn-looking and distracted Hector Senior, with Hector Junior sitting not at the table with everybody else but on a chair in the corner. People will have to address the fact of the moss, the fact that—so obviously, that it takes on a retrospective inevitability (how did we not see?)—it is clearly a manifestation of the apocalypse. "These are *it*," Jacob will say, "the very strands and fibers of *it*, reaching up from under the ground."

"We should never have cut it!" Esther will cry, with a hysterical intensity at least half put-on, like an amateur-dramatic reading of *The Crucible*. "Perhaps by cutting it, with shears, maybe we have *angered* it. We surely shouldn't take knives to the body of—"

A chill is going to scintillate through the room. People, being people, will share an atavistic terror at such a thought. It'll be the real thing. After all, a human being cannot be comfortable with the thought of angering, or—much worse!—*mutilating* their god. Hector will feel this nervous uncertainty too, despite wanting to preserve his rational disbelief. He will succumb to the urge to deny the manifestations of the sublime, and will say: "Hey, so it's allowed to break up our fucking world into little *pieces*, but we can't cut a sprig from its branch, is that it?"

162

But he will not speak in a loud voice. And nobody will pay him any attention; caught up as they are in their own anxieties.

"Let's wait for a moment," Tom will say, in a nervy, high-pitched tone; for, self-selected scientist though he still will be, he will also feel the uncanny terror at the prospect of an injured and angry god. But he will fight his own superstition. "Let's just wait for a moment, we *don't know* that these bushes of, let's *say* 'moss,' as good a term as any, we don't *know* that this moss is a direct emanation of..." He will tail off.

An uncomfortably rustly silence. People will fidget.

"What else can it *be*?" Jacob will demand, suddenly, in his booming voice.

"It could be lots of things," Tom will insist, though in a smaller voice.

But even this mild form of agnosticism in the face of these phenomena will be greeted by derisive tossings of the head and hootings. It will warm Hector Junior's blood a little, as he crosses his arms and his legs, to see Tom, of all people, put in the position of the derided disbeliever. It will please him.

"Are you saying," Jacob will ask, with clumsily schoolyard sarcasm, "that it has *nothing to do* with the events we have all lived through? Come *on*, Tom. Are you saying that?"

"No," Tom will insist, both his hands out, "sure, it has something to do with the events. But all I'm saying, I mean, *all* I'm saying is that," (he will become nervier as he feels the mood of the group shift away from him) "it *could* be something else. Let's say, for instance, that the object, that *it*, carried some *spores* from its last world, caught in its folds..."

"Folds!" Jacob will laugh, as if this is the most absurd thing anybody has ever said. Such scorn in a single syllable! But perhaps Jacob has always thought of *it* as a perfectly smooth sphere, like a black ball bearing of immensely compacted mass and mystery. Perhaps Tom, on the other hand, has always thought of it as a miniature brain, corrugated over its surface with ridges like tangled corduroy. Hector Junior will think to himself, it hardly matters.

"Or some other means, what I'm saying," Tom will press on, "is that maybe this—stuff—is just an alien plant, whose spores have somehow been carried here. Maybe it doesn't matter if we cut it, or harvest it, because the moss is not a direct feature of, of *it*. That's all I'm saying."

But this will not convince most of the group. For, having oriented their lives around the lines of force of this divine intervention for so long, this catastrophe and rebirth, it is only natural that they will read every single detail in their world in terms of it: or, more precisely, perhaps it'll be unavoidable that they will adopt that paranoiac understanding of the cosmos in which large-scale and small all contribute to a map of the relationship between the perceiver's ego and its god-like projection into the world around them. That'll be only natural. That's how people are. Hector will feel increasingly superior to the whole pack of them. Indeed, that phrase will perk into his mind, and he won't be able to place it exactly. Pack, *I'll be revenged upon the whole pack of you.* Is that a quotation? From where? He won't know. It won't really matter.

"And what *I* think," Esther will say, her head forward and her hair veiling her face, speaking in a slightly calmer voice, "is that we should treat it with respect. That's what I think. Res*pect*. It's not growing further out from the ranch—no? You guys went out in the SUV and that's what you saw? That it's growing thickly here, but not so thickly further out? OK. So why else would it be concentrated here, yeah? Why else? It's drawn to Hector. *That's* why it's growing here."

All eyes will turn to Hector at the head of the table. Everybody will want him to interpret this latest sign, to read these entrails and these flights of birds. Everybody will yearn toward his mystic leadership. But Hector Senior will have a vacant, slightly annoyed look in his eyes. He will look more tired than usual. His manner will be even more distracted and absent. Some poignant infantilism will have lodged inside his face, a look of uncertainty, of being in the company of grown-ups and not properly understanding them. His lips will part as if words are about to fly free, but instead the lips will quiver shut again. Hector Junior won't be certain that the others can see it, but he knows his own dad. It will strike him suddenly, in that room at that time, of whom Dad reminds him now: Ronald Reagan. The complex of memory will overlay a transparency over his perception of the scene. Reagan was young Hector's first political memory, his election to the governorship of California back in the seventies (or was it even the sixties?) and its blanket TV coverage lodged him in Hector's young mind as the archetype of the "politician," something that his presidential ubiquity in the eighties had only confirmed. At that time young Hector had taken it for granted, as children will; recalling only that he had liked the cowboy swagger of the new governor, the kindly handsomeness of his face. More than that, Reagan's election confirmed a crossover between the world of the movies and the real world—which for a six-year old (had he been six?) was a thing of almost transcendental wonder. Because of course he lived, as any American boy did at that time, more in the TV than the real world; and Reagan's genius was in confirming the *justice* of that emotional commitment, the *importance* of the lit screen with its cartoons and characters running around. But Hec will remember also the fights between his dad and mom, which were often focused on Reagan and his politics, and especially on his handling of the student riots of those years. He will remember tears, although it won't be clear to him in retrospect whether they were his

165

own tears at his parents' raised voices, or his mom's tears, or, perhaps, both of those things. "He's a Nazi," his mom had cried. "Call out the National Guard on the students today, who's to say he won't call them out on the *hippies* and *Jews* and *Democrats* tomorrow." "You're hysterical," Dad said in a clear strong voice. It was a word that always cropped up during his parents' rows. "So what would *you* do with the rioters?" The rows were frequent, you know. "But they're just *kids*," his mother shouted, and this made Hector's ears sit up, as he hugged his knees on the bottom step of the stairs, for *he* was just a kid too, which meant that his mother was, in some sense, talking about him. And that when his father spoke, it was also about him. How could it be otherwise? "Yeah they're causing some major trouble for *just kids*," said Hector Senior, in his heavily self-certain voice. "They're causing a whole heap of trouble for just kids. They're dangerous—they start this kind of trouble, they'd better be ready to accept the consequences. If a couple of them get shot, that's their lookout, they should have obeyed the *law* in the first place" "He's a *Nar*-tsi, you're a *Nar*-tsi," his mother had called, her voice high and huge, and there had been a crashing noise which Hector had thought was the glass cabinet in his parents' bedroom being smashed to smithereens, but which turned out, after things had cooled, and he had summoned courage to nose forth and investigate the battlefield, only to have been a door being slammed shut.

And, sitting in that room with the rest of the group, years later and after the end of the world, other memories of Reagan will present themselves to Hector's mind, Memories of Reagan mixing up with his perception of his dad. The later incarnation, the President with the doddery avuncular grin, that slightly trembly head rocking side to side on its thick neck. The post-presidential announcement of Alzheimer's, and the retrospect it granted the whole country, the sense that the last years of his grandpappa presidency had been touched by the early onset of that disease. That the country had been ruled by somebody who was mentally absent; as if that made a difference. All of it falling into place, in hindsight: the naps in the Oval Office, the questions Reagan would answer only with a waggly headed levity, the performance as if the presidential role was just one more actor's gig. This will be Hector Senior, in that room. Young Hector will understand that his father's mind is slipping, just as Reagan's did. The spate of life is eroding his mudbank mind, his grasp on things, washing away even his awareness of where and who he is. Old Hector's god-touched mind wallowing in and out of a gray dissolution.

"Hector," his followers will say, prompting him. In fact they will be saying *tell us what to do*. In fact they will be saying *help us*. This will almost be too much for Hector Junior. He will cover his embarrassment with a chortle.

"Yeah," Hector Senior will say, casting a slightly puzzled glance around the room. "What?"

"Have you seen anything about this?" Jacob will boom. "In your visions?"

"Everybody has visions," old Hector will say, dismissively, turning away as if peeved. A *why are you picking on me?* manner.

"But, Hector, that's not true," Janet will chip in. "Only *you* have been having visions lately. We rely on you. Yours are the important ones. You're the only one."

But this will chime obliquely in Hector Senior's head as a rebuke, and he will flash ashen fire. "You can't tell me that. Everybody has visions. You can't pin that on me. Who d'you think you *are*?" His sudden pique will silence the whole room. Anger of the prophet is the reflected anger of god; fire of the sun; lunacy of the moon. The group will fearfully remember

Esther's comments on incurring the anger of *it* by shearing away some of its branches.

"Hector," Dimmi will say, placatingly. Hector Junior will close his eyes. "Hey," she will say, soothingly, "it's alright."

"So *don't* snap at me," Hector will reply. "I didn't ask you to buy my shares. I skellied my *balls* off on this. The market can go down as well as up." Buy his shares?

Perhaps the general mood of the group, the near-cultic anxiety, will have percolated into his muddled consciousness. His brain more radio receiver than thinking organ. It will have made him nervy, and some part of him will find reinforcement in this awareness, a subconscious comprehension that his crossness will be, in one sense, exactly what his disciples want from him—a stern patriarch, the angry god. Standing, he will say, "Just leave me be, all of you. I've got accounts to attend to." And he will exit the room, leaving his acolytes shocked, as if grace has been withdrawn from them and damnation was wagging its finger.

Dimmi will say, "I'll go after him," in an unvarnished voice. And as she gets to her feet Hector will have to watch her. To look again upon her form and figure, the flat z-shaped wrinkles in her jeans at the back of her knees and thigh as she walks away from him. The cool tall grace of her. It will pain him, but he will have to look.

Tom will still be sitting there, holding the wiry sprig of *it* in his hand. *It* in its plant incarnation. "What should we do with this?" he will ask, his voice clouded with superstitious awe. "Would it be safer just to chuck it out the door, you know, to *return* it?"

"Ladies and gentlemen, behold the golden bough," Jacob will announce, nodding his head towards Tom. Hector will be struck by how exaggerated everybody's personalities have become in this socially claustrophobic environment. Tom acting more and more like a caricature nerd. Jacob acting more and more like the ringmaster of a continental circus. Oh I'm *glad* to be out of it, he will think. I'm *lucky* to be out of it. Who'd want to be part of this group of lunatics?

"The golden bough," Jacob will repeat, holding the tinny wreath above his head, as if that were a significant gesture. "To what does it grant us entry?"

"Jacob, show some respect."

"We could wear a sprig in our lapel," Jacob will say, though in an uncharacteristically uncertain voice.

"Wear a sprig in your *lungs*," Hector Junior will bark, uncertain what has prompted these slightly strange words. Jacob will dart a glance at Hec, and hold the sprig further away, as if it really were shedding spores or alien dust that might root in the lesions of his chest and grow something monstrous up through his gullet.

"I think we should return it," Janet will say, not looking at Jacob.

"I agree," Esther will add immediately. "Throw it outside, let *it* reclaim it."

And Jacob will pass the bough to Tom, who, gravely, will get to his feet and walk to the window. Outside, the moss will already have grown high enough to protrude an inch into the bottom portion of the view, like a hedgerow growing close against the house. Jacob will pull the window open and pause, in ritual respect, before tossing the bouquet outside. Then he will close the window quickly.

3

IT WILL BE the day after this that the group hears the airplane: that impossible noise up in the sky. Hector Junior will hear it first, and will cry out, "A plane!" and for once the others will not ignore him. Esther and Jacob will have been sitting in the wing chairs by the front door conversing in low tones. Pablo will be standing in the doorway to the dining room, as if uncertain which room he wishes to occupy.

Hector Junior will be sitting on the couch. A thought will occur to him that has not occurred before. This life-saving couch—what if, instead of landing harmlessly on the couch, he *had* fallen on bald floor? What if he'd died? Knocked, maybe, into a coma? Would that fact explain everything that happened subsequently? "Am I dead?" he will ask, aloud, although this statement will not intrude on Esther and Jacob's conversation, and Pablo will ignore it.

The thought will seize him like a eureka. Am I in hell? Or, more likely: is this all just a coma dream? In fact I'm lying in a hospital bed in Pasadena with tubes puncturing my skin like Saint Sebastian, with nurses coming in to pick the boogers from my nose with rubber bulb pipettes, to change my catheter and sponge me down. *Somebody* must be there to check the bleeping machines that monitor my motionlessness. Somebody out there. Doctors and Dad and maybe even Marj at his bedside, debating whether to turn the machines off—judges involved, maybe a national debate, congress passing resolutions, keep him alive, let him die. But although the neatness of this explanation will appeal to him, something about it will not seem right. The qualia, his actual sensory experiences of his day-to-day, are too precisely delineated. It will feel too wholly as if he is awake and real, not as if he is in a dream. It will be a question of the timbre of his experience, a gritty grubby verisimilitude that convinces him, on some basic level, that he is genuinely experiencing all this.

Still, he will mull the thought over. Had his life hinged, during that bizarre night of the multiple quakes and the great change? Had he taken the wrong turn on the landing in more senses than one? It will be hard to say. The more he tries to pin the memory down, the more mythic and hazy it will become.

What happens after the world's ending? You're dead. What's that like? Like being alive, only less so.

Then he will hear the buzzing of what he will take to be a fly; which in itself will excite him, because he hasn't heard so much as a gnat since the change. He will leap up and hurry to the door, and when he opens it he will recognize the buzzing for something larger. "A plane," he will yell. "That's a plane."

Pablo will join him at the door. Jacob and Esther will stop their conference and leap up also. "I think he's right," Jacob will say.

They will run outside.

The moss bushes will be as ubiquitous as ever, each bush pressing against their surrounding bushes (or whatever they are) more tightly than ever. Even standing on the porch the tops of the growth will reach the height of their shins. To step among them will be to have the fronds reach as high as their stomachs or chests. The four of them will stand on the porch looking into the low white ceiling of the sky, trying to discern what is making that noise.

"Is it a plane?"

"It sure sounds like one."

"Other survivors?" Esther will ask.

"Or maybe," Hector Junior will say, true to his village-idiot role as the skeptic, the unbeliever, "it's some atmospheric phenomenon. Maybe it's thunder, or something." The others will look at him, as if pitying his insanity: to be denying this evidence of other human life! The first evidence of normality, which is the normality he has been proclaiming like John the Baptist in the wilderness to an unbelieving audience. But

Hector long before this will have given up trying to tell a consistent tale about the reality he finds himself in. All he will have is his unbelief. This he will cling to, as his only point of reference in a shifting world. Whatever his dad proposes as explanation for things he will deny. He will put all his energy into his denial.

"This cloud cover," Pablo will ask, his head back. "Is it, like a layer, with clear sky above? Or does it go up and up into the atmosphere, for miles and miles?"

"How can we possibly know that?" Hector Junior will snap.

But they will have gotten so used to treating him as an absent party that they will not register this question. "I'd say," Jacob will offer, in a sage tone, "that it's a thin layer. You can really *see* where the sun is, the light moving over the sky. You can almost see the sun itself through the clouds."

"Almost but not quite."

The noise of the plane will fade and sputter, and then it will be gone.

"That was no atmospheric whodat," Esther will say, looking at Jacob instead of Hector, and then hurrying inside to inform the others.

The sunlight will fade in another swift dusk. People will come and go upon the porch, where Hector Junior will have taken up station, sitting in one of the porch chairs. The air will be warm, moist, a little muggy. There will be a faintly chemical, petroleum or pesticide odor, something that Hector will not quite be able to place. Perhaps it will originate in the moss bushes. Their branches will seem thicker, more purply, like supersize heather, or bolted rhubarb; and a greater variety of blooms will be visible from where Hector will sit: little green trills, scintillations like a thousand brown cilia, stiff little diatoms, feathery outgrowths in gray that look a little like shrimps. The trumpet outgrowths will have broadened their horn-ends, showing a pigeon-chest blend of iridescent blue and green among their brown furred innards. Hector will like the thought that he is staring at an alien landscape translated onto the earth. But at the same time he will remind himself, tapping one finger on the back of the other hand, that it isn't alien, that whatever has happened cannot be explained in terms of his father's strange fantasy.

4

THE PLANE WILL not be amenable of straightforward explanation. Some of the group will insist it is a symptom of human existence, others that it is another creation of *it*, like Hector's visions and the strange, alien plant life. "Perhaps," Esther will say, with the dogged insistence of the true believer, "some portion of it has broken off and is scouting through the sky. Is that so hard to believe?"

"In the form of a propeller-driven airplane?" Tom will counter, in a mocking and disbelieving voice.

Esther will fall back on simple repetition, another function of the stubbornness of her faith in Hector Senior's apocalypse. "Is it so hard to believe?" she will ask.

Hector Senior, once again notionally in charge of this moot, will sit in impassive silence. Only if asked a direct question will he start, puzzled-looking for a moment before relapsing into grouchy snappishness. The group, wary of disturbing their idol, will leave him be. He will no longer be having his seizures, or any visions which he can report; but Dimmi will report that he often twitches wildly in his sleep, as if all the body-shaking intensity of the visions has been concentrated in his five daily sleeping periods. "Maybe it's better that way," she will suggest, in a low tone, while Hector Senior's attention is elsewhere. "Maybe it's less—distracting." But the old man will no longer be able to relate the content of his visions even in cryptically shortened form. Whatever it is he dreams will be a perfect blank to his followers.

People will stay increasingly in the main house; sleeping on the couch and in the chairs, or even on the floor, rather than trek through the chest-high moss from house to dorm and back. Stores will be brought through in larger quantities and stacked in the corner of the kitchen.

Dusk will follow hard upon dawn; dawn will grow slowly out of the darkness. But the night will display no stars, and the days will remain uniform in their polar-spring blankness. The cloud layer will not break, and move over them in white mystery.

The landscape will change, however. The color of the moss will, unmistakably, deepen; a darker blue growing out of the purple and gray and brown. Little fruit-like globes will grow, looking so like blueberries that Hector, heedless of the superstitious fear of blasphemy, will pluck them and even pop one of them into his mouth. But it will taste of dirty water and burnt carbon and a slight flavor of sulfur, and he will spit it straight out.

Surely it will be time for him to leave the compound? Surely—soon?

But questions, even questions of this sort, will no longer engage him. He will have lost the ability to care. He will lie on his bed, in sheets dirty after months of never having been changed, staring uncaring at the ceiling. He will be waiting for something to happen. His skull will feel, beneath the skin, as if crusted by minerals, deposited upon by some hidden accretion. Press *here*, and *here*, just beside the eye socket: can you feel the gritty quality of the bone? Vision, reality, two terms that once seemed thesis and antithesis, will now come increasingly sound like synonyms in his ears. And let it come.

And the time will come, one pre-dawn, in the darkness when only he is awake, lying on his bed with a candle chuckling at him from the floor, and shadows spasming and swaying on the ceiling. He will rise, as if bidden, although the silence will still be as blank, as insectless and bird-cry free, as emptied of the sounds of traffic as ever it has been. He will get to his feet. He will step out onto the landing. This was the path he had taken on the night of the earthquakes. Here he had turned right instead of going straight on to the top of the stairs. Here, at that exact spot, he will stop. The hall below him filled with darkness like a cup filled with coke.

This is what he will be imagining: somebody shooting a small-caliber bullet, a .7 say, at a pool ball. He will mentally sift through the possible colors this pool ball might be, before settling on a blue ball with a white stripe—this the abstract, Mondrian-like representation of ocean and cloud, and the number perhaps diagrammatically capturing the black earth on which the people lived. He will picture this ball resting on dark purple baize, a surface that reaches not to chubby felt-covered rubber cushions but instead stretching out infinitely far in every direction. But from slightly above the ecliptic he will imagine a gunshot, and the little pellet of lead hurtling, distorting to an irregular little oval in flight, towards the innocent ball.

"Hector?" This will be Dimmi's voice.

"Yeah," he will reply. His heart will hurry.

She will be standing at the top of the stairs, a couple of yards away from him. The candlelight through the open door behind him will put out some fitful illumination, and the electric light in Hector Senior's room will plunge through that open door at right angles, to capture the dips and peaks of her face.

"Is it you?"

"Yeah," he will say again.

"I thought you were your dad," she will say, in her accentless English that only very occasionally betrays, through an unidiomatic or overly formal locution, that it is not her mother tongue.

"Isn't he in his room?"

"*I* was in his room," she will say, looking left to right. "I awoke, and he has gone. Have you seen him?"

"He's not turned on any lights down there."

There will be a tone of the slightest uncertainty in her voice; something Hector has not heard before, a wobble in her luminous self-confidence. It will only strike Hector a moment later that *I was in his room* means that she is now sleeping with the old man all the time. This realization will drift over his sensorium like a stroke across his face from a jellyfish tentacle. His smile will become that little bit more rictus. As if he didn't know *that* already.

"We can," he will say, "go look for him." But Hector will understand that this process must involve waking the whole house; for there are dark forms, sleeping, on the couch and the chairs down below who will wake when the lights come on. And once word circulates that Old Hector has wandered off, everybody will want to join the search. And, knowing that this is coming, he will want to preserve the moment between them, this pseudo intimacy of just the two of them, tenuous though it is, if only for a moment longer. *Chère madame, permettez-moi*—

"He's been," Dimmi will say with a slight stickiness in her consonants, as if on the verge of tears (but *her*? in tears? not Dimmi, surely!), "more than a little absent-minded recently. He's been more than a little."

It will occur to Hector to step across the ground between them, to kiss her, to make the connection; but this time the impulse will barely get out before he stifles it. Don't be *silly*.

That would be all *wrong*. He will try: "I was just thinking of the first time we met," although this will be a lie, he wasn't just thinking of that. He wasn't just thinking of anything. "Do you ever remember that? We sat together outside and talked about anything, nothing very much. Do you ever think of that?"

Dimmi's vague face will swivel past him. "No," she will reply, without heat.

"Well," he will say, resignedly, "well, let's get the light on. Let's wake them downstairs. Let's shed some light. *La lumière du monde.*"

This last touch will seem to lighten her mood a little. The creases at the corner of her mouth, amplified in the oblique light, will strengthen minimally, as if almost on the edge of a smile. "Comme vous voulez, monsieur," she will reply.

"Right," he will say, but at once the doubts will again stab. Does she use "vous" in jest, a mock-formality? Or does she genuinely think of him as a "vous"? Her lover's son, her leader's son, the marginal guy, the apostate—how else would you address such a figure except formally? He will find himself craving a comme tu veux. How absurd. How absurd. "Right," he will say, jollily, to cover himself. And they will flick on the electric lights, and cause the sleeping figures below in the hall to twitch and sit up.

"What's happening?"

"Hey…"

"We're looking for Hector," Dimmi will say. "He's slipped out of his bed."

Tom will be one of the figures, asleep in the hall until the lights shone. Hector will consider how odd it is that this boy-eyed, boy-smiled man, this pompous little science major, could sleep blithely downstairs while his wife shares the bed of another man. Has he no pride? And then Hector will swear to himself, solemnly and without any sense of the comic irrelevance of the action, that if

Dimmi were his—*when* Dimmi is his—he will covet her, he will maintain her strenuously as his *own*. He will kill to maintain her as his. But as he stands there a general panic will be spreading through the building. Word will have passed through mysterious channels, that the patriarch has vanished. People, gummy-eyed and stumbly yet panicky and eager, will come through doors and everybody will gather in a nervous knot. "Where is he?" "Where has he gone?"

"He slipped from his bed," Dimmi will say, her voice *plein* with tears, the first time Hector will have heard such an emotional inflection to her words, "and I didn't notice. I should have been more careful. He just slipped away. He's not been himself, he's not been himself on his head, in his head, we all have been seeing that in him." She will put her hands over her eyes, as if ashamed that her grasp of the language is fraying under this pressure. "I am worried," she will confess. "He was talking a little crazily before we fell asleep. I am worried that he has done something crazy."

"The *strain* he's been under," a woman will wail. Of course it will be Esther. Hector Junior will be halfway down the stairs when he hears this piercing ululation, and it will stop him in his tracks. Bacchae.

"We haven't *helped* him the way we should have *helped* him," Jacob will boom. "Helped him with his *burden*."

"Let's find him," Tom will say. "We can still find him, we can make things better." But he will be fighting, in the others, a rising tide of near-hysterical self-accusation, a group half-convinced that their prophet has abandoned them altogether, that the glory has departed.

"He's *gone*—I feel it—he's *left* us." Esther again.

"I knew this day would come."

Somebody will be sobbing.

"Come on," Tom will chivvy them. "Let's not leap to conclusions, let's just not jump to… you, you check the back rooms.

Dimmi, you and I will go through the rooms upstairs. The rest of you, go to the dorm, see if he's wandered off there."

The searching will begin. Hector Junior will take a seat in one of the wing chairs in the hall, and watch as people come and go, and the panic settles into a gemlike frantic despair, a sort of rushing, grim-faced collective mourning. The certainty will come over them all, some more quickly, some more slowly, that Hector *has* gone, that he has left them forever. But however it comes to them the certainty will root deeply in them, because that too is one of the conventions of the cultic leader, the messiah, the god-among-us, that he stays with us for only a while, and that one day or one night he ascends mysteriously and invisibly to the heaven from which he came. Hector Junior will contemplate the circumstance with an equanimity that rather surprises him. He will ask himself whether he shouldn't *feel* more? It is his father, after all. Perhaps his dad is dead. Shouldn't that stir something? But all he will be able to think is that he has drifted above it all, surrounded by a celestial indifference like a spaceship surrounded by a magical force field to ward off asteroid strikes and laser bolts. He will find the scurryings of the group, the people bursting in through one door to run out through another in tears, *interesting* in a vague and unengaging way. The whole thing, hoax, hallucination, coma-dream, whatever it is—all of it will have become a glass-sided ants' nest, and he the entomologist with a clipboard and a distracted sense that his coffee-break is surely due very soon now. Coffee? Anyone?

> *See* if he's wandered
> *See* if he's wandered
> *See* if he's wandered off there

Once upon a time, when the world still existed, he had sat down with paper and a pen in front of a computer. He had spent an hour browsing the Internet, drawing up a list of charities. It had been a time-consuming business, giving away all his money. But, if you persevere, there comes a time when it has all been given away. You just need to keep going with it. And, eventually, you will be free.

After a while Hec will even nod off, sitting in one of the wing chairs, dozing as the world rushes around him. He will wake with a start. The windows will be light. He will get to his feet with that disorienting feeling of not knowing how long he has slept, perhaps through one dawn, or maybe two. The somber hum of conversation will reach him through the door of the dining room, and he is going to walk slowly towards that door, and he is going to open the door.

5

EVERYBODY WILL BE inside, sitting around the table. There will be several tearstained faces, and several more with looks of grim determination such as people adopt when they are trying to convince themselves that they can *beat* this thing, that they can face this terrible turn of fate and *overcome*. But Hector Senior will not have been found.

All eyes will turn to young Hector when he steps through the door. Unused to being the center of such attention, Hector's heart will make several sturdy throbs in his chest, and a blush will brim at his cheeks. "Hi guys," he will say, with a deliberately inappropriate levity.

"Hector," Jacob will say. "Please sit with us—please."

"Okily, dokily," Hector will say, light-headed, as if this is funny. Maybe he will not quite be awake yet. Still riding his own wave of facetiousness. Dad gone, these people will be leaderless, hopeless, but his own doubt and his own resistance to the brainwashing, will have prepared him better for the disaster. If it even is a disaster. Give it all away. He will take a chair at the table.

"Hector," Jacob will say, in a funereal voice. "The news is not good about your father."

"What's the news?"

"He's gone. We've looked everywhere. In every building, and throughout the compound."

"Maybe he went for a drive. Went for a drive with his *hairdo*." He won't know why he added this last zany detail. He will feel a rush of manic-tinged energy. His words will seem less and less his own. He's fidgety with his inner hilariousness.

Jacob will shake his head. "The cars are all still here."

Hector will shrug. "That's nutmeg to sweeten the barium." Where will *that* have come from?

"I don't know what to say about Hector, about your father," Jacob will grumble. "He's not a young man, and his health has not been good recently..."

"Gaga," Hector will agree, nodding over-vigorously. The name is cadavers, reversed.

This will shock the group, another impish little example of Hector's apostatic frame of mind. Esther, at the back, will shake her head mournfully.

"I don't think it's fair to say..." Tom will start.

"We didn't *help* him," Esther will interrupt, in angry tones. "*It* was communicating through him. Latterly, *only* through him—that was a terrible burden, and we did not support him. That's why," she will conclude, her voice splitting with tears, "is why he has been taken from us..."

"For the last time," Tom will insist, anger in his voice too, "we've no evidence that he's been *taken from us*."

"*It* has him."

"We do not know that. For a fact."

"Oh come *on*..."

"Please!" Jacob will half rise in his chair, pleading. "Everybody, please. Let's not go round and round, on this thing. Guys, please." Silence will settle uneasily on the meeting. Once again everybody will look at Hector Junior.

The merest flicker of grief will trouble Hector's thoughts, a candle-flame in a vast and dark chamber. This is *his father* they'll be talking about, after all, who is possibly dead, who is probably dead. Hec may well be an orphan. Hector will remember himself aged ten, and his father tall and handsome in a denim jacket and denim pants, leaning forward to pass across an ice cream. Young Hec will remember the holiday during which his dad had bought him that ice cream. He had desired that ice cream with every atom of his ten year-old soul, and when his father had delivered it to him he had been *so happy*. It had been a week in Tijuana, that holiday: Dad and him in the car driving all the way down, young Hector so excited, for hours, that he couldn't stop bouncing on the plastic seat, and singing, *in come the doctor* and *he said, no! more! mon! keys! jumpin! on the! bed!* Where was Mom? She hadn't been on that particular holiday. Why not? At ten years old, Hector had not wondered, had not asked, not been bothered. Later, looking back on it, Hector will be puzzled at the semi-detachment that seemed to characterize so much of his parents' marriage. That his dad and he could take a week's holiday without Mom, and Hec not even notice that his mom wasn't there? A week in Mexico, on the hot desert-sand beaches, where the oranges and bright greens of the concession stands gleamed impossibly, phosphorescently bright in his boyish eyes, and the sea was a turquoise blaze that ski-sloped up to the blaze of the sky, and every morning he woke with a Christmassy excitement in his belly and he would run through to bounce on his father's bed to hurry him out of the hotel into the sweltering light.

But that was before the world ended. This will be now. He will get a grip. He will think those words, in his head: *get a grip, Hec.*

Everybody will be looking at him.

Maybe his father will indeed be dead. It will seem, to his perception of things, an appropriate fate for the man who organized this whole bizarre end-of-the-world party. And, moreover, Hec will start to feel a tingle of anticipation. All the eyes that will be looking at him. He will think: and after all, if the king *is* dead, shouldn't the king's eldest and only son succeed to the throne? Should he assume his father's powers, and his father's harem? No? And the fumes of power are intoxicating fumes, they're lighter fluid to fiddle with his head, put starbursts into his vision accompanied by a wobbly exciting sense of losing his balance.

Is that, he will wonder, why they have asked him in here?

"So," he will say. "So."

Jacob will be looking at the table. "He was your father, Hector," he will say. "We thought we should tell you."

The mood will have been changed by this event, the disappearance. Hector will sit back in the chair, adopting a more expansive pose. People looking at him, listening to him.

"So what are we going to do?" he will ask.

"*If*," Tom will say, earnestly, still clinging to his own unique and reassuring form of disbelief, "if Hector has gone, *if* your father has gone, then we need... leadership. I've proposed a triumvirate, with myself, Jacob and Pablo as the three. We think that'd be best. We think a democratic process of decision-making is fair; daily meetings of the whole group to discuss what to do over the following five dawns. Parcel it out, timewise, like that."

This, Hector will think, doesn't sound like a ceremony of investiture. But perhaps this will be their way of inviting him back into the group, a voting member. The need to reassert his contrarian soul will be too strong to resist. "I see," he will say.

"Though I'm not sure my dad is dead, you know. And I'm not sure he'd endorse a democratic model, he was no democrat, if you know what I mean." They will all be sitting there, soaking this up, following his words. A mere habit of obedience to the family line, maybe. Perhaps they will be suggesting him as a sort of constitutional monarch, along British lines. "OK," he will say, wanting to truncate discussion for fear of hearing bad things about himself. "I'm going to my room to smoke a cigarette."

"Wait, Hec," Tom will say, reaching instinctively towards him over the tabletop. "We need—it's. The thing is, I have, we've come to the conclusion that communications from it are *keyed* or *tuned* somehow to Hector's DNA. Its proximity to Hector, or the absorption of his DNA, or something like this, something along those lines, that, that have always provoked the visions. And of course, he himself had the strongest and longest visions, those epileptic interludes."

"Those floppings-about," Hector will laugh, unconvincingly. "Dad getting jiggy with it."

The rest of the group will not laugh.

"We know you've had some visions yourself. Vivid ones we heard. None of us have been having any. Which is by way of saying, whereas some of us had visions formerly, nowadays nobody is having any." Whereas? "As the closest thing to Hector, genetically speaking, it may be inevitable that you get them."

"I'll make a note of any epilepsies I experience," Hector will say, offhand, pushing his chair back and rising. "And report straight to the Gang of Three here."

"Be serious," Tom will say, severely, though Hec will hear *B-Sirius* and think it a stellar catalogue name. These little distractions. "Please, Hec. This is a *disaster* for the group, your father's disappearance. A disaster. After everything that's happened—it was only his connection to *it* that's preserved us all so far. None of us can be sure it will grant *us* any visions, any of us... for why should it? But it may very well contact you. You gotta promise, man, that you'll help us. Will you at least *help* us? We're all asking you."

Hector will be flattered by this naked begging. "Sure," he will say, from the door. "But I tell y'all. Dad, I bet you, is sitting in a bar somewhere, outside this zone of weirdness, drinking a beer and watching a game on the TV, and laughing at the whole experience. You ask me, that's what he's done, he's walked clear away from these ten acres of whatever-they-are."

"Hector," Jacob will call, getting to his own feet. "You are an intelligent man." Then, as if registering that this patronizing overture will not achieve the desired effect, he will speak more sternly. "You understand the meaning of the word *denial*, Hector. Psychologically speaking, I mean. You know what an analyst means when he uses the word denial. Can't you see that you—?"

"Hector," Janet will intervene, also standing, and trying for a more pleading tone. "I understand why you cling to a belief that nothing's changed, that everything's the same in the outside world. Do you think we don't all of us fantasize about exactly that? But we have all got to face facts. The world *has* changed."

"It has *ended*," Jacob will bellow, striking the table with his broad fist, big as a bulldog's head. People around the table will twitch, startled at his vehemence.

"Hector—we all need to *pull together*, surely you see that," Janet will say.

"Pull together," Hector will say with a nod, grinning like an idiot. Blinking both eyes at once like a blinking idiot. Then he will repeat: "I'm going to my room to have a cigarette," and then add, "I've got three left." He will be sweating; not profusely, but a dewy spread over his forehead. Filmy. His grin will make an ache in his cheeks. His vision will be a little waverly.

"We need to know," Esther will call, as if dragging reluctant words from some depth inside her, "about the *bushes*, the *moss*, we *need* to know how to handle it, we need to know what *It* thinks, what *It* wants, whether it's a plant we can just cut, or whether it's something *holy*, something it would be a *sin* to—" and she will break off, to cough. Grinning still, Hector will walk through the door, and straight up the stairs.

6

HE WILL DO what he said he was going to do. He will sit on his bed, and light a cigarette, and smoke it carefully, precisely, holding it like a pen between thumb and forefinger and sharpening the ash like a pencil-point against the edge of his ashtray. The smoke will work its usual leavening upon his brain, expansively stimulating and simultaneously calming. The whole thing. An explanation for everything that has happened. On balance, he will decide, he will come down on the side of *some hallucinogenic agent*. As an Art History major, he will think, it's not his business to be more exact than that. Dad will have done business with enough ex-hippies, with enough industrial chemists, to have been able to purchase vats of some pungent chemical or other. Something that promotes hallucinations, of the sort that Hector himself has experienced. Maybe something that Hector Senior, with his in-the-bone self-confidence, could exploit: planting ideas in people's heads, influencing people's perceptions, building up a drug-influenced consensual mass-hallucination. The grainily blue cigarette smoke will eel itself around him, as if urging him on to this conclusion. After all: if this tiny white tube in his hand can so immediately and wholly affect his mood, what might some more potent pharmochemical substance not do? It was probably like this in

Charles Manson's family, reality just warped enough, not so much that you lose touch with the verisimilitude of lived experience, but enough to introduce alien elements and not have your followers reject them out of hand.

He will sit there, and try to fathom why his father has chosen this moment to leave. Perhaps, he will think, the whole scam is about to unravel. He has maintained the illusion for months, yeah, but he can hardly maintain it forever. Perhaps, Tom will speculate, the supply of hallucinogens is almost exhausted. Perhaps the external world, in the shape of a local sheriff in a police car, or in the shape of a curious TV news crew, is about to take an interest in this weird commune. And so Hector Senior has absconded, tired of fucking Dimmi and Janet and who knows whom else, tired of the abject discipleship of these sheep and these goats. Hector will picture him boarding a plane with a suitcase full of euros. Perhaps with a false beard and wig. Not Dad's style, that, at all; but it will be a pleasing fantasy for Hector for a few minutes.

Then, suddenly, he will have an insight into his own love for Dimmi. People, he will see, *have* loves—which is to say, the emotion, that reified crystalline feeling of love for other people—in the same way that they *have* children. Some children are easy-going, tend to themselves, attach their eyes to the TV or sink into the shiny cleft of a book (as he had done as a child, wholly absorbed for hours in the large waxy-smooth pages of *Swamp Thing* or *Dark Knight*). And some loves *are* like that. Loving Marj was so easy-going that, caught up in other things, Hec had for fairly long periods forgotten that he had ever given birth to such a love. But then again other children are demanding, endlessly hungry and endlessly colicky things, loves that cry in the night and keep you awake, that consume your substance and churn in your bed with bruising, spasming little limbs. Individual loves may be more demanding than a whole brood of other attachments. Hec will revolve this conceit in his mind, exploring its points of rightness, the weaker points of its metaphorical fit, increasingly convinced that he has had a profound insight.

He will see himself as a father to his unrequited passion, his mewling and biting child, his love-for-Dimmi. He will wonder how the love itself will see the relationship. Has he been a good dad? But the strange thing will be that this new way of understanding his obsession of perfect-breasted Dimmi, his continual tear-streaked, thirteen year-old-style yearning for her (and he heading for *forty*, for Christ's sake) will bring with it something that approximates to peace. One cannot battle with one's children. One must accept them, flaws and warts and ungovernableness and turmoil and all. One must negotiate a secret compact with them, gleaning what satisfactions one can, and waiting until they grow to their maturity and grant one peace. And, deflatingly, Hec will think: the crackling pomposity of that "*one*!" Why is it so natural an idiom in French, and so patrician an affectation in English? The immiscibility of language.

He will even fold his pillow in half and press it to his breast, in melodramatic dumb show, standing before the window as if to display himself to the universal whiteness. Then he will put the pillow back on his bed.

Dusk will darken the windows very quickly, and Hector will lie himself down to sleep in his clothes and his shoes. And he will sleep.

7

IT IS POSSIBLE to sleep a great deal more than one normally would when external stimuli are disrupted or removed. Hector will sleep through several dawns, and awake with a jolt and a dry mouth. Raised voices. Shouting downstairs. He will wonder if the whole game is up now; if reporters are doorstepping the ranch at this very moment. The illusion shattered. Time to dismantle the sets, and roll the bus out front for the technicians and the actors to get their ride home.

He will step to the window. It will grant him, at an acute angle, the sight of a small knot of people standing outside, among the bushes, bickering. It will be enough to make Hector, still squeezing the sleep from his eyes with his knuckles, leave his room and come downstairs.

Down the stairs, through the front door.

Outside on the porch he will go. There will be Esther, Jacob, a man called Allen, and another man called John, the three of them confronting Tom *solus*. Jacob will have a firearm. He will have this gun in his hand, aimed, pointing. Esther will be weeping. Hector will step onto the porch, positioned a little above and to the right of the group, just as they come to a half-hiatus in their argument, one of those natural downturns that occurs in any heated exchange as weariness and monotony cool the furies of the participants, before a breather gives them the energy to stoke it up again.

"What's going on?" Hector will ask. They will ignore him.

—and he will experience (this is tricky to express, but in his vision he sees a second vision, he finds himself looking forward to a hypervivid looking-back) a memory of the dream he just had, a flashback of such intensity that it will make him think that perhaps the dream had been another vision (sleeping, the hallucinogenic gas seeping in through his nostrils, the lucid dream fooling his brain into believing it was experiencing something from the outside). He will *just then*, just before being awoken by the commotion outside, have been being dreaming of his parents' honeymoon. Before he was born, the two of them in Europe and hiring a car in Rome and driving up along the Italian coast into France. The two of them in a hired car with the windows down in the summer, on those coastal roads that cling to the hillsides and mountains, tight as bindweed, twisty, the air and sea part of a vast continuum of perfect blue, the sky hot and beautifully suffused with light. Both had traveled to Europe before, of course, but on this honeymoon trip it was as if they both became new-minted Americans abroad, like Balboa catching his first sight of the Pacific. Man and wife caught up in a landscape somehow familiar to their Southern Californian apperceptions and yet crammed with these edifices of the most profound and startling antiquity; the continual newness of the sea mocking the crumbling age of so much of the human habitation. The way locals would casually utilize some building *older than America* as a *barn*, or take some ancient house and stick pumps outside it and use it as a gas station. Every time they came across a new example of this, some medieval adjunct of walls concreted up and roofed over and used as a shop, say—they would exchange their astonishment in set conversational gambits (*another one! Christ, that one might even be* Roman—*look, they've put a concrete-brick portico and corrugated iron roof at the front of it—can you* believe *it?*). They crossed the Gard River, speeding over the Roman *pont* with all the other cars and with trucks and buses, and felt the ancient stones tremble under Twentieth-century traffic. And neither of them grew tired with their amazement, "Can you *believe* it?" "Isn't it in*cred*ible," at this cavalier disregard of the antique, as if life could thrust its green stalk through even the most anciently worn-out structures—as if, Hector Senior hoped, even something as worn-out as "the institution of marriage" could contain within it the future, youth, possibility. His new wife wore a green cotton dress printed with a repeating pattern of big-fronded grape-leaves, very bright yellow against a pale ground; and in the heat this flimsy sheath did not so much clothe her body as draw attention to the underneath presence of it. Hector dressed more generically, chinos and check-shirt. Each day they spent in the car trying to cancel the horizon, which of course always reasserted itself, brought with it a hundred moments when she could slip her fingers between the buttons to touch his chest, or tenderly enclose the back of his neck, or simply stand and watch him, trousers rolled to his mid-calf standing in shallow water, gazing at her, during one of the pit-stops in one of the many perfect little bays.

And yet their warmth for one another, their insistent love-making in every hotel room, in the hire car, in lavender fields, and beneath olive trees in the clear heat—even this genuine affection between them contained within it the seeds of their later mutual disaffection. Young Hector looking back on his parents and their precarious happiness of this portion of their youth will be able to see how ill they are fitted to one another. How easily each becomes resentful of the other for imagined slights or actual snubs. And then, like when you close the mirrored door of a bathroom cabinet and its sweep reveals, fleetingly, the whole room behind you—so Hector will feel the vision, or the memory of the vision, slip away from him, although in doing so he will see the whole perspective of his parents' marriage across the many years, the chill coming upon them, the barely concealed infidelities on both sides, or perhaps not so much barely concealed as insolently revealed so as to spark resentment from the flint of the spouse. And then his mother's drinking, and later her drug-taking. Their costive cohabitation of the Pasadena house, a continual cold war that nevertheless managed to last through to the deathly end, and his mother, with the cancer already too far advanced, refusing to leave the house, resisting all efforts to admit her to hospital, as if superstitiously afraid that being removed from the house would be the same as being removed from life. But by this stage Hector Junior was himself on the scene, their wide-eyed and withdrawn only child; a teenager when she died. And the more he had his own memory of the battleground between them, the less this particular future-vision vision-of-the-past was *real* to him. It will be as if his own memories create an interference pattern and destabilize the vividness: such that (for example) his mom deliberately breaking all the plates in the kitchen, *chok*, *chok*, *chok*, one after the other, cracking them with the meat tenderizer, while his dad sat in his comfy chair in the next room watching the game and drinking a beer, not even looking over his shoulder, just sitting there with the most effortfully achieved uninterest in his wife's craziness—as if that was only vague to him (although he had actually watched that scene himself, from the door to the kitchen, scared and uncertain). But his father and his mother on honeymoon, before he was conceived, this thing will fill his mind with gleaming nowness. Not snapshots, but a great multicolored illuminated-glass reality. His dad, unable to find a hotel room anywhere in Monaco, driving from building to building in increasing irascibility, Mom repeating the same phrase every time he returned to the car, "You should have called ahead," and him repeating the same riposte, "Yeah, great advice *after the fact*," until the sun set and the two of them drove out of the town entirely, the anger between them like electrical discharge inside the automobile. Or the two of them in bed together, one hot afternoon, naked, their limbs interconnected. His mom looking through the uncurtained windows at the afternoon sky and the rooftops of Nice (is it?), a large French spider motionless on the top-right corner of the glass like a giant asterisk drawing the attention of the lookers to some qualification or explanation hidden below the sill.

These images will be harder and more perfect in Hec's mind than any recollection. How weird is that?

HAVING COME DOWN with this dream vibrating the cords of his mind, he will stand on the porch, with a more intuitive and lived-in sense of this vision than a chronological delineation such as this can suggest; and he will say to the others: "Hey! I know where my dad is."

But, standing in the fields, they will have gone too far to pay any attention to *his* words. He will have become the absolute outsider, a caste unto himself, a one-man untouchable. They will be wholly focused on themselves. The quarrel will still be heating up. They will ignore Hector Junior.

Tom in the fields, and the others shouting at him. And Jacob pointing a gun at him.

"It's only an experiment," Tom will bluster. "It's only to see if this works. *If* it works, then we can have a proper debate, the whole group, acting democratically, we can—afterwards— to decide what to do then." He will be holding a jerry can in his left hand.

"It's *sacrilege*," Esther will say. Her white face will display two Pollyanna circles of red, one on each cheek. Hector will have never seen her so worked up, so furious. "Sacrilege, sacrilege. I can't—I can't *believe* that you—" She will be trembling tightly in her holy outrage.

"We don't *know* it's sacrilege," Tom will insist, himself trembling a little. "We don't know anything. That's why human beings *do* experiments. That's what fucking science *is about*."

"Don't swear," Jacob will boom, holding his gun up.

"Don't you tell me what to do," Tom will retort, lifting the can and angling it. An aluminum-colored twist of fluid will

193

pour down and splatter through the branches of one of the bushes.

"*Stop doing that*," Esther will shriek, so worked up that she will literally shake with rage, shake wildly as if blown by a sudden breeze. She too will lift a gun—she's got a gun as well!—aiming it a little way past Tom's left side. All this play-acting!

"It's only *gas*," Tom will say, as if this justifies everything. "That's all, come on you guys. We'll just *see*. Just gasoline. It won't take a moment."

"Tom," Jacob will boom somberly, as if he is addressing a whole cavernous cathedral instead of a single person, "don't you think we should treat these growths with respect, at least until we have some more information about them? What if they *are* an integral part of *it*? What if we cause *it* pain when we attack these bushes? What if we anger *it*?"

"You're talking like a preacher man," Tom will say, stepping away from the bush he has just doused. "It's not a god."

"You don't know *what* it is," Esther will shrill.

"Neither do you."

"You have no respect for *anything*," she will press. "Nothing is sacred to you. You're soul*less*."

Tom, ignoring this, will place the can of gas on the ground and pull out a box of matches from his pocket. The others will gasp.

"No!"

"No!"

"No!"

And again, "No!," like a peal of bells.

"Why can't we just *talk* about this?" Jacob will demand.

"We are talking. This is what talking sounds like."

"We can't discuss it with you holding us to ransom like this," Jacob will burly, lowering his gun again.

"Me holding you to ransom? You're the ones with guns, you fuckers."

"We can't," Jacob will insist, strenuously, "we can't talk about it with you threatening to set fire to *it*. You say you want to talk, well let's go inside and talk—but not with you pouring gas and threatening to set fire to—"

"I'm not setting fire to *it*," Tom is going to explain, in his usual pompous schoolteacher manner. "But we *are* going to have to think about clearing some land for crops somehow. We can't cut these things very efficiently, but I'm guessing we *can* burn them back. And if," he will add, fiddling a match from its box, "and if—which I don't accept—but if these bushes *are* a limb of *it*, I hardly think a little fire is going to bother *it*. It traveled through interstellar space and crashed into the Earth with apocalyptic force. If it can survive that, it can survive anything. A little bush fire won't be neither here nor there."

But the others will have passed beyond the rational state to which Tom will be appealing with this last speech. Jacob will say, "We can't go round and round this, just put the match down and let's go inside and have some coffee and *talk*."

"We can talk," Tom will say, with a smugness that even Hector, disengaged from the fury of the others, loitering on the porch, will find infuriating. "We can talk when we've some actual data to talk *about*. Like what happens when I do this."

He will flick the match across its emery board and toss it in the air. It will flare weakly in the bright white light, and tumble onto the bush. Flames will instantly and silently start up. Esther and Jacob, with their guns, and the others, dumb witnesses, will stare down at this, their mouths a dinner-set of perfect Os.

"I can't *believe* you just did—" Jacob will start to say. *Mpaang.*

There will be a gunshot, overwhelming his last word. Esther's gun. For a moment nobody will move. Then Tom will say, in a tetchy voice, "Oh Jesus." He will remain standing, and his face will look annoyed rather than pained, such that Hector, from the porch, will think the shot must have gone wide. But, after three or four seconds, Tom will say, "Jesus that's my *lung*." And as soon as this last word is uttered, Esther will call out, "Oh *no*" in genuine distress, and Jacob will hastily slip the safety-catch on his own weapon and stick it in his jacket pocket. Hector Junior, Medium, Senior. It's cadavers reversed.

Tom will still be standing there, scarecrow-like, and the only sign that a bullet has penetrated him will be a gesture he makes with his left hand, reaching up to his heart and fumbling there as if trying to undo a button. Jacob will stride toward him. "Jesus," Tom will say again, as if this thought is occurring to him for the first time, "that *hurts*, Jesus." And he will sag at the moment that Jacob grabs him, supporting him. And the others will come hurrying out and start helping Tom limp back toward the house, as he repeats "That hurts, Jesus, that hurts."

"It just went *off*," Esther will say, in a strong voice. She will drop her gun to the ground and step toward the cluster around Tom. "Went off. I didn't pull the—I didn't *mean*."

The bush, burning perfectly silently behind him, will not be being consumed by the fire; the gas will burn off completely in a few moments, leaving the branches and their odd buds untouched. But all attention will be on Tom.

"It just sort of went off," Esther will say again, "I'm sorry, I'm sorry. But you were *pushing* us, Tom. I'm sorry, but you shouldn't have done it." She will already be shifting the blame from her malfunctioning gun onto Tom himself. As the knot of people lever the wounded man up the steps to the porch, and on through the front door, Hector will have one clear view of Tom's blanched face, and of a little cluster of redberry bubbles attached to the front of his shirt like a brooch.

8

HECTOR, RATHER THAN go in and join the flailingly anxious group around Tom, will sit himself in one of the porch chairs and watch the quality of light change over the landscape. Behind him he will hear a scream, and think perhaps fancifully, that it is Dimmi, her coolness and grace dissolving completely away under the pressure of her wounded boyfriend. Her dying boyfriend. This thought, Hector will ponder, seems not to move him very much. Perhaps it should. Or will the scream be Tom himself, as somebody attempts to lever the bullet out with a scalpel from one of the first aid packs, the wound slippery with blood and antiseptic cream? That a man in great physical pain will scream a female scream, or a woman in emotional agony will growl and grumble like a man: these things will not interest him terribly much.

But he will *know* where his father is. That'll be something, won't it? That'll be something.

The spread of bushes filling the compound will look, under the westering light, even more blue-purple than it has previously done. By mimicking lavender, although in a distorted and rather alien manner, it will recall Hector to Provence, to Gard and Languedoc. He will ponder the lucid dream about his parents in Italy and the South of France. Did he even *know* that his parents had honeymooned in that part of the world? It had been before he was born. Perhaps the whole thing had been a mere concoction of his imagination. Perhaps Mom and Dad had actually honeymooned in Florida, or Canada, or somewhere else entirely.

Or perhaps, he will think, perhaps he *had* known but had forgotten, and his subconscious had supplied the information in his dream, leavening it with some of his own memories of that part of the world.

Dark will fall with its guillotine suddenness. The ranch house behind him will have fallen quiet. Perhaps—Hector finds himself indifferent at either prospect—in mourning at the death of Tom, perhaps in deference to his need for convalescing sleep.

One feature of the short days and short nights will be that the darkness is warm, a midsummer evening rather than a winter midnight; the face of the worldlet never turned long enough from the face of the sun to really chill. Hector will sit in the darkness feeling almost placid. Calm. Calm. Belong. So he'll think of the South of France, and for the first time the thought will not include Marjorie. He will think, without distress, of his parents fucking on their honeymoon. Of that world, that pre-him world which was therefore as remote as a 1950s Technicolor historical epic, as *El Cid* or *The Rise and Fall of the Roman Empire*. A world under a sky worthy of California, but with buildings made of time-crumbled bricks rather than adobe, and instead of clear redwoods and cedars only these beautifully wizened olive trees, with strangely pronged branches that look as though molten metal has been squirted into cold water, and the weird grasping tangles upended and planted in the shallow soil and dusted with leaves. Late afternoon, the sunlight breaking through the teeth of the branches into many gleaming shafts and beams. As the bushes are shuffled by the wind these beams move and pivot, so that it looks as if the solid light is actually stirring the air and causing the wind.

His parents fucking. It is the intimation of violence in the primal scene, he will think, that makes it so hard for children to imagine their parents making love, making babies, making them. The thought of the implicit brutality of one's father doing that to one's mother, of *le contact de deux epidermis* as the French say, it's that that makes so many people wince. But, of course, it is not the act itself that is so off-putting; for adults have performed that same act, perhaps with many people, and perhaps with a deal more brutality, themselves many times. Rather, it is the thought of the great chasm in the space-time continuum between me existing and me not existing that this parental act bridges. It must have involved some magic of terrifying potency to suture so appalling a gap. It must have happened with thunder cowing the sky and lightning smiting boiled-down smoking tree stumps.

In the darkness of the porch he will find himself singing to himself, softly, *lots of monkeys. Jumping. On. The bed.* Then he will hum the rhythm without the words. A breeze will fidget among the indestructible stalks and flowers of the bushes.

> *One fell off and hurt his head,*
> *In came the doctor and he said—*

When the sky to the east will start the gray and whiten, Hector will get to his feet, and start away to find his dad.

9

IT WILL NOT be a long walk, although it will involve him leaving the compound.

He will choose, for some reason, not to go through the gate, but rather to walk to that portion of fence knocked down by the great rolling ball of stone (now half-submerged by the growth of the bushes around it, like a dinosaur drowning in a tar pit). The crossweave fishnet metal sheet sagging. It will be an easy matter to stride, step, reach over the pendulating wire fence and slip through.

Walking will involve picking a path between the close-fitting bushes, feeling them brush and bristle against his hips as he wades through. But, wiry and nib-ended as the branches will be, they will not scratch or harm Hector as he walks. They will not penetrate the denim of his trousers.

The light will grow, achingly slowly, until it will be bright enough for Hector to stop and survey where he has gotten to. Behind him the fence of the compound will be a pale gray ribbon set in the undulating sea of purple and bile-green growth. The roof of the ranch house will be visible behind the blur of the metal grid, just, although Hector will search his mind for precise memories of how things had looked when he first turned up in his hire car. It will seem to him that the land has flattened, adopted a shallower horizon-to-horizon soup-bowl scoop, than it had possessed when it was blue sky above and red dirt beneath. But he won't be certain of that.

He will walk on.

As the light clarifies the situation he will notice that some of the bushes have sprouted to twice, or three times, the general height. And that some of these sproutings have adopted the manner of bizarre topiary: a grandfather-clock shaped upgrowth, a flat but broad semicircle like a fan, a purple tower that will seem comprised of several bushes together, growing into oddly planar shapes with rectilinear knobs and protrusions, like an organic mockery of a machine.

Up the slope, continually pushing through the foliage, like wading through a drily sticky fluid. And the outgrowths will become more and more rococo, plinths and tongs and hearts and festooning balloon-shapes. He will haul himself up a ridge, and down the shallow far side, and there will be a great wall of growth, bizarrely flat and imposing, twenty yards high. At its exact center will be a door-sized aperture, and through this, as into an unfinished house, Hector will step. The far side will contain more of the tightly packed bushes, although stopping and gazing into the distance will reveal a view of more sparsely scattered growths, and near the foreshortened horizon a few patches of intervening ground will be visible, looking gray-red in the distance.

Hector will stop in that half-grown place. There will be, perhaps, an hour of daylight left. He will be sweating from the labor of walking, and regretting not having brought some water along with him. But this will be the place, this will be, and he will bend forward a little and begin searching between the thrusting boles of the bushes.

On the shadowy and surprisingly clear ground, underneath the layer of thistly buds and branches, between the place where two trunks plunge from the earth, Hector will find his father.

Dad will be lying on his back, his eyes closed, his chest unmoving, his arms at his side. Crouching in the dimness, tired and a little disoriented, Hector will feel alarm sprinkle through his torso. He will have known where his father was to be found, but he will not have expected to find him like this, like a corpse on the slab of the earth. The sheer deathliness of his dad's body will be upsetting. Like a manikin, lying here with his heart stopped and no breathing.

Imprecise notions of medical triage will bother his head, chest compressions, mouth-to-mouth; and he will be so caught off guard, so suddenly desperate, that he will ignore the thought that Hector Senior may have lain here for many dawns, may be long dead, all such emergency procedures superfluous. The mind, used to the living presence of parents, takes a very long time to slow down and stop once parental death has crashed to a halt beside it. It was like that with Mom, and she was dying for several years. Knowing your father dead and *feeling* that he is dead are two different things. He won't really believe it, won't accept the lack of motion in the chest. Breath will surely revitalize him. He will kneel over him. He will insinuate himself underneath the branches of one of the bushes to get at him. His father's lined face will look relaxed, darkened by shadows, and as Hector lowers his own face, bringing his lips close to his father's lips, he will brace himself for the sensation of cold flesh beneath him. But as he kisses the old man's lips he will feel dry warmth, and even the faint movement of air, his own cheek and chin touching the skin of Hector Senior's face. A lifetime of kissing women having prepared him, subliminally, for the smoothness of the other face, he will be startled by how scratchy the face is, how rough and forbidding, like unplaned wood.

He will jerk back, his hair touching the branches above, and say, "Dad?"

"Yeah," his father will reply, without opening his eyes. His voice will be quiet, but steady and perfectly audible in this low-level grove, this shadowy place.

"Dad, Dad, you OK?"

Hector will feel with his hands, reaching to his father's chest, and then round his bony shoulders, and to the back of his neck. There will be a thumb-thick strand, plunging firmly into the earth, and growing directly into Hector Senior's skin. Further fumbling will touch several other strands, finger thickness, like stiff electrical cables, linking the back of his father's skull into the subsoil network of roots. This growth is so tight that Hector cannot lift his father's head more than a millimeter. It will remind him, facetiously, of that old film *The*

Matrix, where people are thuswise linked into some malign computer mainframe. Except that those people could be unplugged, with a twist and tug like uncorking a bottle, whereas Hector Senior will seem as immovably rooted to the ground as an oak.

"Dad?" he will say. "You hurting? Does it hurt?"

"Yeah," his father will reply, his eyes still closed. "Not the head, that's OK. My hip hurts a little. I gotta lie here like this, no cushion. I'm not so young as once I was."

Hector will sit back. His father stony, but a sandstone left in the Californian sun, not cold New Haven granite.

"The others," Hector Junior will say, "think you've gone for good. They're in a state without you, Dad."

"Yeah," he will reply.

"I think Tom got shot. I mean, shot with a gun. They're jittery."

"Yeah."

Hector Junior will settle himself into a more comfortable position beside his father. "You know? Hey, are you plugged in there? That's weird, Dad." And then, as the oddity percolates more thoroughly into his distracted mind: "Do you *know* about Tom? How can you know about Tom?"

"It's all there," Hector Senior will say, with his eyes shut.

This will be marvelous to Hector Junior. "Yeah?"

"It, it," his father will be saying, "it's *spread* itself into a kinda *shield* shape, spread its mass in a more even hemisphere over the habitable side of the planet. Of what's left of the planet. The early distortions, Alaska at seventy degrees, that kind of stuff, that's all been settled down now. It's a longer-term survivability thing. Longer-term existence thing. I think the re-dis-tri-but-ion," up-and-down over this word as if a child were reading it for the first time, "of *mass* has kinda *settled* the orbitals too, a slightly tighter ellipse, but—you know."

203

"Great," Hector Junior will say, uninvolved by this chatter, but wanting to know what's happened with his dad, how these plant roots have grown through his flesh and into his brain. "Good news for all the survivors," to placate him.

"Yeah, oh, there are very few survivors, outside the ranch. Most areas suffered this catastrophic outgassing after the impact. We were lucky, we were in a sort of declivity. It wasn't an accident, of course."

This word, *declivity*, will strike Hector Junior as so uncharacteristic a word, as so completely not the sort of word his father would use, that he'll lean over to check the facial features, to reassure himself that it is actually his dad lying there. Or perhaps it will be only a simulacrum of his dad? And how would he be able to tell the difference?

"A whole lot of death," he will say to his father's supine form, eyes still closed, although the words will not resonate, not carry their weight. Like tin words. None of it real.

"It doesn't really mind the loss," Hector Senior will say, his eyes closed.

"I've got to tell you, Dad," Hector Junior will say. "I'm increasingly doubtful about your explanations for these things." As illustrations of *these things* he will run two fingers either side of a branch of moss bush, the strange new vegetation. This plant life will stand in, in his mind, for everything else, the weirdly shuffled-about day–night alternations, the un-Californian weather. "I mean—I'm not trying to upset you, you know. I know you didn't like it, when I talked about my doubts earlier."

"Earlier," his father will repeat, as if this is a word in a foreign language.

"But, the thing you see is, I don't mean to disrespect you. Want to be a good son, y'know? I'm just not sure I believe the, you know, *extraterrestrial* stuff. There's got to be a simpler explanation, yeah? Not that I'm saying I understand how you've done it. Or how it's been done. Lately I've been thinking, some kind of hallucinogen, maybe." Dad these *pills*, those *pills*, you know the *pills*. But this tightly tangled grove of alien bushes, viewed from underneath, from a toddler's perspective, will not seem hallucinated to Hector Junior. He will be struck rather, by the weird, calm reality of them; the mildly gaping shadows, the hard-rubbery textures, the same Mojave dirt underneath everything. But he won't want to push that thought too far. The reality of this whole thing might tip him over the edge.

"Yeah," his father will say with blank eyelids.

"E.T.," Hector Junior will say. "You see my difficulty with that whole concept?

"I've only come to understand it myself, lately," Hector Senior will murmur. "Fermi's paradox? Yeah? Of course you've heard of Fermi's paradox. But this object, traveling through space, communicating with human beings over centuries as it came closer, I guess we'd call it E.T., wouldn't we? Not what we expected. Not the kinda E.T. sci-fi prepared us for."

Hector will be bothered, at this point, by the thought that perhaps his father is dying. This will not sound like his father speaking, really not at all, not very. Will this be the freaky lucidity of the deathbed, prophecy? There might be insight and promise. Uncertainly, he will take the old man's dry, warm hand between his two, as if to comfort him. But Hector Senior will make no sign that he requires comfort. "Go on."

Hector Senior will say: "Tom liked to think of it as only incidentally sentient, just some kind of freak of the cosmos, an unusual asteroid that happened to punch into us. Dimmi liked to think of it as more thought than matter. You—you refused to believe it was anything at all, you craved this belief that everything that has happened was human thought, and nothing else." Craving. Crave.

"I guess it's fair to say that's what I figured."

"Yeah. Son, but it's both. You were right, and so was I." The shallowest of smiles. "You know what Fermi's paradox fails to take account of?"

"Tell me." Squeeze the old man's hand. Will the light be dying in him?

Something will definitely be passing out of him; a fading away.

"The assumption, that, the unchallenged," he will tell his son, "that *intelligence* would be *alien*. But that's not how intelligence sends itself through the galaxy. It sows, and when its crop grows it reaps, so there's just the *one*, you see?"

Hector will not see. "Very biblically put, Dad," he will say. "Sowing, reaping."

"But it's *all the same*, yeah? It's all part of the same. Animals have brains, some of them as good as humans, some of them better than humans, at doing what the brains are needed for doing. How is a human different? Don't say soul." All this will be uttered in a perfectly unruffled, even amused burble. Soul? The—very—idea. Such jibberjabber.

"I wasn't going to say soul," Hector Junior will reply.

The silence will have a vaguely, distantly creaky edge to it.

"Looking back," his father will continue, after a while, "I should have guessed. *It* was communicating with us from afar, tuning into our thoughts. How? How could it do this?"

"Do you know who you sound like, Dad?"

"How could it do this? Not by being alien. I'll tell you what an old business associate, Charles A. Singleton, what he told me one time. He said if a tiger could speak we wouldn't understand it anyway. Yeah, I was *struck* by that. That's *true*, don't you think? How could we talk to an alien? There'd be no common ground, we wouldn't connect at all. Of course not, of course not." And, as if it soothes him in some sense, Hector Senior will repeat this little phrase, "Of course not, of course not. Of course not, of course not."

"You're rambling, Dad."

"You see? This thing connected with us *immediately*, with our most intimate thoughts and memories. It wasn't alien. It was us. That was how."

"I don't see what you mean."

"Not if you think?"

"I am thinking," Hector will say, noting that the daylight is starting to thicken and darken around him. The fall of night. The fall of the stock market. The fall of the Twin Towers. The *pill* falls down the *long gullet*. Then the night that fell falls away, and it's dawn. Hey! "I'm thinking," Hec says, "and I reckon I'll stick with my hallucination theory, in fact and actually."

Hector Senior supine will make a little *mm* sound, as if to say *suit yourself*. "This thing can't eavesdrop on our thoughts. There's no it and us. There's *only* us."

"Very Zen, Dad."

"But I mean it *lit*erally, seriously. It's a mistake to say that *we are intelligent*. It would be more to the point to say that *intelligence is us*. That's the way round it works. It's got its own life cycle. It came first, laid seeds. It collided with the old world, the one before Earth, and the one before that, because there it found life-forms—who knows what they were, dinosaurs, sewer-rats, whatever, but those creatures were fertile ground to it. Yeah? My. Yeah. It came and knocked the Earth and its moon out of a planet twice the size of both of them together, leaving the asteroids as its rubble and waste. Sure some animals on the ur-world survived. Then it manipulated things, much as it's doing now. Seed became us. We grew, or it grew through us. And now it's come to collect itself. I figure it's going to rebuild this world, and us, to take advantage of the growth. That this time it's going to get itself—or an iteration of itself—ejected back into space; maybe this is the point, or we're nearly *at* the point, when the whole cycle starts again."

There, Hector Junior will think, right there, that's a completely non-Dad word. Iteration. He will be not able to recall a single occasion where his dad has ever before used such a word. Then the phrase *it's not the end of the world* will pop into his head from, like, wherever. Even the actual end of the world is not the end of the world. That's funny.

"You know who you sound like, Dad? You sound like Tom."

"Yeah."

"That's just the way Tom sounds like. It's much more like the way Tom sounds than the way you sound, actually."

"Yeah, I'm Tom."

Hector Junior will think about this for a while. "How do you mean, Dad?" he will start, but his father will be off monologuing again.

"It's a life cycle thing. There is no such thing as alien intelligence. There is only such a thing as intelligence. And this is how it lives, this is how it propagates. That's why they haven't come flying down on spaceships and blown up the Capitol building."

"It's a pretty destructive-sounding life cycle."

"Death," Hector Senior will say, blithe, "life. Can't have newness without—hey I forget the rest. But, yeah, shake things up."

"Can't make an omelet without breaking eggs," Hector Junior will offer.

"Bursting the body of the older generation."

"Right," Hector Junior will say, nervously. He won't like this last image so much. Too much John Hurt and that alien spider whatever-it-was breaking out through his chest. Actor's ribs like rotten timber. Not that.

"And now that I'm physically attached," Hector Senior will say, unseeing, unblinking, "it's really *juicing* itself."

Hector Junior will choose not to ask for elucidation of this alarming-sounding word. Juicing itself?

"The sun's gone down, Dad," he will say, as the dark closes around him like a cloak thrown suddenly. "I'm gonna lie down next to you, OK?"

"Yeah," his father will say.

And so Hector Junior will maneuver his body as far as he can, putting his legs either side of the base of one shrub, and lying in an undulating line as close to his father's body as he can. "Come the dawn," he will suggest, "I'll go back to the ranch, let them know you're out here."

"Yeah," his father will reply, but meaning no. "Carry *on*, go," he will urge. "You'll find her, out there."

Hector will not need to ask the identity of this she.

But here's the thing: imagine it's remaking. Imagine it's, let's say, *rebooting*.

Non tener pur ad un loco la mente. Don't think singly. Here's a way of planting thoughts in another man's head, and it's not telepathy. It's an older and more potent magic. Let's call this words.

His father will fall silent, perhaps sleeping, perhaps being more effectively downloaded like a menu-screen on a computer, please wait, your machine is shutting down. This latest twist to his bizarre sci-fi fantasizing. The darkness will grow total, and spookily intimate. The black surrounds will fill with miniature noises, little creakings and groanings like a house settling at night.

> *Lots of monkeys jumping on the bed*
> *One fell off and hurt his head,*
> *In came the doctor and he said—*

The notion that intellect is governed by the same wasteful principles that has determined the blind fecundity of old earth will quietly, undramatically, appall Hector. The more he will ponder it, lying there in the dark, the more it will unsettle him. All the rubbish shed thoughtlessly by trees in fall. Insects laying eggs in other insects to give their offspring a few bites of fresh meat, at so *total* a cost for the victim. The maw of Nature jammed open, and everything going into the grinder. Cliffs of chalk built from the trillion skeletons of wasted life. But the history of *thought* has not been as pointlessly destructive as that. *Surely* it has not—what a notion. The tenderness of intellectual apprehension, the beauty of communication, the glorious mating-displays of art, painting, poetry. He will want to reject this latest twist of his father's odd apocalyptic theories as thoroughly as he rejected all the previous mad, cultic, lunatic, fuck-blind Old Hector theories. He will want to, and he will do it, although the thought will still trouble him. But he will not shake off the certainty that he will be able to walk out in a few hours, with the new dawn, and walk a little further through the Mojave until he comes to a regular town with regular people in it. And this site of normalcy will confirm what he has always known, that it's all in his dad's head, it's all been his dad's elaborate hoax. Maggots, eggs, bullets. Dad turning a $10,000 bank loan into a million, ten million, by breaking up the initial sum and breeding 0 and 0 in the carcass until they spill out in revolting profusion.

He will doze, and wake suddenly. It will still be dark, although the quality of the darkness will subtly have changed. His father, still lying on his back beside him, is burbling on as if he has been speaking for a while, unnoticing or uncaring of his son's sleep.

"—because values the *doubting* ability of mankind I reckon that's its nature an organism a fly a dog a whale blue jay a bacterium a elephant they have *sorts* of consciousness that respond to their environments in ways that makes it more likely they will survive to pass on their genes *that's* the point of them *caprice des dieux* but those sorts of consciousness lack the, you know, the negative capability. Cannot exist in doubt and uncertainty but hey *we* can because *we are it*. That's the difference don't say soul it's *doubt* it's the kind of attention to the actual texture of things that doubt enables."

The voice won't even be his dad's now. Never mind the strange random abstractness of the vocabulary, the sentiments, a million miles from the sorts of things his dad would ever say. The voice itself will sound like Tom's voice. In the shadows it won't even be possible to see whether anything metamorphosic has happened to his face. Will he be lying down there with a stranger? Alien?

"Sorry, Dad," Hector Junior will say, in the strange darkness, "I nodded off. What were you saying?"

"Dawn."

"What?"

"Dawn's come again." I could only—better than nothing—but.

"It's still dark."

"Trust me on this."

"Dawn, Dad? It's still dark…"

"Trust me on this."

Not wanting a fight: "OK."

"I got another theory. You want to hear it?"

"Tell me your theory, Dad." And then, in an unexpected, ecstatic little spurt of filial affection, "I love that you're so talkative, Dad! We *never* really talked before. I'd rather lie here in the dark and talk this mumbo-jumbo with you than anything, right now."

"I reckon," his Dad will continue, "it was art that prompted the return journey, the harvesting, the gleaning. I reckon it waited the hundreds of thousands of years of brute-like thought, of ape-thought; and then eighty thousand years ago, or whenever, human thought stepped up a notch, and started religions and started art. I think that's when it swerved its trajectory back on a collision course, and starting tuning into the intellects it had sown. Like mine. On the other hand," he will continue, "maybe its course is predetermined, Newtonian, and it was always going to come back when it did. But I like the idea that the fruit of us is art, and it as the farmer squeezing the fruit to see if it's ready to pull down fro' the bough. Poetry—painting."

But, although Hector Junior will have meant what he said about the sunburst of love he feels, he will find himself again repelled by his father's monomania, by him continuing this arid fantasy with such an uncompromising single-mindedness. Maybe it's time now to walk back to normality, to ground himself after his monk-like spell of seclusion from the world. With this walk, and the appearance over the horizon of a tan-colored town, whitewashed adobe, cars, gas station, police station, everything would come back into focus. Then he would finally see where he was, see how the bizarre interlude had been effected. "I'm going to get up and stretch my legs a bit, Dad," he will say.

"Yeah," his father will reply. "Go for a walk. Go find. It's dawn already."

"Alright, Dad. Whatever."

And, standing, Hector will discover that his father was right after all, and that the dawn has come. The foliage will have grown over their heads as they lay there, will have made, in fact, a rather spookily exact replica of a room, complete with spaces for the door and for two windows. Light will be flooding through these apertures, and staining the shadow inside with radiance. In one corner one of the pseudo-room bushes will be in the process of growing into what looks like a table.

Startled, Hector will pick his way through the bushes and through the doorway into the white light outside. The doorway itself, as he passes through, will be half filled by a rough-edged block, as if the door itself is growing *into* the aperture. Like a scab over a wound.

On the street outside, turning and turning about, he will look up at a half-completed pastiche of the Pasadena house, the first floor sketchily complete, the second floor in the middle of growing into place, the third floor still to be done. It will not be possible to mistake the identity of this simulacrum house. It will not look like just any house; rather it will have the dimensions and the particulars of the very house in which Hector grew up; except that the walls will be spinach-colored and rough, like close-grown hedging.

And to turn away from it and survey the land around will be to see a strange sculpture park of alien topiary, bushes sprouted into the forms of towers and walls, and one, a hundred yards upslope from the imitation Pasadena house, in the shape of a car. Hector, walking over to examine this, will find in the rough nubbled surface of this shape, a memory of the car he and his dad had driven down to Mexico in, many years before. Rectangles of bluer growth will already be growing like isinglass at the places where the windshield and windows should be.

213

10

WHEN WE HAVE usual dreams, the memory of the dream is most vivid immediately upon waking; the dream itself fades away to almost nothing within a few minutes. But Hector will increasingly find, as he lives on further and further into the future, envisioning this in his proleptic future-sight, that this human truth will become reversed. Dreams will be blanks to him immediately upon waking, and then will fix and develop photographically into precise memory a short time later. Walking through this organic approximation of old Pasadena, he will remember that during his brief sleep inside, lying next to his dad, he had dreamt of Mary Wyckoff, a girl he had known at high school. A girl perfectly pink and blonde and slight and opposite in every way to Dimmi as could be imagined.

Thwack, and bang. Knocking the pool ball of mind into higher consciousness. Swooning away into emptiness and purple space, and disappearing while that higher consciousness stewed and cooked, before returning with another thwack and crack to smash it higher up. How many collisions could this cycle countenance before it broke the world into *Petit Prince*-style planetules, fragments of rubble only a kilometer across, or less—house-sized, car-sized, man-sized pieces of former world? It was crazy. But where did it come from, the poetic image netted in Dad's mind? Hec will wonder. The way collisions happen.

Back at school, Pasadena High. He had been in love with Mary Wyckoff, he will remember that. He always sat at the rear of the classrooms, and she always sat near the front, but he had spent tremendous mental effort on looking at the back of her head, where her hair was sometimes plaited and tied with gorgeous complexity, and sometimes hung free,

something tickling and exciting-obscene about that uncon-
fined hair, something to do with *nakedness*, or something.
He had never had a girlfriend, however hungrily he yearned
for one. But it was difficult, because he existed outside the
main flow of the school's social hierarchies. He was too solitary and tinged with bookishness (comics in his satchel, a
fondness for the quiet of the library) to be accepted by the
popular crowd. But neither was he a nerd. He was too vague
in his likes and his dislikes. He was too unengaged with *Star
Wars* or *Rush* or whatever the shibboleth happened to be
that month, to fit in with the nerds. There were several others like him, who loitered at the edges of the class, who sat
alone to eat, Michael Robertson was one; Virgil Hopper
another, whose port-wine birthmark spread like a maple leaf
over his forehead had long ago marked him for solitariness.
But it was the nature of these kids that they did not band
together. When the whole class went on trips to out-school
locations, to a county fair, to a headily ink-smelling print-
works, Hector sat by himself on the bus there and back.

Mary, however, pulled him out of his placid unengagement.
She was so pretty. It smote Hec deeply and directly. She was so
pretty. He daydreamed immensely complex and erotically
charged, though physiologically vague, daydreams about her.
He imagined intense frottage, and the smoothness and honey-
flavor of her skin. He told himself, trying the phrase out, that
he loved her. He tried, rather self-consciously, whispering her
name to himself in bed at night.

And this love was clearly something that had to be communicated. He had to find the right moment to tell her that
he loved her. And one day, without foreplanning, he found
himself standing next to her, waiting in the corridor for the
principal to finish a tête-à-tête with Mrs. Griffin. The kids
all milling in the corridor, leaning on the wall, or standing in

knots of two or three. He had happened to find Mary Wyckoff standing next to him, hugging her schoolbooks to her new chest. "Do you want to come to the prom?" he asked, without preliminary. She had looked at him with her neatly squared-off face, her big, slightly overcurved blue-eyes, and had said simply, "Jimmy Kruppman asked me." So that was that. At the moment of rejection Hec didn't even feel anything particular, neither upset nor shame. The principal had come out, and they had all filed into the classroom for geography, and Mrs. Griffin, slightly flushed and quicker to disciplinary anger than usual, had flicked through rain-shadows and mountain ranges with slides on the white screen. But later that day Hector had become aware of a sense of shame, and palpable injustice, in being turned down by this girl. The asking-out had not gone the way it was supposed to have gone.

Swallowing his resentment, he had chanced upon Deirdre later that day, Dirty as she was called, a nickname supposedly grounded in her habit of not washing. A nickname that neither a whole term of more-than-usual scrubbing and perfume nor crying in the study hall had been able to dislodge. Now Deirdre was a lanky, broad-faced girl, with a small mouth and two small eyes close together over a broad nose. But she had a noticeable figure, and she dressed well in lavender and black, and when she laughed her face became much more attractive. So he asked her, and she said yes, a little too surprised and obviously delighted for Hec to be truly gratified by her acceptance. But at least he had a partner, for all that he was a nobody and lurked in the shadows, and for all that Mary Wyckoff had turned him down. And, like the earlier rejection, the effect of this acceptance sank in only slowly, such that by the end of school he was disproportionately elated by the thought that he had somebody to go with, and that she was nice, and that she was obviously really into him.

On his bike home that afternoon he had planned in his mind how best to use the fact of his new girlfriend in order to retort Mary Wyckoff's rejection back upon herself. To bring her down a little. He fantasized possible conversations with her the next day, in which he casually brought up the fact of his having a girlfriend now. And in his mind these conversations always brought the horror of her missed chance to Mary Wyckoff's face, which led, as he pedaled leisurely and glanced behind him to turn right, to a related fantasy conversation in which she begged him to ask her out, or promised to be his secondary girlfriend. A car burlied past him, wobbling him with its aftertrail of wind, and he came to the left turn into the road where his parents' house sat, placid and broad in its row of placid, broad houses.

There was a wall on the right side of the road opposite the turning, tall and redbrick veiling the large garden of one of the area's mansions—for there are always more wealthy people, with bigger houses, even than one's own wealthy parents. It was Hec's habit to rest his right shoulder against this wall, angling the bike a little with his feet not leaving the pedals, to stop here while checking behind him prior to pulling across the road. There were few enough cars in this affluent network of avenues. He was already thinking about how best to tell his mom that—hey! he had a girlfriend now! Imagining her pleased, and he glanced down rather than behind him, checking the exquisite pattern of tarmac with its starmap inset of white chips. Then he heaved himself upright on his two wheels, and weighed down on the right pedal and then the left and he steered the bike through its turn across the road.

The collision impinged upon his consciousness, at first, as a clatter of chaotic disorientations. Never having experienced anything like this before in his short life he could not, in the first instance, string together into comprehension the breath-punching pressure from the left, the iceslip rightwards of both bicycle tires, the mixed soundtrack of tinny clattering and a human-voice warble of alarm. The pivot up into the air. The tarmac angled on an imaginary hinge up around Hector's head and down towards his shoulder, tracing out a black halo of astonishment. Then he crunched into the road, left shoulder bruising against the stone, and he skidded and rolled. He got immediately to his feet, but his legs were skittish and he fell down again. Then he pulled himself into a sitting position and simply sat for a while, simply stared in horror at the painless scratched-up palms of his hands, red striations crisscrossing the white flesh. Looking at them, as if the sensation was called into being simply by the looking, these grazes began to throb with first pain. Then he became aware of a second pain, in his left shoulder. Only then did he look up, along the road, to see his own bike, the steel tubes of its frame bent like pasta, its back wheel and saddle flat on the ground but its front wheel raised at twenty degrees and the tire spinning clackingly. Then, panting, he was able to place the next element in the narrative composition: a second bike, lying a little further on, the crescent of its supine front fender bent into a crook. And further on still a human form, kid-sized, lying face down on the road and making half-hearted attempts to draw its arms in and lever itself up.

As he tried a second time to get to his feet, his breath increasingly frantic and the grazes on his hands starting to sting, he saw who it was: Mary Wyckoff herself, turning over onto her side and looking up at him with surprise and pain on her face. Her nose was scraped red in a thin rectangle from tip to bridge. She open her mouth, and blood spilled out. Hec sat down again. He felt giddy.

Helped out of the road by a motorist, and then by neighbors, he was too startled to be upset. Stunned. But Mary wailed and wailed, and when she was sat on the floor and somebody peered into her open mouth, an old woman who lived three doors along, the announcement was made that her two front teeth had been knocked clean out. People even went back out onto the road, and stopped the passing cars, to look for them, but to no avail. That was when Hector began to cry. He was already thinking: I shoulda looked behind me before turning left. But when his dad, in a severe voice, demanded to know what had happened, he instead insisted, his voice tautened and reined back by sobs and the tightness of his chest, "*She* shoulda looked where she was *going*, she knocked me clean *over*" and "She was going *crazy* fast."

Hector's shoulder was bruised, but the E.R. doctor told Hector Senior that he needed neither cast nor bandage, although in the weeks that followed Hec Junior came to wish that he had some more permanent badge of the accident, for purposes of display. He sought out schoolfellows to whom he could tell the story, embellishing it with each retelling. Inevitably he encountered Mary Wyckoff herself at school; her face somber, her nose increasingly pretty with its fading engraving of black-red crosshatching, and her mouth gleaming with silver, the top-brace she had to wear until her new artificial front teeth set and grew hard in her gums. Every time he saw her, in whichever lesson, or watching her practice cheerleading with her girlfriends, he could barely suppress the urge to rush over to her and grasp her and hug her and somehow *extract* from her the truth that *they had shared something*—that fate had brought them together. That they had connected. But of course he never did this. The closest he came to this passionate outburst was a mumbled apology while they loaded up their lockers in the morning. He came over and said, "Sorry about the bike."

And she had said, "Alright."

But one of her friends, who was right there, Ruth Conant, had leant over and said, "It don't surprise me you didn't look where you was riding, you don't hardly look where you're *walking* when you *walk* about the school." She didn't say this with any spite or force, just as a simple observation. But Mary nevertheless tried to quiet her with "Ruth" and a slight shake of the head. Ruth finished with, "Always reading a comic and walking at the same time, you're going to walk into the lamppost" and pulled away again.

He skipped the junior prom, and withdrew further into himself at school. His dad bought him a new bike, and a cycle-helmet (something of a novelty for the early eighties, even in California) and Hec Junior cycled about with an exaggerated care. But he was moving through a world defined by the tart intensity of anticlimax, and even in his youth and callowness he knew it. No later contact with any woman, he thought to himself, would match the *force majeure* of that encounter. That was then, of course. Then is the past. Now is the future. When is the future.

11

IN A SINGLE two-hour night the whole world will have been changed again, adorned with spectacular growths that will imitate the myriad aspects of Hector Senior's past life. Some of these growths will be in more advanced states than others, the buds and stalks knitted into nearly wholly smooth surfaces, like scratched and pitted plastic, or like the flat thorns and spines of a painted canvas seen up close. Hector, stroking these rugged protrusions, will not doubt that in time the scuffs will smooth away and perfect themselves.

He will wander through this rough approximation of his father's life, the sights and the scenery, with an increasing sense of the hard *materiality* of it all. Perhaps a little disoriented he will find himself back at the original house, making his way back through the tight-packed scrubby bushes to find the mimicry of the Pasadena house almost complete, except only for the color. All three stories, with windows and ledges in the right places, and a door grown over the gaping doorway through which he had exited only half an hour earlier. This door will not work, its handle just a feature of the façade not connecting to any internal mechanism of lock or bolt, but the pseudo-window will have cleared enough to allow Hector to peer inside. He will, hazily, just be able to make out a lumpy couch grown of the stuff, with a body lying placidly upon it. A dead body, or an alive body, as if those distinctions will mean anything any more. As if there will be a way of distinguishing between the one and the other, any more. Evermore, nevermore. More ever, moreover, more than never, more than any.

He will hunker down below the wall, like Tiresias, Hector Junior will; and he is going to think, soul and oblivion are the same word, the end of the world is a meticulous process of replication and simulation, honey and money and their rhyme—

He will know that, should he return to the simulacrum of the house in another half hour, the door handle will work just as a door handle should. Should he return then, he will be able to open the door and walk inside. His father had been a world in his own right, as all human beings are; but a child must see that world as a Jupiter, not a Pluto, not an asteroid: as a globe inevitably larger and more real than their own subsidiary existence. His dad on honeymoon, shooting out his miniature parcel of genes, firing it off with great bullet-shot force, such that it smashed into the globe of his mom's egg, that globe of

Hector's own non-being, and splintered it into existence, broke the pure curve of nonentity into two cells, four cells, eight, sixteen, an iteration, the word for speaking words and for passing DNA through the hoop of itself to magic more from nothing. He was a tight little bundle of fragments before he was a fetus, but he's a tight little bundle of fragments again now. Then everything else. But that's OK, that's the way of things, we become habituated to living on the sizeable splinters of our parental worlds, floating away into space, sometimes very far from the original location. How happy they look! From Petit Prince to Petit Roi. It will always be better for a child to stage the funeral of their parents than for parents to stage the funeral of their child.

And so he will and is going to and shall get to his feet and will stroll away, with this curious inarticulable feeling inside him. There will be an odor of smoke and marsh gas somewhere, faint. The whiff of distantly burning tires, maybe.

The simulacrum city will not follow cause-and-effect the world it will imitate. The Pasadena house will not have grown itself among a replica of the Pasadena street upon which Hector grew up. Instead, the buildings around will be gathered from all around the country, all the different physical backdrops to Hector Senior's life. Hector Junior will recognize the blocky San Francisco brownstone that had been grampa and gramma's house, where his own father had grown to adulthood. He will see a smaller house which his dad had co-owned with a business partner in downtown L.A., and where he had lived before he had moved inland and bought the Pasadena house. There are other buildings that Hector will not recognize, and which he will presume relate to other aspects of his dad's life; one that will look like maybe a bar, several business premises, one huge block, still not completely grown at the top, with a large Ω standing proud on the frontage.

Walking through this jumble of streets will remind Hector not of Disneyland, not that sort of simulated reality, but rather of those generic SF flicks in which a hero ranges through a post apocalypse, or post atom-bomb, city, in which the buildings reach only up to rubble-fringed decapitations and the streets are wholly overgrown by vegetation. Wherever a building will require more than three floors it will be incomplete as yet, and the ever-present bushes of moss pack street, alleyway, and entrance hall equally.

Stopping for a moment, and looking up, Hector Junior will feel a thrill in his gut. The level of cloud will be thinning and from where he stands the sunlight breaking through the high mist will be strong enough to scatter a careless broadcast of mini-rainbows, bent lines of multicolor such as are thrown off by lawn sprinklers on a sunny day, scintillating and shifting in the air directly over his head. He will be so struck by this pure color that he will almost cry. It will have been such a very long time since he saw such color. For long minutes he will let the sheer possibilities of his father's vision possess him: the weed, this outreaching of the intelligent supermassive object lodged beneath his feet spread into its subterranean curving aegis, can clearly grow to anything. So why not to rocket ships, or sleek saucers, or whole cities that will fly off the world altogether and—who knows? (Hector will be vague about the details)—who knows, journey off through the cosmos gathering mass, scooping dust or assimilating some other function of space-time, to grow over many millennia into another planet-smashing object. Perhaps those alive now, whose environment will now be minutely built by the bushes, will inhabit it as gods, not to die, the fruition of a life process, the single sperm that survives the spermatic holocaust of conception to go on to a greater life?

He will not really believe it. None of it will chime with his sense of how the universe is ordered. A pretty dream, though.

Turning a corner, he will find a hill covered not by the bushes but by grass, or rather by the bushes' close approximation of grass. Standing on the top of this little hill will be a figure, a human figure, and Hector Junior's legs, freed at last of the thigh-chafing obstruction of the bushes, will hurry upward towards this person. At the top of this hill, where the view of the mock city randomly (or not randomly) accreting all about is clear and beautiful, Hector will reach the distinctive shape, and he will recognize it immediately even though it will not yet be completed; a Body Snatchers-style humanoid shape of compacted vegetable matter. But before his eyes, before his very eyes, Hector Junior will watch the tiny fibers knit and smooth themselves out into the shapes of cheeks, chin, neck, and chest. He will stand amazed beside this evolving simulacrum, and then he will sit himself down on the mock grass, discovering that he has the patience within himself to wait and see how well, with what losses and with what gains, this being will grow into full adulthood. Perhaps it will be only an elaborate toy, and not a person at all. But perhaps it will grow to such levels of detail and precision, with moss-grown neurons and downloaded memories, with pores and wrinkles, that the simulacrum will be indistinguishable from the real, in which case it will *be* real. Won't it? It will only require time and a little patience to come to discover the answer to that question. Hector will have the time, and the patience. He will wait.

12

A CHILD SEES the baseball diamond, and sees the green grass browned and singed by so many white boots, and can believe that the passage of a child's foot over the earth that creates such friction, like dry stick trembling hard against dry stick to father fire, could rub away the world itself, in time, and reveal—what is beneath the world.

At first the new woman (he will have forgotten her name, although he recognizes the beauty of her face and limbs) will not move, will not speak. Above him the visible sun will skeeter like a bright roulette ball across a blank blue bowl and will be gone. He will sit down next to the naked and warm shape of the *lusus naturae*. They'll sit together. Then he will cry out when she sits up suddenly, levering up like an actor playing the vampire with a board up her spine being heaved by a hidden stagehand. Hec Junior will yelp *serow!* and start back. The woman will look limpidly at him, open her mouth, and start speaking; an instantaneously unrecognizable babble of vowels and consonants that will chime like no language Hec has ever encountered. "I don't understand what you're saying," he will repeat, three or four times, each sentence unable to cut across the rush of nonsense words, or full-sense words, Hec really won't know. She will not become frustrated at his non-comprehension, but will gabble on.

To the left there will be a glimmer among the streets of the topiary city. A car will be coming, headlights glowing white. The people from the ranch (he will have forgotten all their names) come to explore the strange new-grown town. He will stand up, and start toward them, but the new woman (he will have forgotten her name) will touch him on the shoulder, and he will turn. She will be standing right behind him, naked, her face quizzical, and will suddenly step forward to kiss him. This kiss will be a complicated sort of unexpected: since he will already have had the vision of the future (this vision) in which he sees that it will happen, and so might reasonably think that it cannot surprise him, yet it will surprise him for all that.

There will be some tart kind of short-circuit, with the smell of singed rubber and a tingle in the nerves. Her mouth on his mouth will prevent him calling to the others in their car, although he will be able to hear the engine coming nearer. Her tongue will encroach into his mouth, reaching all the way to the back of his throat and making him gag and widen his eyes. It will have a strange texture, part human tongue and part a stretch of compact felt or moist bristle.

He will break away coughing, and stumble backward, tripping over a bush, or a half-grown bench, or an approximate railing, or something. The taste, mucus mixed with smuts, will be going down his throat, and he will feel heady, a little drunk. The lights of the car will be dissipating among the narrow alleys of half-grown buildings; the occupants (he will be entirely unable to remember any of their names) presumably goggle-eyed exploring this strange new conurbation. It will hardly matter to him. Hector will look up and see the towering naked form standing over him, like the divine Hertha (he will not be sure where that image comes from), or the goddess Artemis. The Muse herself. But he will not see her face in the darkness. Instead he will see the shape she makes against the stars behind him. And, his mind singing like a cello string under the influence of some new and powerful intoxicant, he will open his eyes wider at the stars, the stars, stars which he has not seen for months. Stars he has not seen for the longest time. An enormous population of stars filling the blueberry-colored sky from end to end. No moon, of course. Neither moon, nor the space where new moon blocks out a circle of blackness against the starfall, nor a single cloud, nothing to interrupt the run from horizon to horizon. Lying on his back looking up, Hector Junior will wonder where it is now. Now. Now no moon relentlessly clear in her blueberry vastness, not a spotlight-shaped pool of whiteness, not a crescent like a cut in the skin, a nick, a slipped sliver of white nail. It must still be there, shining over some mere vacancy now, rubble spinning, crumbs where a world was.

The world is small now. You could probably walk around it in no more than two months. Two months and a number of days.

SPLINTER THOUGHTS

1

HECTOR SERVADAC, VOYAGES *et aventures à travers le monde solaire* ("Hector Servadac, journeys and adventures around the solar system", 1877)—a title sometimes translated into English as "Off on a Comet"—is not one of Jules Verne's most famous titles. But it is certainly one of his most intriguing: bizarre, compelling, creatively unconventional, it's the book of all of Verne's output (and yes, I can say—not without a certain weariness—I have read pretty much *all* of his output) that has stuck most in my mind.

I wrote *Splinter* under the spell of, and as a gloss upon, this little-known Jules Verne original. Why? Actually I'm asking two questions with that one little word—both: "why did I write it?" and "why does this novel, of all of Verne's output, fascinate me so much?" The bad news is that neither question has an easy or single-sentence answer. What I *do* know is that *Splinter* is one of the most carefully worked-through of all my novels; a work that has stuck persistently in my conscious and subconscious mind for many years. Whence this persistence?

A good question.

Of course, some people insist that it is a fruitless business, interrogating a writer about his or her own writing. Imagine that I could write down a block of prose that fully and lucidly explains what *Splinter* is "about." Shouldn't I, at the very least, have written *that*, and not this novel? That might look like a facile thing to say, but actually it's a point that touches on the taproot of the writing process itself. If I could fully and lucidly explain what *Splinter* is "about" then I would not have been able to write it in the first place. This much I know: writing—*true* writing—is a process of technically controlled self-distraction. In my case it involves the cultivation of a writing state: loud music through headphones, strong coffee through the mouth and into the bloodstream, an absorption in the mere process of tapping at a keyboard that it would not be *wholly* wrongheaded to call trance-like. Naturally, a writer must maintain some degree of rational and intellectual control over what he or she is writing, but where the first draft is concerned I prefer to favour the absence-seizure model of writing practice, and I bring in Enlightenment Reason only to judge the rewrites, the second and third drafts, the reconsiderations. The damage it can do, at this secondary stage, is limited, you see. No writer wants to produce mere splurge, of course. But no writer, I would submit, can write with somebody *staring hard at them whilst they write*, even (no: *especially*) if that person is themselves. You get self-conscious. You get embarrassed. The words come awkwardly, or stop coming at all. You feel like shouting, "Leave me alone! Get out of my study! You're putting me *off!*"

I have a day-job at the University of London, and people sometimes ask me my opinion on the notional "Death of the Author" still taught in literary academies around the world. Which is fair enough; I've taught this doctrine myself. Roland Barthes coined the phrase in 1967 as a facilitator for critics: the author should die, he said, so as not to impede the passage of the text into the world. Once a book is written it doesn't belong to the author any more; it belongs to the readers. "Biographical criticism" means that our attention is on the unimportant thing (the life of the author) instead of the *important* thing: the text itself. This, I think, is both interesting and right. What is less well known is that this authorial mortality is a vital part of the creation of the literary text as well. Lookee here. *I'm* an author. Am I dead, though? See—I breathe, I cough, I stand up—no George Romero creation could be prouder of his power of independent locomotion. But no, take a closer look. Of *course* I'm not alive! Say something to me. Anything you like. Ask me a question, tell me to raise my right hand, politely enquire after my opinions—nothing. Nothing at all. You'll get nothing out of the man or woman behind whichever book you're holding. It's exactly like talking to a corpse.

The truth is that it's neither that *I write the novel*, and nor that *it writes through me*, although both of these are statements I've heard from writers at one or other stage (what's "it"? The Muse? Culture-and-Society? Genre? Who knows?). No: it's that the novel gets written. Think, for a moment, of the phrase "I write the novel." Who's this "I" being invoked here? The ego-function? The part of me that is self-aware, conscious, in control? That's got vanishingly little *to do* with it. Writing, like laughing (something with which the process of writing shares more than most people realise) is driven and therefore determined subconsciously.

Because everybody has a subconscious, everybody can write. They may write *badly* (a word which here means "inhabiting the idiom of cliché"), they may write *fluently* (a word which here is used to indicate "automatic writing"), but they can only write *well* if the stairway between their inner crypts and their inner naves is wide enough to permit a passage from one to the other. This, in turn, is easiest of all if the author is already dead; and, truly, far from being an impediment to the process of the novel getting written, it's a real boon. Buddha said that we must get out of the house of the Self, which is on fire. But that fire can be a distinct bonus for the properly committed writer. Immolate, ashify, scatter, watch the crop start to grow.

All this may seem like a long-winded way of saying that I do not know what my novels are about. But I don't mean to say anything so categorical. I do have my theories as to what they're about, as a matter of fact; and considering them has, actually, clarified for me some of the things that I am about, as a writer. But these interpretations are after the fact, as interpretation always is. Its belatedness does not disqualify it; and, indeed, when reading the Literature of Belatedness (as I like to call non-SF, "mainstream" literature) a belated analytico-critical intelligence can be a very illuminating thing. But for a visionary literature though, like SF, it works less well. This may be why SF/F has as yet been only relatively poorly served by its criticism.

So I can guess, now that I look back on it, why *Hector Servadac* made such an impact upon me, and why I was moved to write the novel you are now holding in your hand. Those guesses I shall put down here, in this place, for any interested party to read. But guesses is all they are, and some of them are fairly abstruse. Moreover, although they touch on some larger questions (viz., the nature of science fiction as

232

a whole, the place of happy endings, life and the universe and every-something-I-forget-how-it-goes) they may put a strain upon the interest of even the most interested party. But, you see, this is writing from the conscious mind. That's one of its drawbacks.

A place to start would be with the material circumstances of the composition. What happened was this: in 2004 Eric Brown and Mike Ashley approached me, amongst many SF writers, to contribute to a collection of original stories: *The Mammoth Book of Jules Verne Adventures*. The brief was for each author to riff on one Verne title; writing perhaps a sequel, or an alternate-version, a pastiche or in some other way to let his/her imagination run. I heard the call but dillied, as I sometimes do. Then, fatally, I dallied. Having dillied and dallied, I was constrained by the pressure of other work to revisit the process in reverse, via dallying *to* dillying again until the cart was lost and the way home uncertain. By the time I added my name to the project all the more famous Verne titles had been snaffled by writers with names like "Stephen Baxter" and "Justina Robson" and even, implausibly, "James Lovegrove," a name which sounds like a pseudonym but in fact isn't.

Actually this didn't matter. It so happened that I had recently read *Hector Servadac*, and although my metaphorical knee-jerk had propelled my foot in the direction of more famous Verne titles, the more I thought about it the clearer it came to me. It had to be *Hector*. I thought it over, and sketched out in my mind the pages that now form the opening section of the present novel. The modern-day Hector landing in LAX, rejoining his father. The story came to me, then, as a modern take on one of the most stalwart of SF-storytelling warhorses, the end-of-the-world tale. I wondered about it: a collision striking the world and splintering it into planetecules, life continuing upon one of these (How? By what means? To what end? And so on). It was clear enough to me that this was going to be a narrative about the process by which something larger breaks up into something smaller. That it was going to be, in other words, about family, and specifically about that awkward three-way transition from childhood to compromise adulthood to full adult independence. This last state is something which (of course) occurs at different phases in different lives, but which seems to be happening later and later in our era. So: Hector, a late-thirtysomething, occupied with those pastimes (university study, travel, relationships) with which young adults keep themselves busy during that awkward transition from being part of a family to becoming their own separate world; all those things that seem simultaneously so grown-up and so time-consuming, but which are actually avoidance strategies, the screens that eventually we set aside to actually begin our adulthood.

There is a mordant Jewish saw that one is never an adult until one's parents are dead. That's too severe a judgment, I think; the truth is messier. For some of us true adulthood comes when, habituated as we all are to thinking of our parents as the carers, we have to come to terms with caring for them. They used to make all the arrangements for us; now it devolves upon us to arrange the care-home, to handle their affairs, to sort them out. Then, I think, we can actually call ourselves adult. For others it is estrangement, or geographical distance, or change of faith, or sheer selfish isolation that can make that break. But for Hector in my novel it has not yet happened. He is, chronologically speaking, a grown-up; but he is not an independent adult.

So I wrote a brief story for Mike and Eric. I updated Verne's premise, and therefore his style, adopting some of the mannerisms of the *hommes moyens sensuels* American School of Updike and Roth and DeLillo. The relationship between son and father was at the heart of it. For reasons that felt right to me (though I wasn't quiet sure *why* it felt right) I made the son not just a student but a student of History of Art. The father, naturally, had to be a stonier, larger (although not *physically*: that would be too obvious), solider and *realer* individual; a world with enough heft to endure a quantity of collision and splintering off. The practical day-to-days of the ranch on which they meet were determined by the physical constraints of the circumstance. The world ended. Things carried on. I titled it "Hector Servadac Jr," submitted it to Eric and Mike, and they accepted it and published it, and that was that.

But it wouldn't leave me alone. I kept thinking of it, pondering it, wondering how the story continued and soon enough I came to the realisation that it had set hooks in my mind that wouldn't come out without a deal of tearing and wrenching. As to why it had done so, I refer you to the preceding paragraphs and to the section below that is folded beneath the division number "4" below. But at the time it made itself present to me predominantly as a series of practical problems that needed addressing. I couldn't let it go. It needed to be written through. So I sat down and wrote more, over a number of months, picking up from where I had ended the short story. Soon I had written a short novel. When I looked at it again, it needed to be longer, and accordingly I rewrote it longer. I discovered that, amongst many other things, I had written the first section in the past, the second in the present and the third in the future tense. That also felt right, although at the time I was not certain why. (I have a better idea now, I think.) It seems, on the surface, a simple tale, and perhaps even flirts with banality; but of all the novels I have written it is the one to which I have found my mind reverting most often. Now, why might that be, I wonder?

2

THE FACT THAT there are lesser-known Verne titles is a function of just how many books he wrote. Even when we list the very many of his titles that enjoyed enormous international popularity (he remains the world's second-most translated author; only Agatha Christie has seen more copies of more titles translated into more languages) there are still some left over. For most of Verne is Very Well Known Indeed, and the consistency of quality of Verne's writing means that only by a process of crowding-out could a work be "lesser known" in the first place.

Hector Servadac is late Verne, and it is his earlier works that are best known. More than this, it's a novel that entailed obscurity perhaps by being so atypical. The standard Verne adventures are of course very familiar to us: the subterranean wonders of *Voyage au centre de la terre* (1864); Phileas Fogg circumnavigating the world in eighty days in *Le Tour du Monde en quatre-vingts jours* (1873); the early moon shot narratives *De la Terre à la Lune* (1865) and its sequel *Autour de la Lune* (1869); and perhaps most famous of all, the varied adventures of Captain Nemo's fabulous submarine "the Nautilus" in *Vingt mille lieues sous les mers* (1869) and its lengthy sequel *L'Ile mystérieuse* (1874).

Verne worked in close collaboration with his Parisian publisher "Hetzel" (his real name was Pierre Jules Stahl) who was not shy about suggesting improvements and changes to Verne's manuscript. It was Hetzel who came up with the evocative series-title "voyages extraordinaires" under which Verne's fictions appeared. The contract Verne signed required three volumes a year (some of Verne's novels were published in three volumes, some in two), and although this was later reduced to two a year it still placed tremendous pressure on the author to produce. This in turn necessitated certain compromises. Verne's productivity owed something to a willingness to exploit collaborators (who usually went unacknowledged), and a certain brazen willingness to copy chunks straight out of a range of scientific textbooks and sources directly into the narrative: what we today call "infodumping" and which we might also, if we were feeling severe, call "plagiary." The typical Verne-Hetzel product combines an encyclopaedic didacticism with wide-ranging adventures in a forcefully propelled narrative, usually structured around a journey that is driven by some external force—escape from pursuers, the urgent search for the solution to a mystery or some other specific goal; more rarely the motive is simple exploration.

But the primary appeal of Verne's books is not in "finding stuff out"; if that was what his readers were after then they might as well have simply read an encyclopaedia. Verne's genius lay in the field of narrative. He mastered a fluid, onward-moving narrative technique that is always intensely readable.

Verne was a writer of motion. The *voyages extraordinaires* are all, without exception, formally *in*, as well as *about*, movement: a form of literature that is (to quote Captain's Nemo's motto) *mobilis in mobile*, "mobile in the mobile element." Verne's novels are all about the restless urge to move on, to go further, to seek, to strive, to find and not to yield: and they all, to one degree or another, articulate this impetus in their *form*, their narrative structure and style, as in their subject-matter. This restlessness very often takes a circular trajectory—in *Vingt mille lieues* the journey is *around* the world with no destination in mind except a continual return. The journey *De la Terre à la Lune* turns out not to be to the moon, but around it (*Autour de la Lune*) and back home again.

But there's more here. Sarah Capitanio, in an insightful reading, points out that the constant to-ing and fro-ing in his books actually circulates around a sort of *stasis* at the heart of Verne's imaginings. "Situations tend to be played out in isolation and the characters then return to the world 'as we know it' which itself remains largely unchanged and unchallenged." This is connected to the fact that "the characters themselves undergo no fundamental evolution as a result of their extraordinary experiences... At the end of the novels the speculative objects and marvellous machines are destroyed, the world returns to comforting order, and the reader... is encouraged to accept an unproblematical status quo."[1] So whilst *travel*, in both a literal and metaphorical sense, is at the core appeal of Verne's appeal, his novels always dramatize a recirculation and a reassurance, a resettlement. His speculations were grounded at all times in contemporary discourses of "the possible" and "the known": Verne almost never extrapolated or speculated, his imaginative realm was not escapist, and in fact it was continually being brought back to the world with which his readers were familiar.

This is what makes *Hector Servadac* so extraordinary. It is one of only two works in which characters leave the surface of the Earth (the other is *Autour de la Lune*, a book so cautious

---

1. Capitanio, Sarah, "'L'Ici-bas' and 'l'Au-delà'... but Not as they Knew it. Realism, Utopianism and Science Fiction in the Novels of Jules Verne," in Smyth (ed), *Jules Verne: Narratives of Modernity* (Liverpool: Liverpool University Press 2000), 70

about ungrounded speculation that it does not even land its characters on the moon, just swings them about and hurries them home again). It's the only novel Verne wrote in which characters leave the ambit of Earth wholly. In *Servadac* Verne seems to have permitted himself unusual imaginative liberties, and the book is the better for it.

The story starts with a meteor crashing into the Earth and carrying off a sizeable chunk of northern Africa, upon which happen to be not only the titular Servadac (a French military officer) and his servant Ben Zoof, but various other European characters: a Russian Count, the crew of his yacht, a group of Spaniards, a young Italian girl, a Jewish merchant and a French professor. It is this latter gentleman who first understands the precise nature of the catastrophe that has overtaken them all, that they are now travelling through space on a cometary object. He even names it, patriotically, "Gallia." This new mini-world (still possessed of atmosphere and, apparently, full gravity) passes into the outer reaches of the solar system, freezing as it does so: the humans survive by retreating into volcanically heated caves. Eventually, and after observing many interesting astronomical sights, the meteor's orbit swings it back in to the inner solar system. The humans construct a balloon out of the sailcloth of a ship and leave their world hoping to transfer themselves to the atmosphere of Earth and so return home. And in a bizarrely dreamlike conclusion they do just that, finding the world exactly as they left it. In fact Verne wanted to portray a world devastated by the catastrophe, but Hetzel demurred, pressing upon his author the need not to leave too tragic a taste in their readership's mouth. The result is a book in which, after seemingly taking the reader on the most fantastic of fantastic voyages, and apparently having dramatised the end of the world, Verne ultimately reveals that they have been literally nowhere, and nothing has happened.

This is one of the most abrupt and wrongfooting endings that Verne ever wrote, and this is saying something. Verne often ends his stories with a startling and rather unsatisfying abruptness. Take, for example, *Voyage au centre de la terre*: Professor Lidenbrock finds a set of runes that after decoding reveal themselves to be the memoirs of a long-dead Viking called Arne Saknussemm. The prof then leads a party following in Saknussemm's footsteps consisting of himself, his nephew and a Danish guide. Verne expertly fills these subterranean adventures with incident, atmosphere and suspense: what will they find at the centre of the Earth? Did Saknussemm truly precede them? Will they survive? But after discovering a vast inner sea ("un océan veritable... desert et d'un aspect effroyablement sauvage"), voyaging across it and seeing dinosaurs sporting in the waters, Verne suddenly drops a narrative guillotine across the wonders. Suddenly the voyagers are swept into a shaft, elevated rapidly by exploding lava, and cast alive onto the surface of the planet, on the summit of Stromboli in Italy. O most lame and impotent conclusion, as Shakespeare once wrote. But on the other hand, this is the dilemma of any narrative conceived of as *in motion*: stopping the motion will inevitably seem anticlimactic. There are dozens of examples of similar endings in Verne's fictions.

3

So, Verne's *Hector Servadac* ends with an improbable and even dislocating happy ending. But then again, who's to gainsay Hetzel's judgment in this matter? People *like* happy endings. The Novel as a form of art (a bourgeois form of art— I use the descriptor technically, not pejoratively—that was really only a century-and-a-half old by the time Verne started writing) exerts a sort of gravitational pull towards happy endings. Unlike the theatre, tragic endings in the novel often feel forced and unsatisfying to us. It's woven into the form itself.

Now, of course, we all know that unhappy endings are more prevalent in life than happy ones. *Our* narratives—your story, and mine—will end not with a happy wedding, but rather with a long stint in a hospice followed by a deposit into a coffin-shaped trench in the ground. This is the "so-it-goes-ness" of things. Nevertheless we don't need to accuse the novel of mere escapist wish-fulfilment to notice the forcefulness with which the novel reorients this fact of life around its own lines of force. Fredric Jameson notes that the novel's predominant happy endings assume their own aura of necessity, neither fairy-tale optimism nor cynical pessimism but a third quantity.

> It is the reality principle that must be joyously discredited [by these happy endings]; yet it is the test and the obligation of the form of provincial realism to outwit sheer wish-fulfilment and daydream, to overtrump both fairy-tale endings and naturalist certainties with a new form of necessity.[2]

Jameson is talking mostly about classic novels from the likes of Fielding and Dickens and George Eliot. But SF, by essaying a knight's-move leap over provincial realism, finds itself more not less likely to revert to this new form of necessity. Tolkien's "eucatastrophe" is one example of this, very common in both SF and Fantasy (a definition of eucatastrophe: disaster impends, *impends*, IMPENDS!, but *at the very last minute* is

---

2. Jameson, "The Experiments of Time: Providence and Realism," in Moretti (ed), *The Novel* 2:125

averted—hurrah!). But although it often gives form to myths of Resurrection, as it does, actually, in Verne's *Hector Servadac*, it would be a mistake to assume that this is a merely religious impulse. As Jameson says, "the salvation [of the happy ending] is not a religious but a *philosophical* category... resurrection expresses the euphoria of a secular salvation otherwise inexpressible in material or social terms." My own perspective on the relationship between religion and science fiction is complicated, and cannot easily be summarised here. Nor, when I published a lengthy critical study devoted to embroidering it, did it find a welcoming or persuaded audience in the world of science fiction criticism.[3] So I should probably leave that hobby horse in its hobby stable for the moment; except to say that it seems clear to me Hector Servadac's happy ending is not a mere publisher's imposition. It's integral to The Verne Novel, and actually to science fiction itself.

I'll explain what I mean.

Above, I kick around the notion of Verne as a *recirculating* sort of writer. Science fiction is often exactly this sort of genre. Brian Aldiss coined the neatly needling phrase "cosy catastrophe" to describe a kind of 1950s British Science

---

3. The study is *The Palgrave Critical History of Science Fiction* (Houndsmills: Palgrave 2005). Copies are still, I believe, available, if you're interested in the ins and the outs of my argument. In nutshell form that argument is that SF begins with the Reformation, as a cultural response to a complex of problems, amongst which are the new Science's monstrous expansion of the size of the universe and man's place in it, which separates out a Catholic (magical) form of the fantastic tale—which we nowadays call Fantasy—from a Protestant (non-magical) form, SF. Accordingly, I say, SF carries to this day the natal imprint of certain questions; to do, in particular, with atonement, incarnation, Will and the Sublime, that date from those days. But don't worry if your eyes glaze over as you read this. You're not alone.

Fiction where global disaster strikes (a new ice age; a blinding comet followed by ambulant lethal vegetation, the death of all grasses) actually in order to provide an environment in which an upper-middle-class hero can have a series of jolly adventures, drive fast cars, get the girl, and ultimately restore the status quo ante. A surprising amount of SF disaster fits that model, actually; not just stuff written in Britain in the 50s.

It is, in other words, precisely one of the *cool* things about *Hector Servadac*. It starts with a catastrophic event of unusual magnitude; a planet wounding and perhaps killing event: a major cometary collision (precisely the scenario that must be *averted* in movies like *Armageddon* and *Sudden Impact*). Then it follows a group of survivors on a lengthily circumlocutory journey that brings them back to a world that—without explanation, and without so much as the waving of a wand—is miraculously restored. It articulates the form of the narrative serial, the mode that has come to dominate contemporary narrative, most especially in televisual form. *Star Trek* or *Battlestar Galactica*, *Buffy* or *Lost* may flirt with ultimate catastrophe, the deaths of all the characters, the end of the world; but they must always return the story to the place, more or less, where it started, in order for the next episode in the series to be able to go ahead. Verne and Hetzel's *Voyages Extraordinaires* was not a narratively sequential series in exactly this sense, but it shared the basic narrative inertia. Readers needed to finish where they started in order to be able to start again on the next instalment.

Verne's novels are all, in fact, narratives of return, and of repetition. And this too is deeply science fictional. It's one of the ironies of this wonderful genre that, despite the fact that it's predicated upon radical novelty—the newness that Darko Suvin famously called "the novum"—what we find in practice is that each new instance of science fiction, each new SF novel or film is deeply familiar. Reassuringly so. Whatever it is, the SF text will almost always rehearse one of the hoary old tropes of space travel, time travel, technology gone mad, Hitler winning the war, robots on the rampage, slinky catlike aliens, and so on. SF will almost always be formally conservative, unambitious about (or at least uninterested in) prose style, characterisation, structure, narrative focalisation or the various other technical processes of putting a story together.

So, what exactly does the average SF text have to offer by way of newness? By what means will it live up to Suvin's proud promise of novum-osity? Well, often it will offer us a *blip* of newness: a single or perhaps a cluster of ingenious ideas, or technical devices. It'll be a standard crime story, except with robots in it. It'll be a standard Western, except with Green Martians instead of Red Indians. But these blips will not disturb the larger flow of time. People in the year 1,000,000 will still talk, act and in essence *be* pretty much as they are now. People will still marry and be given in marriage. They will still love and laugh and get excited over their adventures, and cry, and perhaps even despair. But the human spirit will still triumph. There are exceptions to this statement of course, but they're rare; after all, what ordinary reader would want to read about human beings radically different to themselves? Where would they gain empathetic purchase on such characters? Why should they care?

I don't mean to sound snippy, but this *is* to miss the point of newness. The Twentieth-century French philosopher Gilles Deleuze got it right, I think, on this important subject. He argued that "to think of newness as a 'blip' within time is to think of time as a sequence that has its disruptions but then flows on." But this just is not right. "The new does not occur *within* time; true time *is* newness itself, the eternal production of transformation."[4] What's needful, I'd say, is a literature that can encompass *that* profound observation.

The travellers in *Hector Servadac* return to repeat. Novels generally return to repeat. The default mode for novelistic discourse, the third-person past-tense, always already implies the existence of survivors knowledgeable enough, and interested enough, to relate the adventures. (This is one reason why my particular end-of-the-world story gears up through the narrative tenses the way it does: past, present, future.) It's a reassuring thing, a repetition; and it is by way of reinforcing the satisfactions of repetition that the SF fan continually seeks out new-old genre writing, SF that supplies via novelty all the satisfactions of the familiar and comfortable. It's also why SF fans will watch their favourite films and shows many more times than most TV-watchers or film-goers will watch *their* favourites. Fort-da, fort-da. Again? Fort-da, fort-da. We want it over and over. Over and over. What am I doing in this novel except repeating Verne's novel with variations? Except repeating (with variations) the SF mode of novels about the end of the world? Except having an image in my head—Hector breaking blindly through the first-floor banisters and falling to the floor, say—and obsessively, repetitively elaborating that image? Writing *is* a profoundly repetitive process after all: tapping the same keyboard buttons over and over, coming back morning after morning to the same study, the same computer, the same story, until you've finally finished. It's perhaps no surprise that writers find themselves fascinated with repetition. And

---

4. This summary of Deleuze's position is quoted from Claire Colebrook's deft introductory study, *Gilles Deleuze* (Routledge New Critical Thinkers, 2002), 63

then what? Fort-da, throw the manuscript over the side of your cot, and reel it back in by writing a lengthy endnote (you're *reading* it now!). Over and over. This, I hope, is a book that recognises the immanence of repetition, not just in form (part 1, part 2, part 3) but in subject, in the understanding that not even the end of the world puts a stop to the repetitions.

Look over there—Lady Macbeth is still scrubbing at her hands. For her it's not a problem; it's a routine. It's how she feels comfortable. You might stop her doing it, forcibly, and save her fingers from blisters; but to do so would only result in more severe blisters on the skin of her mind. Leave her alone. Obsessive compulsions, most of them minor, are surprisingly ubiquitous in society.

Repetition. Servadac, as my Hector notices, is *cadavres* backward. The journey into death and out of it again is the major theme of Verne's novel. The journey of the seasons, summer to winter to summer. You can go down, but keep hold of your golden bough so you can come *up* again. Newness is always coming into time, and death is always a newness, and of the most unexpected sort. I'll confess I like Deleuze the Philosopher, in part because he is one of the few properly SFnal philosophers. Not that he wrote much about SF (he didn't); but because, where conventional philosophers have so often conceptualised their work as getting at "the truth of things," Deleuze unembarrassedly declared that a philosopher's job is the *creation* of *new* and *cool concepts*. In the same way, where Realist novelists may flatter themselves that they provide insight or nuance, SF writers know that the proper business of an author is the creation of new and cool worlds.

4

THIS ALL, I fear, sounds rather abstract and rebarbative. It's worth stressing what we all know already, that stories don't work that way. Stories parse people through events, not theories via thought-experiments, or even sense-of-wonder via generic convention. Even extreme events (let's say, the world ending) serve mostly to intensify the way people go about ordinary things. I always loved those lines from the old REM song "Belong" (it's on *Out of Time*):

> *Her world collapsed early Sunday morning*
> *She got up from the kitchen table*
> *Folded the newspaper and silenced the radio.*

Is her world collapsing in a personal, emotional sense? (Her husband has left her, say?) Or has she heard something catastrophic on the radio, that her world is literally on the point of collapsing? (Nuclear war, asteroid collision, neo-birdflu? Probably the latter, because the song continues, "*Those creatures jumped the barricades and have headed for the sea, sea*".) In either case her reaction is deeply human. You do the next thing that comes to hand. You don't, by and large, sit in the corner and wail or rend your hair or even tell sad stories of the death of kings. You make the supper.

So, yes, *Splinter* turned out to be a story about families, or to be more accurate it is a novel about a particular pared-down family dynamic. Now it so happens that women have loomed so very large in my life (and continue so to do) that my fiction almost always orients itself around female characters, or more precisely around male apperceptions of female characters. But I have a father, whom I love; and I am a father, to a child I love.

This was a story that enabled me to write about father-child relations. And this I did.

Love is a difficult thing to write about, not because it manifests itself in the world in impossible ways (I mean, impossible to apprehend, impossible to reproduce in the novelistic idiom—although there may be something in this) but because love by its nature inflects so large a quantity of desires that its representation gets pulled out of shape by desire itself. Love in fiction becomes the textual expression of how we desire love to be. In simple form it becomes wish-fulfilment erotic-romantic fantasy, where you get the guy, and he's a splendid fellow; or you get the girl and she's a doll. But more complex forms do not escape the black hole-tugging ellipses of desire mapped onto lived-experience; even tales of the woe in marriage, of desperate affairs or exploitative relations tend to represent sex as mind-blowing, love as life-consuming. This is the shape of our desire for desire.

If you need to find a way of representing that in fiction, then that very desire needs to be thinned by the addition of the writer's turpentine. So I brought my own ideas to a representation of the way love is shaped—determined and limited—by family. But (and it's a facile thing to say, but no less true for that) family is a nexus in which desire bites at its own tail.

One of the symptoms of modern times is the way that, especially in recent decades, love as a general quantity has become very thoroughly personalised and sexualised: it's about me and the person *I* want to fuck. It's there to fulfil *me*, and it finds *expression in* my fucking, because that enables passion, excitement, danger, piquancy, ego-reinforcement and sexual pleasure; it's, frankly, hard to beat. Most of us would acknowledge that family-love is also an important part of life, of course: but it is something that seems to have been very sharply separated out from the eros-love. This leads to a number of awkwardnesses—for most of us come to sexual maturity *within* families, and therefore find ourselves experiencing the sometimes uncomfortable frictions of different and incompatible modalities of loving working upon us. Best get the hell out of *there*, maybe: find yourself a girlfriend/boyfriend, find your own space and get down to it. These are the times we find ourselves filled with a disproportionate and rather nameless dread at the prospect of our own parents having sex (ugh! I don't want to *think* about it!). On a cultural level, and lancing more sharply into the tender spots of the collective psyche, a mass hysteria has accumulated around the distressing subject of child-abuse. Sex and the family become increasingly *so* immiscible as to begin actively threatening one another. This really is not a healthy state of affairs.[5]

You start life as a member of a family. You end it, as every creature that breathes ends it, alone. Life, in the largest sense, is the transition from the former to the latter state. That's no easy trajectory to follow. So you die alone, just you and the Prime Objectivity: but you start in a state of compromised (or if you prefer, buttressed) multiple subjectivity. In other words, the major trauma in most lives is not the prospect of one's own death, but the wrench when we separate ourselves out from the group-units into which we have been born. For

---

5. "Love has been personalised and sexualised in the past 200 years, and that process has been in part responsible for cutting the ties which bind individuals to a social sense, and an understanding (and acceptance) of her or his part in society. When we started to think of love in terms of romance, of sexual desire, and above all of a lifelong entitlement to both experiences, then we effectively turned away from engagement with the intimately *social* question of the impact of our actions upon others. Thus we can (and obviously do) theorize extensively about the 'breakdown' of the family and the rise of the single-person society, but until we address the beliefs that motivate and inspire these changes we examine only the consequences rather than the causes." [Mary Evans, *Love: an Unromantic Discussion* (Polity 2006), 123]

some of us this wrench is impossible, and we carry on living in the pockets of parents until we are ourselves so old as to be embarrassed at our inertia. For most, though, there's a long-drawn-out period where we experiment with independent living—when, for example, we have a flat of our own in one city, but still talk unselfconsciously about "going home for Christmas" to another city—that is capped by an event, or a series of events, that shift us over to *another* mode of living. This event might be a Saul-Bellowesque death of parents; or the begetting of children of our own; or some other breach. But it's a major (I'm tempted to say *the* major) breach in the longer-term emotional life of most of us.

Why is so little literature concerned with this important subject? I've no idea. Such examples as occur to me are few enough. Brian Aldiss's neglected but superb *Forgotten Life* (1988) is a mainstream novel that addresses precisely this subject. But what else is there? Lawrence's *Sons and Lovers*, perhaps? There are certainly novels of characters stuck in the stasis of being *unable* to move beyond a parent (Saul Bellow's brilliant little *Seize the Day* is one such; on a much bigger scale Proust's *Recherche* is another). And then again, as if psychopathologically attempting to cut the Gordian knot, literature is disproportionately stuffed with tales of orphans, David Copperfields and Harry Potters who start life already severed from the comforting-stifling familial embrace. But that's an artificial sort of strategy, I think. Or (for setting a story in and after the literal end of the world is also an artificial strategy) it's a less legitimate artificial strategy than some. It's too clean-cut, too abrupt. Life isn't really like that. Life is like the *Prelude*'s sixth book: it's like Wordsworth marching out happily to cross the alps, getting lost, having to backtrack, looking forward to the moment when he'd be crossing the Alps! (like Hannibal!)—only to stop to ask a local directions and to find out that he'd crossed over hours before without noticing. This isn't to say that life is about anticlimax, for although sometimes it is about anticlimax, sometimes it isn't. But it is to assert that events we anticipate as sharply defined and defining almost always turn out to be fuzzy-edged, diffusely defined, enveloping. A fog rather than a lightning strike.

Isn't that what life is like?

Don't you think?

That's what I wanted to do with *Splinter*. The metaphor does not work in the straightforward way that perhaps you think it does: I mean, it is not that Old Hector is the Old Earth, and that some single event cracks him apart and leaves Young Hector to float off on his own life. It's not that. It's the trope that the world might end and that we might not even be sure it has happened. We surely wouldn't be wholly oblivious (this is the *end of the world* we're talking about, after all!). But we might not be wholly certain, either. There would be a lengthy transition period during which we would become increasingly convinced that something substantial had changed in our lives. *That's* the passage out of family into independence.

5

EVERY ANIMUS HAS its anima. A dislike of conventionally written derivative novels finds expression in a novel that is more, not less, obvious about its derivation (Verne). All these SF family sagas (from *Star Wars* to *Battlestar Galactica*, from *Frankenstein* to Heinlein) feed into a novel that is precisely about the family, and about that Saga moment of retirement and supercession. If events in a novel are constrained, in terms of place, character, possibility, then it becomes not less but more important to channel the story between well-made embankments of the process of time, its onward-going-ness: let's say, for instance, one section written in the past, one in the present and one in the future tense. Constellate: love, father-hood and sonhood; family-love and love for others; sex and solitude; the end of the world; atonement and rebirth. Do that.

All this, I now think, was in my mind as I wrote this novel, the one you are holding in your hand. I just wasn't *aware*, as I was writing, that all this was in my mind. That, you see, is the technique. That's the way it goes, which is to say, that's how a novel gets itself written.

—Adam Roberts, November 2006

PUBLISHER'S NOTE
If you are intrigued by this discussion of the inspiration behind *Splinter*, head to the Solaris website. There you can freely download the complete text of Jules Verne's novel, *Off on a Comet*, in a newly edited translation prepared and introduced by Adam Roberts. Point your web browser at **www.solarisbooks.com**

ABOUT THE AUTHOR

Adam Roberts is a writer in his forties.
He lives a little way west of London with his
wife and daughter. *Splinter* was written as
his seventh novel. Seven is a highly symbolic
number in many belief-systems.

The Solaris Book of New Science Fiction
Edited by George Mann

ISBN 13: 978-1-84416-448-6

The Solaris Book of New Science Fiction is a short story anthology of the highest order, showcasing the talents of some of the world's greatest science fiction writers, including Peter F. Hamilton, Stephen Baxter, Jay Lake, Eric Brown, Adam Roberts, Paul Di Filippo and Ian Watson. The eclectic stories in this collection range from futuristic murder mysteries, to widescreen space opera, to tales of contact with alien beings. All stories are original to the collection. This is truly a book for all lovers of science fiction and is a fabulous introduction to the world of Solaris Books.

Deadstock
A Punktown novel
Jeffrey Thomas

ISBN 13: 976-1-84416-447-9

Punktown, crime-ridden metropolis on the colony world, Oasis, is home to the scum of countless alien races. Stalking its mean streets is Jeremy Stake, the private detective with chameleon-like abilities he does not want and cannot control. There's his wealthy client, Fukuda, whose company makes synthetic life forms as playthings for the rich. Then there's Fukuda's beautiful teenage daughter, whose priceless one-of-a-kind living doll has been stolen. And there is the doll itself, growing in size and resentment. The destinies of all these individuals will converge, and collide, in Punktown.

www.solarisbooks.com

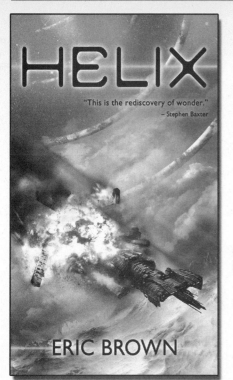

Helix
Eric Brown

ISBN 13: 978-1-84416-472-1

Eric Brown, critically acclaimed author of *The Virex Trilogy*, *The Fall of Tartarus* and numerous short stories, has penned an exciting new novel for Solaris. *Helix* is a grandiose space opera, a story of exploration, alien contact and desperation. It follows the plight of a group of humans who crash land on a desolate alien planet. Daylight brings the discovery that the planet is merely one of thousandsarranged in a vast spiral wound around a central sun. The group set off to discover a more habitable Earth-like world, encountering bizarre alien races on the way. But they must also find a means to stay alive...

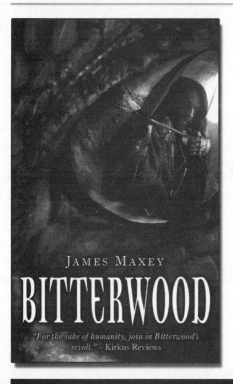

Bitterwood
James Maxey

ISBN 13: 978-1-84416-487-5

Bitterwood, the famed dragon hunter, is growing old. His desire for vengeance on the dragon–soldiers who murdered his family finally beginning to wane after many years of bloodshed. A disastrous encounter that leads to the death of the royal prince dragon, however, incites the king's retribution and brings terror and death to the world. For the king sets out to eradicate the human race, and only Bitterwood, trapped inside a doomed city, can try to lead his people to salvation.

www.solarisbooks.com

 SOLARIS SCIENCE FICTION & FANTASY

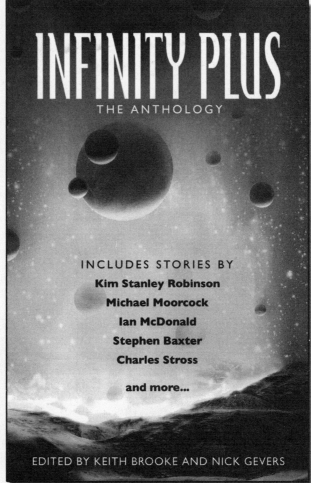